Skoob Books Publishing Ltd.

Skoob *PACIFICA* is contribu
disseminating regional literatu
understanding between cont

At the turn of the last century, Europe developed a penchant novels set in lands afar which had a tendency to look **at** the colonies whereas the Postcolonials view from within themselves, experimenting with the deviation from tradition and affirming the aesthetic of the sublime as against an aesthetic of the beautiful.

"The reality of cultural entity should be the simultaneous act of eliciting from history, mythology, and literature, for the benefit of both genuine aliens and the alienated, a continuing process of self-apprehension whose temporary dislocation appears to have persuaded many of its non-existence or its irrelevance (= retrogression, reactionarism, racism, etc.) in contemporary world reality."

Wole Soyinka, *Nobel Laureate*

"Storytelling, to the readers of a *genre* of novel, written by a particular writer for a small group of people in a large and fragmented culture, still survives in those places the English like to call the Commonwealth. This idea of narration, of the active voice is in the calypsonian as the ballad singer, the narrator, the political satirist."

Derek Walcott, *Nobel Laureate*

As the *fin-de-millenium* approaches, the colonies have a voice of their own, a new *genre* has developed. Ironically, this diachrony is written in the language of the Imperialist. Behind the facade of tropical, sandy beaches and factories of video games lies the cross-cultural and interliterary tradition of two continents.

Skoob *PACIFICA: THE EMPIRE WRITES BACK !*

SKOOB *Pacifica* SERIES

Joint Series Editors: Ms. C.Y. Loh & Mr. I.K. Ong

SKOOB *Pacifica* SERIES

No. 2003

IN A FAR COUNTRY

By the same author:

Prose
The Return (1981, 1993)
Plot, The Aborting, Parablames & Other Stories (1989)
The Third Child & Other Stories (late 1993)
A Hundred Years After & Other Stories (late 1993)

Drama
The Cord (1983)
The Sandpit (1990)

K.S. Maniam

IN A FAR COUNTRY

Introduction

by

Dr. Paul Sharrad
University of Wollongong
Australia

Afterword

by

Dr. C.W. Watson
Department of Social Anthropology
University of Kent at Canterbury

SKOOB BOOKS PUBLISHING
LONDON

First published in 1993 by
SKOOB BOOKS PUBLISHING LTD.
Skoob *PACIFICA* Series
11A-17 Sicilian Avenue
off Southampton Row and
Bloomsbury Square
London WC1A 2QH
Fax: 71-404 4398

ISBN 1 871438 14 4

Agents:
Skoob Books (Malaysia) Sdn Bhd.
11 Jalan Telawi Tiga, Bangsar Baru,
59100 Kuala Lumpur
Tel/Fax: 603-255 2686

Graham Brash (Pte) Ltd.
32 Gul Drive
Singapore 2262
Tel: 65-861 1336, 65-862 0437
Fax: 65-861 4815

Typeset by Pearly Kok . Tel/Fax: 603-255 2686
Printed by Polygraphic, Malaysia. Fax: 603-905 1553

For
Saroja, Ramajuna and Usharani

"For the truths which the intellect apprehends directly in the world of full and unimpeded light have something less profound, less necessary than those which life communicates to us against our will in an impression which is material because it enters through the senses but yet has meaning which it is possible for us to extract."

Marcel Proust

INTRODUCTION
By
Paul Sharrad
University of Wollongong
Australia

K.S. Maniam's first novel, *The Return*, is a classic account of psychic displacement induced by migration and cultural assimilation under the impact of British colonialism. After some successful plays and a collection of short stories, Maniam here returns to the novel form, investigating the 'far countries' of the mind and dreamed of homelands. The ideal is not recovery of a country of cultural origin, but the discovery of a meaningful connection to the place one inhabits. *In A Far Country* works with similar material: memories of childhood amid the Indian indentured labour of Malaya's rubber plantations, of a dying and bitterly unhinged father and schooling's promise of escape from poverty and meanness of spirit to a bright and increasingly alienated young man. We witness a drama staged inside a man facing the existential void. Anchoring private scenes in external 'reality' allows them to be significant for us as well. The narrator's struggle to find a balance between being 'his own man' and being part of the world he finds himself is an old problem, and it is the particular dynamics of the Malaysian context that give it new interest.

Maniam is a Malaysian. His novel is about trying to become a Malaysian. This paradox of being and becoming is expressed throughout the book in philosophical terms, but it also represents a social reality. Mr. Rajan, a successful businessman in a developing country marked by ethnic division, enters a mid-life crisis. Secluded in a room, his thoughts start "straying to avoid the blackness" of his soul and his lack of commitment to the people who have moved through his life: his father, the disillusioned drunk rubber-tapper from India; his obsessive doomed colleague on a jungle development site, Lee Shin; the orphaned vagrant philosopher, Sivasurian; villager Zulkifli, in quest of the spirit of the land; Rajan's wife, Vasanthi, isolated by ingrained patriarchal tradition. The book is Rajan's compendium of notes, letters, memories and meditations: its discursive abstractions tend towards the didactic but are enlivened by dramatic snapshots of memory, jerkily and briefly flashed up, often intense in their imagery.

Most readers today, in this world of shifting populations, will recognise the general problem facing Maniam's protagonist. How does the individual pull up cultural roots and retain a sense of life's significance; how can one *not* divest oneself of a specific group identity in this modern age of levelling multiplicity? Moreover, how do you hold to the supports of ethnic identity while affirming nationality, especially when your nation defines itself officially in terms of another race and culture? *In A Far Country* asks these questions, seeks to bring the far-off ideal into the imaginative country of the here and now. If the quest is broadly familiar, the specifics of this novel's setting may require explanation.

By comparison with India or Africa, Malaya has not loomed large on the popular imagination of the world. Its current national and social formation is the result of colonialism just as much as those other places, but connection to the global network of imperial image-production came relatively late. Also, with the exception of Penang and Singapore, for almost a century Malaya was ruled indirectly through local princes and administered at second hand through India. Kipling and others had said what had to be said; here was merely a repetition of less fabulous proportions which, because of quietly entrenched Islam, denied the West even the vicarious excitement of heroic missionising.

The Malay peninsula and surrounding islands did receive sporadic attention. Clifford tried to evoke the mystery of the jungle, the romance of sorcerers, were-tigers and court intrigues (as in *The Further Side of Silence*). Conrad created moral dramas out of the atmospherics of a brooding tropic coastline in *Almayer's Folly* and *Lord Jim*. Rajah Brooke carved out a personal fiefdom while suppressing piracy and served briefly as a focus for European literary dreams of power and adventure. The region hit its peak in terms of overseas exposure when the rubber boom was on in the twenties and Somerset Maugham captured the sordid 'good life' of plantersand civil servants. As his stories make clear, however, plantations were boring places and their managers rather declassé. Despite the historic efforts of a few enthusiasts like Francis Light, Stamford Raffles and Frank Swettenham, Britain remained only half-hearted about this part of the world and let it go quietly to Independence in 1957 after a somewhat shame-faced collapse upon Japanese invasion. When the Commonwealth directly intervened in post-war counter-insurgency measures, literary PR varied from the cynical naturalism befitting guerrilla warfare to the sardonic comic-opera of Burgess's *Malayan Trilogy*.

One lasting effect of Malaysia's desultory but significant colonial history is its multi-racial population and the structuring of it as discrete communities. Malays were left largely to their own cultural devices once they proved amenable to British influence, and when reforms leading to self-government were instituted, it was the Malay elite, both traditional rulers and modern professionals, who took political power, not unnaturally legislating their favoured status as 'sons of the soil' in the new nation. Since most Malays had been rural farmers and fisherfolk, their control of land ownership and the eventual monopoly of the Malay language over national affairs meant that they could continue on unchanged, save by the inevitable impact of modernity.

Through the character of Pak Zul, Maniam gives credence to the Malay villager's strong attachment to the land. One of the most powerful passages in the novel occurs when Zulkifli attempts to bring Rajan into contact with the tiger spirit embodying indigenous authenticity. (The compelling treatment of this 'tiger hunt' is a direct counter to colonial fixations on hunting and on Malay 'magic' as colourful 'native superstition'.) The author is careful to resist the appeal of a romanticised induction into this cultural circle. His character, Rajan, can come to learn from his partial encounter with the 'tiger', but he cannot 'convert' totally to that experience: he must accept his otherness, yet find a way of understanding that is more than merely intellectual assent or visceral repulsion. Maniam also shows that despite privileged national status, the ordinary Malay is as vulnerable as anyone else to cultural alienation. As Pak Zul knows bitterly and Rajan comes to realise, Malay youths like Zulkifli's son are 'sons of the soil' only as a political slogan. In the modern city it is this identity that leaves them at the bottom of the economic ladder and prey to despair. The son acts out an old colonial stereotype of the Malay who runs amuck, but this time it is not because of the insidious tropics or some supposedly inherent instability, but in response to 'development' - a development that Rajan has played a part in, but which, ironically, has been orchestrated by the Malay political elite.

The novel portrays individuals from other major groups in Malaysia. Chinese had traded for centuries with the Peninsula on a small scale, some having settled in Malacca in the fifteenth century and adapted to local customs. Others were encouraged by the British as traders and were, anyway, already attracted by the money to be made out of tin mining. Since they were organised through Chinese societies and labour bosses and then by special British administrators, and since they had their own schools and remained largely concentrated in towns and mines, they too, were able to remain ethnically autonomous, attuned more to the politics in China than in Malaya. Their almost exclusive involvement in the communist insurgency after the War reflected this as well as their dismay at being squeezed out of the political arena in the emerging nation, but it served to drive a wedge between their people as a whole and the other racial groups of the Federation.

In A Far Country looks for moments in both village and town when inter-racial harmony is attained, but admits that they are both fragile and fleeting. A Chinese shop-keeper is held to be self-interested and stingy, but breaks free of his reputation to support his neighbours, only to enclose himself in the family circle under the stress of Japanese Occupation. Lee Shin, isolated in a forest camp, retreats to a dream of securely stereotypic Chinese traditionalism as an expression of his artistic temperament and a defense against insensitive work-mates. In doing so, he counters popular images of Chinese as clannish, family-centred and interested only in money-making. Rajan observes him as a strange species whose music is incomprehensible, but he does manage to establish a rapport on the basis of a common sense of alienation. His attempt to help his colleague by asserting their common manhood on a 'dirty weekend' with some prostitutes downplays ethnic difference and attacks another stereotype of the Chinese male as lusty epicurean. This only drives Lee Shin further into neurosis, but it is his death that eventually forces the narrator to confront his own attitudes to women.

The other major influence on the history of the peninsula was India, whose southern empires in particular wielded immense cultural influence over the ancient kingdoms of South East Asia. Britain brought Indian convict labour to Malaya to build roads and cities, and then indentured large numbers of plantation workers to cultivate coffee, rubber and palm-oil. Again, with a few exceptions who became merchants, police and clerks, these people lived a feudal existence in rural barrack-lines with access mostly only to Indian overseers and a couple of years of Tamil schooling.

The narrator strives to escape this restricted life through a colonial schooling that gives entry to the decultured materialism of the modern professional class. Rajan's sudden sense of rootlessness drives him to remember his father's tormented dreams of ancient Indian trading voyages and then the crowded holds of indentured labour ships. When these prove too disturbing, the son recalls Deepavali celebrations, but that leads to childhood memories of goat slaughter, and so his thoughts break to another temporary escape route. In each flashback there is a passing reference to some ritual suggesting hope of peace or fulfilment. The narrative itself becomes a ritual of "pulling yourself out of passivity and despair by telling a story", even if it puts Rajan in the artist's role of the scapegoat whose sacrifice will keep the nation from complacency.

Segregated communalism was, no doubt, a convenient system for colonial management, but it was hardly a sound basis for nation building; sectional interests and mutual suspicion have continued to strain - sometimes violently - against the otherwise peaceful prosperity of modern Malaysia. The narrator's career in land and housing development reflects both the collective rush towards 'progress' in the early phases of Malayan nationalism and the personal anxiety of a second-generation, upwardly mobile migrant seeking some way of belonging. The novel shows the increasing difficulty of this as communities grow apart under the action of war and independence politics (when "people become peoples").

But if anti-colonial nationalism forces people into ethnic enclaves, it also forces some at least into greater social interaction. Rajan's coffee-shop circle is multi-ethnic and breaks up when he asserts his *individual* opinion. Rajan strives to escape from the stereotypic roles for Malaysian Indians; not only does he move away from a 'coolie' existence, but he constantly alters himself, shifting from a businessman contrasted to the unworldly Sivasurian to someone influenced by his metaphysics. Rajan's existential quest after something deeper than cold rationalism and economic drive implies the nation's need for more than fixed superficial links across class and ethnicity. Maniam's 'far country' is one in which public and private identities are always shifting. The changes occur around given cultural axes, but while these supply frameworks for meaning and direction, they are not themselves immutable. It is this very possibility of painful 'alter-ation' that creates recurrent possibilities for human community.

In A Far Country is remarkable novel for its experiment. It moves beyond early Malayan writing in English which sought to establish a local literary imagination in opposition to an imposed colonial one. It resorted to 'slice-of-life' sketches of a fairly limited world and to the self-conscious introduction of local idiom. Such nationalist realism found its end result in the official assertion that Malay was the only medium for national culture, leaving writing in English marginalised with an increasingly elitist or overseas audience. *In A Far Country* seeks to free itself from this literary ghetto by addressing national issues and departing from realism to do so. Maniam's venture into dreamscapes and metaphysics is important, and, while it works mostly through Hindu-sounding phrases, it offers a point of contact with literature in Malay - the animistic world of Shahnon Ahmad's villagers, for example, or the strong moral tone of Malay poetry. *In A Far Country* builds on the fictional quest after a multicultural national belonging instituted in Lloyd Fernando's *Scorpion Orchid*, but it avoids that book's pessimism partly because it manages not to rely on ethnically representative (potentially stereotypic and therefore imaginatively ghettoised) characters.

The book's texture may suggest the opposite; dreams, recollections, bits of writing and dialogue leap forth and cut off in disconnected fashion. But there is a logic in the narrative that eventually intimates a degree of hopefulness for a more integrated community. Maniam's style relies on 'dead-pan' declarative sentences that seem to imprison the voice in flat objectivity. This is appropriate to Mr. Rajan, the pragmatist who resists enlightenment, but it is set against poetic passages of heightened emotional intensity. Modulation between styles is handled skilfully via shifts in tense that take on a connective rhythm. Another integrating technique is the repetition of rhetorical questions. This can be a dangerous ploy in that we may get tired of the constant deferral of an answer (spiritual truths have a habit of sounding obvious). But religious consolation, whatever its cultural form, does not come easily in real life. The narrator struggles amid separation from his past and his fellows to build a fabric of wisdom, finally learning enough from the wider community to begin improving his own marriage relationship.

A major organisational device is Maniam's use of light and time as motifs that link the 'disjecta membra' of the narrator's memory and connect the character's personal obsessions to general metaphysical questions about truth and appearance, about history as a series of discrete events versus the continuity of experience across everyday action and timeless epiphany. It is this dimension of the book, coupled with a social background carrying legacies of colonialism that suggests comparison with Raja Rao's Indian metaphysical comedy, *The Cat and Shakespeare*, Australian Randolph Stow's *To The Islands*, or, closer to home, the late Lee Kok Liang's ironical *Flowers in the Sky*. K.S. Maniam has given us a challenging new work, solemnly alert to the historical limitations of humanity yet compelled by those dreaming moments when genuine selfhood and community seem possible.

CHAPTER ONE

THERE has hardly been a time in my life when I've stayed in a room, looking outside, doing nothing. Here I am writing - for which I see no immediate value - and watching the light come into the room and mix with the brightness inside and become indistinguishable. There are no shadows, either inside or outside the room. There have been many rooms I occupied, in houses or offices, that were filled with such even brightness. I hadn't felt uncomfortable in them; I didn't feel disturbed as I am now. I look past the roof-tops of the neighbouring houses and see a clear, blue sky streaked with white. Such plainness, I find, is suddenly unsettling. It was on such a bright morning, some time back, that I left my office premises, abruptly, and shut myself up in this room in my house. My wife and children didn't know what to make of my behaviour the first few days, then fell into a routine that emerged from the crisis.

It was another stroke of light, I think, that brought me into whatever I am trapped by now. Even language denies me plainness, straying this way and that to avoid the blankness that has come into my mind. Fortunately for my generation, we had a good dose of it in the schools during our younger days. I mean the English language. But since I left school and university, where I read economics, the English I used has had to do with adding up and avoiding subtraction. But now there is only a zero in my mind.

It was that blade of light I saw one evening which has brought me to this pass. I remember coming back to an empty house. My wife and sons had gone off to some shopping complex - there was a note with this information- and it was the servant's day off. I went into the kitchen, had a cold drink, and as I was coming into the hall, I noticed the door to my right slightly open. I wouldn't have seen it if the sunlight coming through the crack hadn't struck my face with the warm sting of the *lallang* grass.

The room is a sunken one, which an architect friend specially designed for my sons as a playroom. Located next to the kitchen and opposite the servant's room it is well within reach of the fridge, my wife's arbitration responsibilities and the servant's help. But over the years I had forgotten about its existence.

I pushed the door open and entered the room and was, for a while, blinded by the sunlight. After I had grown accustomed to the brightness, I saw nothing in the place that made it a playroom. The windows were wide open as if the occupant wanted the room aired and the curtains were made out of old *saris*. I drew them across the windows and recognized that the saris were the ones Vasanthi had brought from her home and must have worn after her puberty rites. There is a photograph of her wearing one of these saris, taken just after she came out from her menstrual isolation.

I looked around at the room and was struck by the frugality of its furnishing. At the opposite corner from that occupied by the photographs is a wide plank bed covered with a mat and a thick blanket. On top of the single pillow is a folded, white coverlet. Near the window, not far from the bed is a bronze statue of a beggar boy, hands held out and face appealing for charity. I've since returned to the room in my wife's and sons' absence and notice that nothing has changed.

I've stayed in this room as I would have in my office, at the end of the month, to track down any miss-entry in the accounts ledger or try to trace some non-entered item. But that

---

lallang - Malaysian tall, wild grass.
saris - Long textile worn by Indian women.

kind of procedure hardly seems to work in my present situation. Most of the time my mind is blank and to get rid of the blankness, I've been reading, off and on, when I'm not staring out of the window, whatever books have been lying around the house. My wife, true to her sense of duty, has brought in supplies from the public library and bookshops. But nothing seems to replace the drive that I've lost, the drive that brought me to my present status of house and property owner, with a solid bank account. The fire that I had in me is simply spent.

During my most idle moments, when I'm off guard, events and people I had thought hardly worth paying attention to, come into my mind. My father's face and his last days in the estate house keep coming back to me. (Is it possible for despair to be inherited through the blood?) Though in his early fifties, he looked old for his age. Perhaps he felt harassed by his wife and eight children. I don't know. All I can recall is that he would lie like a covered corpse on the long, wooden bench outside the house in the mornings. Later in the morning the corpse sat up and blinked at the bright day. Somehow it found the strength, some hours later, to go to the cooking place, make gruel from the previous day's rice and pour the mess down its throat. Then the corpse straightened itself some more and put on a shirt and shorts.

Though I scoffed at him, how strange it is now to almost look and be like him. At least he could eat a morning meal; I merely look at the food my wife puts on the table in my room and move away.

That breakfast prepared my father for the toddy drinking for the remainder of the day and most of the night. When he returned, late, my mother, sisters and brothers would be fast asleep, having scrambled and fought for whatever food and space they could get.

I couldn't understand at that time why my father never shouted back at my mother when she scolded him. One of the highlights of estate life was to see and hear husbands and wives go for each other almost every day. Other men beat their wives and abused their children under the violence toddy brought on in them. But my father was worse than the stiff corpse he had been in the morning and early afternoon.

The kerosene hand-lamps danced all over the long row of houses when the men returned. The women's faces, under the dim lights, took on heightened anger and indignation. In my house, only I came out, my mother being too exhausted to care. Seated on the steps beside the lamp hung on a nail, I watched my father. Perhaps he had grown used to my presence or he was indifferent for he didn't notice me.

The stiffness that had held up his body during the day, disappeared. He was a mass of pulp; his head lolled from side to side. His stomach was caved in; his shoulders hung down as if at the end of invisible strings. In short, he was collapsed like a puppet put away in a box when the show is over.

As far as I can recall there had been only one great adventure in his life - his escape from India to Malaysia. There were times when he muttered and mumbled during his toddy-soaked carelessness, and it was through these moments of indiscretion that his story came through to me. Thinking back, I realize that that was how he tried to pull himself out of his limp helplessness.

The faint, flickering light and the night silence created shadows and echoes that could have been of another man and another place. The place was another country, India; the time, another era that comes through to me in a strange way. Can memories be inherited? Can repetition make actual the past?

When my father returned home, his uncertain tread brought me out as if to a rescue. Also the duty of handing him his blanket every night had fallen upon me. He received the furry thing as if it was an animal, with unconcealed disgust. He sat wrapped up in it for a while until even I began to feel the cold bite into my flesh.

Then he spluttered and growled and chuckled.

"What animal brought me out here?" he said, falling into a steady stream of words. "You prick me everywhere as if you want to pickle me alive. Remember those nights I came home straight, steady and serious? You didn't sleep turning your back on me. Now you don't even know I'm alive."

At first I thought he was addressing my mother but as he talked on I began to feel he was flinging his words, frustration and anger at something invisible.

"You kept me from sleeping the whole night. Through the open window I saw the stars up in the sky. Did they shine on a better land? Was there drought in those other countries?

"My great-grandfather told me many stories. About those stars. How they had guided our travellers, the bold ones in the family, over lands never trodden by feet before. Ah, those men carrying their boats overland, passing through sandalwood-scented forests! How many were there to carry the boats? How big and heavy were the boats?

"The ship we came in was crowded and foul. The hulls were rusted. When I drank water from the taps there was only a taste of rust. And the human dung - all over the place. The men not even closing the door. The door too rusted to be closed. The women with just the saris over their thighs, to hide their shame. Sometimes no water even to wash, to flush away the human filth."

The months and years of such talk overlap and has become its own reality. Such occasions made me forget who I was and to whom I was listening. The lone voice in the half-darkness removed my self-consciousness - I was about thirteen when these confessions began - and allowed me to escape from brow-knitting thought. There was a certain yearning in me for visions and mysteries that could destroy, even for a short while, the bareness and harshness of my surroundings.

My father carried me away with him when he talked of those early voyagers who either carried their boats across vast tracks of jungle to launch themselves once more into a fresh sea or build another one to reach the land of their dreams. What country could match the complexity of their dreams? How could frail boats transport them into their dreams? My father drew from his memories the discovery of a fabulous kingdom by his forefathers.

"They were not right in the head, those travellers. Why didn't they continue to stay in the land where they built their temples? Go and see them. As good as the ones in India. A little India just here. Were received with respect and honour. Given the chance to lead and to rule. What did they do? Lost their dreams. Went again on their unquenchable travels.

"Those temples. Nothing like them nowadays. Clean and upright. No need for rich men to donate bells with their names inscribed. Even when dug up from deep inside the ground, they were not cracked. Could make a sound that holds together the whole world."

Where was this kingdom and the bells that though buried for centuries retained their pure music? My father was an avid reader of Tamil newspapers, that was, until drink overtook him. Had he read about some archaeological discovery? There had been passing mention of some diggings, somewhere in the north, in the English papers. But he gave me such details as to make me wonder if the source was not himself. If he hadn't invented that glorious, utopian reign of his ancestors, why was such a find suppressed? And who kept it from public notice?

He went on: "People coming together like brothers from the same family. Not strangers from different countries. Look where we are now. Shadows in the darkness, not even hearing the other person breathe. Not even caring.

"Those stars were wrong to bring us here. But how can we stop ourselves from following their pull? Everything is joined together. One land's grass dies, another land's jungle is cool and full of fruits. Like blind bats we come to the fruit trees. Then we're caught in the net."

He wrapped the blanket more closely round his shoulders and sat there rocking himself. He turned his face once or twice in my direction and seeing me there on the steps, seemed to be reassured.

"Wife and children. Just cycle after cycle. Can't break the turning of the wheel. I tried. Yes, coming in those peoples' dung-filled ship, I looked out at the water rolling past us. How vast and clear it looked! Going somewhere deep down. Had its own life. Our lives just small handfuls of dirt. Dropped into the ocean, they just disappeared."

There was one terrible night when he didn't even talk to himself. He wasn't bunched up and formless. Had he swallowed a different kind of drink? He had risen out of his helplessness like a ferocious giant. He stormed there on the cement verandah, his arms raised like huge axes ready to chop down anything that came in his way.

"So what do you want me to do?" he railed. "Build a diamond palace for you? Cut down the hills and plant the flat land with honey-dripping bushes? I took you away from that dry, gossip-diseased family and land. Yes, I thought I would find heaven. But people can be wrong. A man can be wrong.

"The price has to be paid. I'm paying it with blood. With all this suffering. Ah, you're laughing. Saying, 'A fool for following the stars! Fools sometimes walk into hope-giving things. Fools sometimes fall into insect-gnawing ravines. Do you understand?

"I've tried to understand but my mind is all mixed up. The knots are too many to untie. You're not helping, only laughing at me. Getting angry, spitting on me, making me suffer some more. Why must there be suffering? We suffered there in India. Now there is only suffering. No escape like the last time."

He withdrew deeper into that blanket, slid down and went to sleep on the bench. I sat on, watching, waiting. There was only the strangled breathing that came from the huddled figure under the blanket. The oil lamps had already been taken into the houses and what remained was a starless night. That brought on in me a helplessness almost like that of my father's. A world was blotted out. There remained in the darkness only a voiceless, faceless being.

Fear embraced me like a big-pawed, furry animal. Was that only a young boy's imagination playing tricks on him? I sat there on the steps for a long time, unable to move. My body became slowly covered with sweat. I breathed against the fear, trying hard to regain some confidence, some sense of security. The figure under the blanket offered me no help, only lay still as if its suffering had turned it into stone.

In the distance, through the fearful darkness, I saw the slaughter house. A light came through, somehow, from beyond, like memory recreating a forgotten incident or encounter. The slaughter shed, open on all its sides, stood out there clearly. No goats were tethered there but they would appear when Deepavali was about a few months away.

When I came into adolescence, Deepavali was, for me, held within a circle of mystery. My father's drinking seemed trivial; my mother's suffering was hardly worth the attention. People seemed to be taken out of themselves. The estate lines were transformed. The songs that came from the valve-set radios reached into a more complex and deeper harmony. Somehow the dingy, green plank houses did not rest just on earth-bound stilts; they cushioned themselves on an invisible axis of enchantment. They were unusually clean and neat. The children did not have to be told anything; their faces were washed sober by an air of responsibility.

All this happened after the goats appeared. The older boys roamed the plantation late into the evening with the goats. They returned home with the herd, not scratched or bruised from a fight with each other. Not one of them was bitten by snakes or had to be rescued from wandering away too far. An uncanny kind of order took charge of the lives on the estate.

My own preoccupations and forming personality were held within a stillness and calm that went against the self-centered turbulence I had seen in boys of my age. While they were boisterous, their energies didn't take them into destruction. They didn't swing a cat by its tail. They didn't stab sharp sticks into the anus of a dog. They didn't throw stones, hidden behind hibiscus bushes, at a passing car. They didn't twist and snap the stems of flower plants in the office grounds. They were all curiously self-restrained and loyal to some ordering force outside themselves.

The goats they herded were tied to iron stakes beside the slaughter shed. When it rained, the boys scurried like a wave of ants to these stakes, untied the goats and housed them inside the shed. Their parents watched them, filled with pride and a sense of awe. They too, appeared to be ruled by an awareness beyond that of the ordinary selves.

The goats munched ceaselessly on whatever was pushed into their mouths. They were given grass, banana skins, drum-stick tree flowers and, on occasions, rye cakes. When *pujas* were held on Fridays, the women hurried out to the goats with whole bunches of bananas and rice boiled in brown sugar. It therefore came as a surprise to me to see their behaviour change a week or two before Deepavali.

Nights grew darker than in the previous months. The stars, shining above an awed estate community, now steadied their light as if for a demoniac scrutiny of the world. These were not the stars my father spoke about. They didn't shine an encouraging and benevolent light upon the inhabitants of the earth. They were withdrawn, unsympathetic and mysterious.

The estate population reached a frenzied climax on the eve of Deepavali. The nights before the eve seemed to be plunged into deeper darkness and the households lighted hurricane lamps as a kind of defence against the unknown. Even then there were scarry patches of shadow between the houses. From where I sat, on the steps, I saw the houses appear precariously

---

pujas - Special prayer session.

out of nothingness and I felt when morning came they would have vanished. But there was certainty in the actions, speech and gestures of the tappers, weeders and gardeners. The clerks, typists and accountants, though removed from the estate lines by a short distance - they lived in small, wooden bungalows - adopted the remote air of the cautious and uninvolved. Perhaps, having watched the annual ritual for years, they preferred the detachment their British masters had impressed upon them.

I don't know.

The morning had an unusual calm about it - the calm the condemned feel before their execution. The men, women and children were silent and restrained like the tethered goats beside the shed. As the morning progressed there came to me the thought that we were slowly being drained of our blood. The light was parchment thin, like the bloodless skin of a man who has lived too long in an icy cavern.

I walked about the estate, lingering under the cool shade of the trees. There was a restlessness inside that forced me into some kind of action. The walking didn't help for it seemed to carry me towards the slaughter shed. And I didn't want to be there at all. Yet I knew the mystery that I longed to confront waited for me beside the cement floor with its little drains and tall pipes. The water would gush and wash away the year's dust and dirt before the awful ritual of slaughter began.

My father, as did most of the men, went out early and returned by mid-afternoon, primed with toddy. In their absence the women and children squatted down to an early lunch. There was an expression on my mother's and sisters' and brothers' faces I couldn't quite place. It was a kind of despair or some secret joy or perhaps it was just desperation. Why should my brothers, so much younger than me, feel cornered and fearful? The men's absence, even if only for a few hours, carried the sense of a final betrayal.

The men returned. The afternoon sky was already tinged with a rusty glow. The children ran out to grab from their hands the little bundles of *vadais* and *murukus* that would prevent them from paying too much attention to the killing of the goats. Already long knives and shorter blades were being sharpened on whetstones. Women ground, gratingly, the chillies, coriander, cummin and poppy seeds in anticipation of the cooking to be done for Deepavali. The day stretched before them like a long vigil.

All over the estate men moved with the weight of habit and determination. The children hung about in knots of curiosity and eager expectation. As they watched the younger men bring down coils of seasoned and well-used rope from hidden stores beneath the rafters, they felt they were entering a ritual that would take them a step further towards adulthood.

Other men cut down banana leaves, the juice from the stems spiking the air, and piled them up without cracking the spine or shredding the edges. These the boys helped to carry to the shed hearing behind them the command: "Don't tear any of the leaves! I'll cut off your tail before it can grow!" The girls who stood watching the boys at their tasks, giggled. They had seen the "tails" when they went to the communal bathroom and caught, unawares, the boys bathing naked. They would see the "tails" again this time that of the bull-goats, when the broad shouldered men slaughtered the animals.

In the late afternoon, time seemed suspended. The goats bleated and their cries dispersed quickly in the emptiness under the now red sky.

Women's voices, issuing orders to the older girls, reached my ears as faint distortions. Between me and these waves of activities came a clamouring silence. Now and then insects ticked loudly as if they would split their tiny throats in some mad sacrifice. Then the silence overpowered them and they were lost to my consciousness.

Somehow at this point, I find myself stationed at an old well in front of the shed. The covered up well provided a slab-like

---

vadais - Indian doughnut.
murukus - Indian spicy tidbits.

11

seat and I sat on it, quiet and remote, watching what went on. The men who would slaughter the goats were old hands at the job but had beside them younger men who were apprentices. These slaughter-trainees merged themselves with the more experienced men as if they were their shadows. Inside the shed waited the skinners and dismemberers. They shuffled, whistled, sang old Tamil songs and drank toddy from dirty flagons while waiting for the carcasses to be brought to them. The two teams taunted, jibed, provoked and abused each other.

There were about eight goats tied to separate stakes at a site a few yards from the shed. The slaughterers had thought it unwise to let the goats smell their approaching deaths. This precaution became necessary after an incident a few years back. Among that batch of five or six, there had been a dappled bull-goat. During the months that it was bred for the slaughter it acquired a personality and a name, Mani. The estate women had fondly tied a brass bell to its neck and, therefore, its name. Mani was not tied up for the night like the other goats; nor was it led on a rope for its grazing. Mani was too gentle to rebel, too courteous to steal food from the pots and pans.

Mani's lustrous, spotted, black-and-white body hung like a charm in the doorways of the estate house kitchens. Sometimes Mani gave in to the whimsical tenderness of a woman and allowed himself to be stroked. He let some of the young girls brush his coat until he shone like their unviolated virginity. But he was there all the time, the faint yet unriddable scent of a hardly understood nostalgia. His bell tinkled, awakening memories that had nothing to do with the struggle for a living in an estate far from a motherland.

Where did he come from? They bought him in a neighbouring estate but he came whole and fresh from the centre of a mystery. To this day he puzzles me. He lived briefly among us and then he was slaughtered. He was an animal but he saw life differently. How was his behaviour the days before his dying to be understood? Was there another kind of deep-seated awareness?

Some three days before Deepavali, Mani disappeared. The women and the young girls became distracted. A few of them joined the boys in looking for Mani. They clucked and called out seductively, "Mani! Mani! Mani!" The boys had banana peels and one young girl even took the trouble to make brown, sugared rice, Mani's favourite. But Mani was not to be found. The people were forced to call off the search.

Mani returned by himself the next morning. There he was beside the shed, on his haunches, an unfathomable expression in his eyes. He didn't so much look at you as beyond you. Into those smoky eyes there came to be crowded all the space that lay beyond man, far from his reach. This vastness terrified me, made me shiver and withdraw into myself. There was, I thought, a subtle insult in that look. Man, he was saying, go ahead. Lock yourself up in the narrow prisons of your making. Me, I'm going out there, into the incomprehensible mystery you can't grasp.

So I shied away but still watched him from a corner of my consciousness. He got to his legs and strutted about, glorying in some discovery only he could have made. His shaggy body - he had not been brushed since his return - tensed against the light that filtered through the jungle, rubber trees and more domestic plants, down to the roof of the shed. His eyes glinted with the fire of a smouldering anger.

Most remarkable of all, at that stage in his life, was the ease with which he lived in complete isolation. He didn't come near the kitchens any more; their doorways were filled neither with memory nor with nostalgia for him. This behaviour not only intrigued the women, both young and old, but also drew from them a respect that verged on reverence. Though Mani indicated he valued his solitude, they never left him alone.

He was approached, besieged and clamoured around at all hours of the day, particularly in the mornings and evenings. They didn't seek to tie a bell at his neck though he had lost the previous one. Instead, they garlanded him with a variety of

13

flowers. Mani neither looked at them nor acknowledged the flowers around his neck. His indifference bore the awesomeness and ferocity of the goddess, Kaliamma.

The women thronged like supplicants around him. Did they want another god in him? One old woman even went so far as to anoint his forehead with sandalwood paste, *kumkum* and holy ash but Mani kicked so violently at her that she had to abandon the attempt. But the other women would not give up so easily. They tried to get through to whatever he represented for them in subtler and more persistent ways.

They talked to him.

"Mani, why're you behaving like this?"

"Yes, tell *amma*. Everybody here wants you to feel happy. Remember the *kanji* water you used to drink? With just a pinch of salt and onion slices? Not too watery or too thick. You drank it like honey. Come to amma's house, Mani. Wear your bells again. The sound makes me glad I'm living."

"Don't listen to her too much, Mani. Listen to me. My words are sweeter. And my palms even more sweet. In some peoples' palms whatever they hold goes sour. In my palm they become crystal sugar. You always came quietly to my house. Like a saint. Look at you now. You've become too proud. Be gentle and simple again, Mani."

This woman went towards Mani with rice boiled in milk and honey, but he only turned his head away.

"That's right. You're too good for our food. Show us what you really want. Something special that only gods and goddesses can prepare for you. Take us and show us. Might be good for us too. Cure our blindness, take the evil away from our tongues. Make us see what you see."

---

kumkum – Red powder worn as a dot on women's forehead.
amma - Mother.
kanji - Rice gruel.

14

This was the philosopher-woman. Whenever anyone had problems, he or she ran to this calm, knowledgeable woman. The philosopher would chew her *sireh* and betel nut shavings, spiced with lime and dried *kerambu*. She had a melodious voice and just listening to her drove your problems from your minds and hearts.

Mani, after listening, made a noise in his throat that resembled a man's hawking just before he spat.

They turned aggressive towards him and finally left him to his own devices. Mani used this freedom to wander all over the estate, it seemed to savour and relish whatever was not human. He ran with the dogs and hid with the cats. Once he got a black cobra to open out its hood and, to the tapping of his hoofs, sway in dance. As the days drew nearer to Deepavali, he gave up all these treats and rested, without eating, beside the shed. His eyes were dull and smoky with a despair man could not even know.

That Deepavali eve the slaughterers were in an unusually savage mood. Was it because Mani had been given too much attention? They didn't give him a glance though he lay docilely waiting for his execution. They only had to reach out and they would have got him. No, they had to reserve him for the last.

The killing began in the late afternoon. Two men held the legs while the slaughterer turned the head until the throat bulged like a tube. The long knife went to work, moving up and down until the bleating at the first slitting turned into a rasping whistle and finally into just wind struggling to be released. The blood gushed into the yellow, enamel basin an assistant held under the neck. Then the lifeless body was thrust aside and the next goat brought to the knife.

All this while Mani had been quiet and complacent, a mass of rough and shaggy indifference. Though flies had begun to

---

sireh - Leaf eaten with betel nut shavings.
kerambu - Indian spice.

buzz over the offals now piling up on the shed floor and settled distractingly on his ears and snout, Mani didn't shake himself free from them. He turned stony eyes on the meat workers and looked away.

There was too much nakedness, fat flesh, mutton and blood everywhere. Skins had been cleanly removed from the goats' bodies as one would take off deep fur coats in readiness for spring. There was just too much neatness and reduction. A goat didn't seem worth its killing: a pile of chopped up meat on a banana leaf and a bowl of blood.

As the goat before Mani's turn shivered and lay still, an unearthly sound made the men abandon their activities and listen. No man or animal could have drawn such a deep moan from a throat. Is it an exaggeration to say, in retrospect, that the rasping boom came from some horn in the earth's centre? We were startlingly put off our tracks. Confused and surprised, we stood there in the post-afternoon light like half-formed creatures, the life-force yet to be triggered off in our bodies.

There was gritty granite dust in the air - a sudden obscuring of everything we had known. In that still, unexpected confusion we saw Mani bare his teeth in a devilish grin. Then he stood up and gazed at us through eyes that held in its fires a millenium of innocent anger. Then Mani turned and bounded towards that immeasurable green, the jungle.

Something broke and the men released from their trance, gave chase. Knives, thin blades and scrappers fell behind them like so many useless instruments of pillage. Someone grabbed a coil of muscular rope as he joined the mass that scuttled towards the disappearing animal. Shouts, cries and curses, only half-human, pursued Mani faster than could lean, young legs.

A sudden silence descended upon those remaining behind. We didn't look at each other, mesmerized as we were by the lightning disappearance of Mani. Flies, now a thickening blue blanket, clamoured voraciously at the mass of uncleaned offals. The buzzing monster seemed to consume itself more than it

16

did the hidden intestines, stomachs and livers. The severed goats' heads looked down from a cement shelf, their expressions sculptured by death. One head, the eyes open, looked mockingly at the entranced people. Another, the eyes closed too tightly, stretched its lips into an impossible line of scorn. A third had both eyes slightly open and jaws that seemed to have been wrenched apart by surprise.

The sky had dipped into a greyer shade when the men returned with the struggling Mani, his legs trussed up with rope.

"You can't run away from us,

"We'll deal the final blow," the younger men sang as they marched with Mani to the slaughter block.

Mani stopped struggling when he saw the shed, the flies and the goats' heads. He didn't go limp; there was only a strained quietness in his body. His head was held erect, an amused indifference in his eyes. As they placed his neck on the wooden block, he made a guttural sound that resembled a human voice. The men left him tied up at the legs as they held him down for the knife.

The burly slaughterer, a peculiar viciousness filling his movements, sharpened the long knife again. His thrust against Mani's bulging neck was more than professional: his knife drew a trickle of blood even before it moved. Mani took the sawing blade without flinching and those of us whose nerves had been heightened by Mani's escape and capture, heard the knife cut into the animal's bones behind the throat.

"So you'll run away from us, will you? Try now!" the slaughterer said and pushing away the men pinning down Mani's legs, he loosened and flung away the ropes. Then, with one blow, he severed the head from the body and held it up for the people's inspection.

Mani's eyes had not closed and I thought they looked in the direction of his body. Could there be communication between the dead mind and the dead body? We almost jumped out of our skins when Mani's body stood up and tottered, shakily, towards the slaughterer. The children screamed and ran to their mothers. The burly man, still holding the head, took a few steps backwards.

"Close his eyes! Close his eyes!" the older men and women shouted but the slaughterer was too dazed to obey even such a simple command.

Then Mani's body turned and trailing blood like splotches of vengeance, hobbled towards the jungle fringe. Midway it steadied itself and now that it was just a body, all the muscles strained and stood out so that we got the impression that Mani, in death, grew in stature. The body circled - the children screamed again - and came towards us. The raw flesh at the neck looked like an eye in the severed throat and Mani cried blood as he took off into a last, spasmodic gallop around us.

"Close the eyes! Close the eyes!"

Some elderly man seized the head and massaged the eye-lids shut. Almost immediately Mani's body whirled, leapt and fell to the ground beside the slaughtering block. The man who was still holding the basin got out of the way, spilling globs of Mani's blood on his shorts and knees.

That was many, many years ago. The slaughter still continued every Deepavali eve but I didn't go near the shed. On that particular night when I watched my father's drunken form, I bristled with a vague restlessness. There come to my mind other incidents and episodes which had nothing to do with goats or their slaughter.

I am reminded of another shed, this time the smoke-house of the estate. And another man, Muniandy. Andy, for short, also for the dirty brown shorts he wore. He wore nothing else. His bare body sprouted greying hair on the chest and in the small of his back. There hung about him a perpetual burnt rubber smell and he was darker than the other workers because of being 'smoked' in his work place.

When I began to notice him, he was already in his early fifties. He was remarkable for the way he made himself inconspicuous. If he spent a long time in the smoke-house, you could hardly separate him from the smoked rubber sheets. I suspected that he often lay on the piled sheets not only for the springiness of a mattress but also for the criss-crossed lines he got on his back. Walking behind him, you imagined a smoked rubber sheet was going to some rendezvous in the dark.

Though he occupied a house not far from my own in the same row, I never knew when he came home or if he did at all. Something must be said about the way my mind worked at that time. It couldn't shut itself off to subjects and areas; it could only focus itself on something of its own choice. This shut-and-open habit carried my response to life, spasmodically. This went on until I took over conscious control when I was older.

Perhaps my mind fixed itself on Andy for no reason at all but when it did he became the most absorbing subject. So I became a follower of his movements, a sort of secret or private eye and began to work out what he was doing at all hours of the day. But the man could be elusive. Even when I kept the strictest watch, he escaped the net of my vigilance and would be in the house when I thought he was at the smoke-house.

From discreet inquiries, I came to know a little of his past. Like my father, he had come to Malaya with only a wife. For some mysterious reason the wife - a traditional Hindu woman if there was one - withdrew completely into herself and died only a few years after her arrival in the country. For a time it looked as if Andy would follow in her footsteps but recovered sufficiently to volunteer to take charge of the smoke-house. From then on this dark shed next to the estate factory became his entire world.

What went through his head? So many ideals and desires clamoured in mine, I wondered how he could live through an enforced suspension of all ambition. The smoke-house rose like a squat stake to which he allowed himself to be tethered. Had his mind become clouded by all that smoke inside the shed?

There were occasions when I went to the estate factory and helped my mother to flatten the thick, coagulated latex into lined, thin sheets. To escape the stink the chemicals and the rubber raised in the factory, I walked up to the smoke-house and stood about for a while looking at the rubber saplings that would, in a few years, produce latex. Usually Andy would be inside the shed but there were times when I caught him seated on a rough, wooden bench outside. We never talked but some communication was made when our wandering eyes crossed paths and we looked into each other briefly.

At such moments I became aware that he wasn't all that empty inside. Andy as a person was lost to my sight. He was replaced by a vague, dark shape - sometimes a lion, at other times a dragon or a muted sea or all three together - which I had no power to understand. I turned away quickly, dissatisfied with myself for at my post-adolescent stage I was being looked up to as a sage by the estate.

There were other times when he looked beyond me and into a vastness that made me feel diminished. Then I was no more than a speck of dust in that infinite conception that was his world. Was I making up thoughts for myself, having read H.G. Wells and Jules Verne and their preoccupations with space? There appeared before me, when I gazed at his sightless eyes, a billowing yellow fog behind which teemed incomprehensible shapes and bright gleams of an unknowable universe.

Did he exist only for these and for the sprawling universes *The Ramayana* and *The Mahabharata* created? (At that time I didn't pay much attention to the estate story-teller who narrated portions of these epics; they have come to figure more importantly in my thoughts only now.) I saw Andy then, a passenger in one of those time or futuristic machines, returning to his planet where eyes were not necessary and seeing was done with the whole being from some centre within oneself.

His fleeting, ghost-like existence certainly pointed to this invisible centre. I sometimes wondered if he was in occult, secret communication with his dead wife. (Superstition was so

The Ramayana - Indian classic.
The Mahabharata - Indian classic.

rife on the estate that such a view wouldn't have been unorthodox.) He entered his house, the door opened swiftly by eager, waiting hands. The door then closed on a silent, intimate relationship for the duration of Andy's stay within. He seemed to need no one's company or reassurance. The cooking and the eating were conducted silently, the spirit of his wife all the time beside him. We never heard him grumble, mutter or talk to himself - signs that would have shown he needed and understood the language of our world.

And then moving, waif-like, he was at the smoke-house. He was to be found there at all hours of the day except for the one time he went into town. That happened on pay day, when he wore a white *vesti* and shirt to receive his salary and then go off to buy the month's provisions. When he returned from town, he smelled faintly of toddy. On his shoulders he carried his hemp bag containing his rations for the month. His vesti was a little crumpled at the knees as if caused by his kneeling at the temple beside the road leading to the town.

Mostly, he dissolved into the smoke and shadows of the smoke-house. Soon I began to associate that shed with his presence. If it was a bright afternoon, he was the sunlight that lay spangled on the rubber-tree logs and the grass. He was the dark grey shades on the smoke-house walls on cloudy, rainy days. On festival days such as Deepavali, he was the colourless solitude that fell on the silent smoke-house.

Andy, the smoke-house man and the smoke-house became inseparable. One gave the other life and the other robbed one of life. Wood turned into flesh; flesh turned into wood. And the two went up in smoke. Andy led an invisible, separate existence in the smoke-house. His life was consumed by the coconut-husk and rubber-tree log fire that produced the smoke. The years became ashes and the man rose out of the ashes as the bony remains of an incomplete cremation.

---

vesti - Cloth worn from waist downwards by Indian men.

A younger man was needed for the job and retirement was thrust upon Andy. He had to vacate his house - not that he seemed to have lived in it - and the bonus and his savings were so meagre that he couldn't rent a place in town. He stayed for a while with his neighbour but the wife had such a virulent tongue that Andy was forced to take to the streets of the town.

There we saw him wearing his white vesti - later this garment turned into an unapproachable and dirty black - and lying on the cement walks fronting the shops. Andy soon stank so much that the Chinese shopkeepers had to kick him so as to be rid of him. I witnessed one such kicking and saw Andy receiving the blows in his mute, unprotesting way. He shuffled away to another refuge. The last I heard of him was of his body being found beside the large furnace where the town's rubbish was burned.

What I registered at that time was the indignity of Andy's and my father's deaths. Though I never noticed my father and Andy talking with each other or going out anywhere together, Andy's departure from the estate further deteriorated my father's condition. He fell more frequently into his depressed moods. He talked less and whatever he said hardly made sense. Andy's death worsened his depressions; they became prolonged. One morning he coughed up blood and the verandah was tarnished by those thin spatters of fatigue. Within hours he was dead. During the final spasms, he kept his eyes closed on a world in which he had found no home.

Andy's and my father's deaths strengthened my resolution to leave the estate but escape came only years later. There was school to be finished and a profession found. These were the years of loneliness which schoolwork wasn't enough to banish. I became a scavenger and a parasite: I fed my mind with visions culled from my reading. I read voraciously, defying the noise and the poverty of my surroundings. Sometimes my mother sat in the doorway, watching me, and there was that look in her eyes that said I too would be lost to her.

CHAPTER TWO

ALL this recollection seems like a futile exercise but which stirs certain feelings and recesses of thought that must have lain dormant within me. What I recognize now is that at that time in my life, I was a kind of voyeur, a looker-into other peoples' lives in order to reinforce my own need to escape. I seemed to view time as if it was a gravel road leading out of the estate and into the towns and, progress. But childhood, as they say, experiences time in an immeasurable way. Perhaps there wasn't any childhood in me to be experienced. My family made many demands on my time even before I reached adolescence so that, in my thinking, it, time, became an accountable and precious commodity. But something happened one day that collided against this notion of time.

It was late afternoon, just after I had returned from school. There was hardly anything to eat in the house. Hugging my barely-filled belly, I went into a doze on the wooden trestle in the smaller room I shared with my brothers. My brothers and sisters must have sensed my irritation for they left me alone. The doze had deepened into sleep when I was shaken awake by my mother. Her haggard face hung above my dazed eyes. She put a folded paper bag into my hands and sent me out to buy, on credit, rice, dhall, sugar, oil, milk and salt from the sundry shop in the small town.

Trudging along the laterite road - my father had taken the bicycle for his drinking session - I felt an otherness accompanying me. Perhaps it was the heat, my half-alive mind or even the stretch of road that put me into a glazed state.

That bit of winding, red-gravelled stretch always had a strange effect on my senses. All along the road there stood skeletal, frugally leafed trees. Their brown, speckled trunks could sometimes, if the light was not sharp and clear, be mistaken for stiff boa-constrictors planted into the ground. The thin, springy flowers reeked with a death-filled odour.

All that I had known seemed suddenly to be dying. The air took on a weightiness, a solidity difficult to associate with its usual, breezy thinness. The irritation of that young boy at being sent to seek credit to survive, disappeared. Survival didn't matter any more.

My sweat-stained shirt and the folded paper bag were inconsequential details. They belonged to personal history. One was smell, the other just grained matter. The otherness gained dominance. The trees were no more boa-constrictors nor the flowers spines of odour. They lined the laterite road well within a pattern of their own making. The space between them reflected a light that only the first morning on earth could have radiated.

There was no time; there was no place. There came a muffled booming sound from beneath my feet. Startled, I let the paper bag fall. But it would not fall with the speed with which gravity pulled down objects. The paper bag sailed down the breezeless air. The barks of the trees rustled like silk, the dusky, speckled layers sliding over each other. They flaked and then floated to the ground, parchments inscribed with an indecipherable code.

The sound, the boom, scaled and let scatter, layer after layer, a radiance the ordinary eye could not look upon. The laterite road thinned into a pencil line, then spread out as a red beam and hung like a canvas, attached to the trees. A flower detached itself from the stalk and, following mesmerizingly the arc of the boom, traced a fateless journey downwards.

I fled from that pure sound which interlaced road, tree, flower and sky into an unimpressed and unmarked fluidity.

At the shop, I wasn't the meek estate boy but an aggressive individual out to make a mark in the world. That ambition continued to support me until the present. I've been, until a few months ago, a successful businessman with my own firm. But now I'm filled with a terrifying emptiness. Everything has come to a stand-still. It is as if I can't find the strength to go on. In fact, the opposite is happening: my mind keeps going back to the past. And I see, like a helpless witness, a terrible thing that happened during my first posting, and the last one.

I was posted to a place in the north of the country, a few miles into the interior from a seaside town. The first few days - I had come earlier just to acquaint myself with the place - I stayed in a dark and dank hotel room in the town. It wasn't really a hotel, just a shop blocked off into rooms. My room, at the back, wasn't far from the bucket latrine. A musty odour crept into the dimly-lit room. But in the evenings this presence was displaced by another. It wasn't a smell at all.

I would sit on the hard bed and listen with all my being. After a time I heard a quiet but clamorous clawing behind the wall. The wall was plastered with the covers of popular Chinese movie magazines - I thought - to hide the cracks and holes in the planks. I peeled off a few and found that the timber had been recently planed and fitted in. The possibility of a termite invasion was thus ruled out. But the subdued noise of a million claws at work on the solid foundations of the hotel - and even beyond - persisted.

My presence in the room suddenly seemed precarious. I decided to investigate the source of this danger. Hastily putting on my clothes, I stepped out of the room and looked down the passage. I needn't have been so cautious for I found myself to be the only occupant, at that hour, of the building. The noise became even more clamorous as I reached the front door and was confronted by an empty road.

Affected by the solitude - I had remained, perversely, in my room most of the time - I saw the emptiness as a vastness that couldn't be crossed. But the sound, like the keening of ancient sirens, lured me on. Looking beyond the road I saw, for the first time, the broken down embankment of the sea. The boulders that had formed the wall now lay on their sides, slabs eroded and darkened by history. There still stood a monumental slab, leaning skywards. I made for its half-reclined safety.

Just before I reached it, the crackling and keening rose to such a pitch that I thought the lone, standing portion of the wall was going to plunge into the sea. Instead, there came an abrupt silence. The waves splashed against the shore as softly as memory laps against the consciousness, awakening vague fears. I crept up the inclining wall and stood for a while before peering over the broken head.

While I had been busy coming to terms with my curiosity, the sun had dipped. The world I had been trying to sight removed itself from my knowledge through a few layers, covered as it was now with a sudden darkness. In that dimmed setting the slanting slab jutted over like a ledge into another plane.

Beyond the wall I sensed, as I stood in its shadows, lay another reality. The silence was disrupted by a faint but audible clinking and clanking, it seemed, of tiny swords. The sound transported me to the time of the crusades when soldiers had crossed swords in the name of religion and chivalry. I feared that if I looked over the wall I would witness awesome deeds and unmatchable heroism.

The thought drew me up the inclined stone, worn away into a primeval shape by the sun and the sea. When I was almost at the top, I was struck by a sudden wave of protest in a language I didn't even know existed. The metallic clashes rose into a pitched fury, whipped up by that clangorous, resentful complex of voices. Sitting crouched on that stone ledge, I peered into the semi-darkness. Almost at once I was confronted by milling eyes, legs and bodies.

The dark bodies clambered over each other until the mass took on the shape of a monster. It slithered and heaved as if it would reach out to the rock on which I perched. I withdrew a little but didn't abandon my place on that broken-down wall. My feet found holes lower down and wedged themselves in. All the while I didn't take my eyes off that growing monster.

It too couldn't leave me out of its sight. The strange thing was that those massed legs and bodies scrambled, stood and adjusted themselves so as to form a huge eye. This eye glittered there in the dark for a while, dissolved, disappeared and then suddenly was there again, staring at me. From within this large eye there shone like phospherescent specks, little irises. To this day I can't decide from where that eye, with its numerous stares, came. Perhaps a horde of besieging, keening crabs from some dark swamp formed this collective eye. Suddenly as the sound and the eye had appeared, they disappeared.

Though I didn't notice it at that time, the external siege of destruction turned inwards and resided within me as a quiet force, dislodging, scattering and dispersing, over the years, whatever centre I possessed. 'The centre is all,' someone I knew years later, used to say. He even wrote a whole book on the subject and presented it to me. 'You'll read it one day,' he told me mysteriously and as mysteriously vanished from my life. The book is somewhere in this room - I've never discarded anything I collected - and one of these days I'll dig it out and, as he predicted, read it.

At last all the personnel - clerks, officers, administrators - assembled on that land, specially marked off, which came to be called the settlement. It was a distance off from the town and faced the interior, which was all jungle. Why did I like being nearer the land than the sea? The sea, on recollection, seems to have been there in my blood, a phase in a forgotten evolution: that part of a process when the human spirit was lost in all the seas and the oceans and only yearned for land, for a home. Was that the shiftlessness and the desire I had seen in my father's eyes before he died?

The work on the settlement was finished by late afternoon and we were free for the rest of the day. The other staff usually went fishing, either in the streams or in the sea, or to the town to socialize. I stayed mostly at home as did Lee Shin, my neighbour, but for different reasons. The more I observed Lee Shin the more I felt I was part of a left-over dream. The memories of my father must have shaped, unconsciously, my relationship with Lee Shin and my existence on the settlement. I felt my stay there was a kind of training for the real life I would lead later on. I was prepared to go through privations and isolation for the sake of a better future.

The mornings and evenings were the best parts of the day for us. Even though we led separate lives, we seemed to be joined together by some deep-seated desire for a home. In those days when he kept the hall windows open, I saw the bright aura of the fluorescent bulb presiding over his breakfast. He had some book he read while he ate and he would glance in the direction of my house. We were both book-bound and table-bound and took great pleasure in these activities.

As the light of the appearing sun eclipsed our electric lights, we witnessed, as if they were our private possessions, the hills and the jungle come into existence. I don't know about Lee Shin but something like nostalgia awakened within me. The source of this feeling still escaped me though the fragility of the scene didn't. The light showed me first my hands, cup, saucer, bread and furniture as if these objects bore no significance and had to be quickly revealed. Then, as I lifted my head and looked out, I saw, faintly, the early colours of a perpetual creation. They were pale, thin signs of the tones to merge when the white shroud covering them, lifted.

As the sun rose higher somewhere behind the hills, the paper-flat colours too mounted into slopes and gradients and tall, furzy trees; mounted into birds that took to the sky; mounted into leaves that opened to the thick green that flooded them. The earth where the contractors had cut into to bank our houses, glistened with a brown rawness. Tree trunks stood out, quietly displaying their intricate and runnelled barks, black lines cutting out tiny grey or dark blocks. Then the grass came up at us, each blade chiselled into green curves that would wilt and flatten out as the day advanced.

Some kind of recognition passed between us as we got our work materials together and prepared to walk the short distance to the cardboard erection of office buildings. (The morning sunlight splashing on the unpainted walls, constructed out of hollow, grey bricks, covered them with a transparent flimsiness.) Perhaps we recognized that as we left our houses behind us for the working day, we also left behind some secret part of ourselves. I recall we only nodded to one another during the early days of our acquaintance.

The days, filled with routine, threatened to dissipate our energies and we had to cling to whatever dreams possessed us in order to revitalize ourselves constantly. My contact with the rest of the personnel was minimal: in the coffeeshops or at the rest house. Though there was a mess in the settlement, most of us preferred to eat out in the town. I ate my meals hurriedly so that I could be back at the house before it got pitch dark.

This happened around the hour when the morning reversed itself. As the sun went down, the sky glowed with a red rawness, not always, but often enough to touch me with the mystery of a universe putting itself away. All petty prejudices, jealousies, resentment and suspicion fell away. There was no 'me' left. The fading light gradually erased from my consciousness the familiarity of my body. The mind became space that slowly diminished with the disappearing light. And when there was only darkness the mind became comfortably blank.

I must have sat there, in the verandah, not seeing for there was nothing to see. Then a clatter came from my neighbour's house. Lee Shin was preparing himself for the night's vigil; he invariably filled the hours before sleep with, what appeared to me, strange activities.

While I had immersed myself in withdrawal, he had crossed the dusk into his other world. Sitting in the darkness, I watched that world take shape on the slope above me. It was like spying but Lee Shin gave me no other choice. The darkness concealed me and gave me the confidence to observe him fully. Perhaps, like my father, he knew he was being watched but couldn't be bothered with the intrusion.

Lee Shin was like that. He never let on, at least in those early days. He and I went through different routines, physically, though we were within reach of one another. I took my time putting on the light so that I could break down this barrier between us. The night helped. It diffused my thoughts and reserve and allowed me to enter, sympathetically at first, into Lee Shin's preoccupations and activities.

What was he? The question obsessed me for a long time. But as I went on watching I understood only a little of what he was and wanted to be. He became such a focus of attention for me that I kept, in writing, a study of his movements, behaviour and final developments in his life. I'll reproduce it here so as to see if it can throw any light on my present predicament. The language appears stilted and pseudo-scientific but that was what I was at that time. I've tried to keep myself as much as possible out of the account. Sometimes I've written as I followed his behaviour; sometimes I've written in recollection. This record is extensive in the beginning when we hardly talked; it comes to an abrupt end just before he met his death.

CHAPTER THREE

The Lee Shin Study

This study attempts to understand, in detail, Lee Shin's behaviour, thoughts and motivation. While it cannot be exhaustive, it can, nevertheless, be an honest record of what was seen, heard and observed. In this place, after work is done, there is more than enough time for such activities.

Men can be put into two categories: the independent and the dependent. Lee Shin is an independent. The other men here mass together: in the mess, coffeeshops, rest house and the houses of nurses and salesgirls. They clearly belong to the second group. Their code of ethics is based on mutual support. Thus, they support each other's opinions, attitudes, idiosyncracies, actions and the ability to put down those outside their circle.

Lee Shin seems to have come to the settlement with a fierce desire to safe-guard his freedom. From the beginning he has kept to himself as if he mistrusted people. It has been more than a month since Lee Shin came under observation but he has not said a word to the observer. As a neighbour, he is uncommunicative and sits by himself in the verandah, late into the evening. Now and then he whistles a tune which has no resemblance to any that the observer has heard. Sometimes the whistling rises to such a pitch as to sound inhuman. Then he breaks off suddenly.

No sound comes from his house throughout the late afternoon. When the observer wakes up from his nap, the house next door is still quiet and looks uninhabited. The observer who has had lunch in town and is preparing to go out for his tea, wonders what Lee Shin has eaten for the afternoon meal.

When the observer returns from his tea, he finds Lee Shin dressed in white shorts and T-shirt. He is out on the slope of grass beside his house ready to begin his exercises. This is the part of Lee Shin's behaviour that the observer finds strange. He never carries out any of the regular exercises young men pick up. Instead, he creates a slow-paced pantomime with his trunk, hands and legs.

Sometimes his movements are so painfully slow that the observer wonders if Lee Shin has entered some sort of a trance. There he stands, within an invisible centre, his body defying gravity and the backbone's flexibility, arms stretched out in a kind of farewell. Then he bends low and holds himself temptingly between sinking down to rest and rising up to fierce combat. But he does neither. He just remains in that position for a long time. He is rivetted to the earth and sky with an invisible bolt. To the casual onlooker he may be a bronze statue balancing itself between life and death.

Perhaps it was that moment that had attracted the observer's attention to this lonely individual. Lee Shin then lifts himself up as if by the hair. The head goes up, followed by his shoulders, waist and thigh, all in slow motion. He does something with his shoulder blades and they spread out like a cobra's hood poised for attack. He dips his head and brings up his hands so that the fingers curve rigidly, as if they were the snake's fangs. He advances slowly, and the fangs come down viciously on some invisible enemy. Lee Shin straightens, relaxes, and resuming his usual slouch, whistles his way to the verandah and sits down on the steps.

The evening is mildly warm and Lee Shin remains seated there for some time, almost immobile. As the day recedes, he acquires the dimension of a granite statue. His body, carved up by shadow and light, appears to be supported by an emaciated purpose. There is dignity in that posture but little else.

When the observer returns from his evening meal, Lee Shin has already bathed and changed. He is once again seated in the verandah, on a chair, and he has started something new. There is a bright object in his hands; he polishes it with a yellow, velvety cloth. Then Lee Shin puts the shiny object to his lips and the sound it emits confuses the observer for a while and then only amuses him. As Lee Shin launches into a full melody, the observer becomes more and more disoriented. He has never heard a harmonica produce such strange strains. `Yankee Doodle' comes to his mind for that was what was traditionally played on that instrument or it was `My Bonnie Lies Over the Ocean'.

The days now are a torment for the observer for he does not know how to stop Lee Shin from playing the harmonica. On the silent grounds of the settlement, the music from the harmonica booms like some unearthly sound. What restrains the observer, however, is the objective he chose when he undertook this study. Once he interferes, the subject will be robbed of his peculiar habits and personal circumstances. So the observer has to bear his discomfort and adopt the attitude of a detached recorder.

As the days pass, Lee Shin plays furiously but stops now and then to look in the direction of the observer's house. In the company's offices he casts shy but significant glances at the observer. Is some change imminent in Lee Shin?

The past three days the harmonica has been reedy, desultory and cautious. No blaring, pungent thrusts come to provoke; instead, Lee Shin looks more and more towards the observer's house. The attitude of the other personnel is becoming clearer and is, sometimes, distressing. Obviously, they would like to be elsewhere, in some of the brighter towns but the money here is good. Perhaps this recognition makes them quieter but beneath the calm lies a latent viciousness.

All this makes the observer view Lee Shin differently. He is so self-contained nothing seems to touch him. Can the observer be affected by the observed? It is certainly so in this case: Lee Shin's self-sufficient existence gives the observer a strange sense of confidence. Some of the restlessness the observer felt earlier is gone.

Some weekends Lee Shin tramps off into the jungle nearby, haversack on his back and a butterfly net in his hand. Returning in the evening, he sits in the hall and mounts the specimens. The observer sees him bent over the butterflies, the syringe in his fingers sucking out the insides and, later, pumping in the formaldehyde. What is there about the posture that says neither the activity nor the interest will last? Two or three weeks later Lee Shin has shifted his attention elsewhere. He has taken to pressing leaves, flowers and rare plants. Then he is back at the verandah railing, barehanded and listless.

Then one evening he signals to the observer. It is not so much an invitation as a command, the hand waving imperatively. The observer, taken aback, wonders whether to comply or not. But he is curious and crosses the short distance to Lee Shin's house.

The observer mounts the steps and stands beside Lee Shin. The man makes no move to acknowledge or greet him. Lee Shin's gaze is still turned towards the house down the slope as if the observer has not left it. Then, suddenly, he snaps out of his reverie and looks at the observer.

"The harmonica music has brought you here,"Lee Shin says.

"In a way,"I say.

But Lee Shin does not say anything else. I stand there for a while puzzled by his behaviour and then thoughtfully return to my house.

One day the observer returns from dinner later than usual. It is already night and as he parks his motorcycle an eerie sound almost makes him jump. For a moment the observer thinks the darkness itself is the vibrating, shrilling disturbance. Then the two separate: the shrilling and the darkness. The observer reaches the living room and puts on the light. The sudden brightness reveals the world anew to him. It is no more the world of the evening; now there is a subtle crack in the old familiarity. Caused by the darkness or the shrilling? The demented wailing is still out there. The observer knows where it is coming from but will not look up at the house on the slope.

This is not a matter of weakness or courage, only one of exerting the powers of observation. It takes time for the observer to compose himself into a receptive state of mind. He does not like rushing off into matters without thought. A cup of coffee, which he makes on the gas stove, helps. Then the observer opens the hall windows and, placing a book on the table, sits before it preparing to read. He is a bit wary of Lee Shin and does not want to be caught watching him.

But his eyes and attention turn slowly and surely towards the figure, now dimly visible, seated in the verandah. The light from the observer's house catches Lee Shin only in a zigzagged half so that the man is not fully revealed. Because he is holding a tubular instrument to his lips and his cheeks are blown up, he resembles a gargoyle removed from a foreign frieze. There is a kind of half-formed deformity in the way Lee Shin bends down to blow into that instrument. He is raising a weird, defiant strain of sound that almost chills the listener.

On normal, silent nights the observer finds it difficult enough to sleep. He usually closes the doors and windows to the happenings outside. The vents above the windows allow the cold, mountain winds to come in, so there is no fear of stifling or suffering an airless, hot discomfort.

There were nights when, not turning my mind outwards or interesting myself in any person, I lay there in the bed, reading. The light in the room threw, in the beginning at least, unfamiliar shadows on the wall. Then as I got to understand what these shapes represented, I became more comfortable with myself. Then I would read or just lie there thinking how strange it seemed that at the prime of one's youth one was forced to lie supine, trapped in inertia and a kind of death-in-life. But these thoughts soon left me as I began to work out a plan to rid myself of such depression.

No, I'm not slipping back into a personal view. Just providing a contrast, studying myself as somebody else. Not to lose myself within myself but to stand outside and examine all the thoughts and feelings that cause attachment and misery. There is another point as well. Lee Shin's playing on the flute - that is what it is - is certainly connected to time and its many disturbances. Lee Shin is trying, deliberately, to destroy time. My activities did not attempt any such thing. I let time work itself out. It did not always happen. The light helped. After a duration - nothing to do with time here - the sense of the clock was replaced by something else. Maybe the shadows also played a part in all this.

Through all these nights there were only light and shadows. Some nights the light was overshadowed. Some nights the shadows were overlighted. In that room, away from signs of human habitation, the light wrapped you up in a thoughtless warmth; the shadows mummified you in a breathless security. One night the warmth and security disappeared under a wild beating of some live thing outside the room. The wall thudded again and again under the desperate assaults.

The observer scrambled out of the bed, flinging his book into a corner. He took the torchlight from the bedside table but stood, arrested, before the window. The grey, wooden walls had always given him the feeling that nothing could get through them. They had kept out unwanted night intrusions and kept in a familiar cosiness.

The observer listened intently to the shuddering walls and the penetrating squeaks that came with each attack. The air outside swarmed with thick menace. His heart beat louder than the thuds on the wall. Then he controlled himself: the intruder would have swarmed in if he had any intention of doing so by then. The observer waited a while longer, then flung the window open.

The brightness outside surprised the observer. The sky was suffused with a light of its own. Against that translucent sky everything else looked opaque and impenetrable. The trees clustered behind the house on the slope, just as much as the house itself, were meaningless blotches on the landscape. Other, darker objects filled the air. At first, their shrill clamouring did not allow any identification. Then one came, a furry, musky creature and almost crawled into the observer's face. He ducked in time and then raising his head cautiously, he made out the bats now winging away in clumps and then returning to dash against the walls, in frenzy.

Were they on flight to somewhere else? And had lost their way? They continued to swoop and hit against the walls. One detached itself from the irrational formations and came for the observer, whizzing through the open window. It flew so close, screeching, that he was able to study its features for a fleeting moment. The observer found it a compulsion to arrest the creature in flight and examine the reasons for its presence in the neighbourhood that night. But the power of ordinary rationality was useless under these circumstances. He could make no sense of the monkey-like bat's and its companions' actions.

The comparison seemed irrelevant. No, it was not monkey-faced or any faced. Rememberance of Mani, that irrational animal, stirred in the observer. But, instead of the distant expression Mani acquired in his last days, there was in the bat's eyes a piercing, disconcerting stare. It seemed to prick like needles into the vulnerable flesh of the observer. Then a strange thing happened: the bat was trying to communicate with the observer. Its soft throat bulged in nodules of urgent messages; it fluttered at the window sill and then squeaked away. Was the observer seduced into imagining happenings that were not there by the unexpected effulgence in the sky and pleading, sorrowful voices in the air?

Lee Shin's window had not opened and any noise he might have made could not be heard above that plaintive ruckus. What the observer noticed that night was the sudden transformation of the whole scene into a nightmarish landscape. He had always kept away from such exposures by simply jamming his window to and throwing himself into the timeless world of books. But that night realities of a different kind shook at and invaded those premises he held inviolable.

This is what the observer feels now listening to the interminable squeaking and hissing of Lee Shin's flute from across the slope. One night, after his dinner, the observer goes across to Lee Shin's house. It is a ridiculous sight but there it is: the observer standing there on the steps and Lee Shin straining away, unconcerned, at the flute. He may not want to acknowledge the observer's presence but his entire effort at the instrument reveals a total immersion in something the observer cannot, for the time being, put his finger on. He listens and his attention is arrested by the flute's appearance.

The observer has never seen its kind before. It is an amazing, intricately decorated piece of bamboo the like of which certainly cannot come from this country. It is a long, slender tube not so much varnished as some art having

38

preserved its natural veneer, heavily tasselled at one end. Such bamboo instruments, so Lee Shin informed the observer later, if made out of local materials, would only have a fragility and shortness that come from unrootedness and shallow skills. He does not make sense; nor does the Mandarin inscription along the length of the flute.

Lee Shin suddenly stops playing and looks at the observer. He puts the flute carefully on the small, low table beside him. His hair, normally straight and combed rigidly into compliance, is now all dishevelled. There is a haunted look in his eyes from which he detaches himself to stare sceptically at the observer. The observer moves and Lee Shin cringes in his chair as if recoiling from the observer's advance.

CHAPTER FOUR

I broke off there not wanting, for the time being, to continue reading what I had written during those immature years. I am afraid too, of my interference in his dreams and ambitions, which comes later, and in my present state of mind, I simply can't be confronted by that.

What astonishes me is that I didn't notice the similarities between Lee Shin and myself. He was haunted by desperate dreams, consciously, and I came under their forces, subconsciously. How else can I account for my excursions into the country, at that time, in search of some elusive rootedness?

Now I sit in my room - if I recall correctly - as Lee Shin did in that verandah, so long ago, without the will to do anything. There is even an unwillingness to think about the will. What I feel at this moment is that there is no such thing as will. It is only artificially created by man as he does determination, tenacity, ambition and goals so that he can feel secure. More than anything else in those days that I observed Lee Shin, I wanted security.

No one could be held responsible for another man's life or death, I thought at that time. Now I'm not so sure. Something happened to me - or became extended - during that excursion into the country, apparently to study and evaluate the land. But there must have been, inside me, a secret ambition.

Wali Farouk, our guide, took us deep into the country. No one knew how and when he got to the settlement. He did all kinds of jobs, most of the time, jovially but there were days when he turned sullen. (Why didn't I pay attention to the way he treated Lee Shin? He was, I remember, unnecessarily vicious towards him at least on one occasion.)

Chinese New Year had come and gone; Lee Shin didn't return to the family house for the reunion dinner. Though I remember going to an estate conductor's house, some miles away, I only vaguely registered Lee Shin's presence. The doors and windows were opened and closed but the flute remained silent. When the other staff returned from the holidays and prepared for the expedition, Lee Shin didn't join them. He wanted to remain to finish a backlog of paper work.

From Wali Farouk, I realized that the land was different from the one I had seen with my father when we happened to stray beyond the estate boundaries. The rubber plantation and the numerous weeds that grew between the trees were familiar to us. In a way we reduced them to familiarity by praising them, cursing them and, in moments of desperate alienation, by even scarring them with the tapping knife. My mother, while my father lived, went at the trees with a secret vengeance so that the latex spilled outside the cups. At the end of the month she found she was poorer by about twenty dollars; the next morning she attacked them with even greater ferocity.

"You want to cut up something," my father said, learning about her destructive moods, "cut me up. Yes, I brought you to these trees. Made you their slave. Put the wounds on me."

So when he started coughing up blood during his last months, I thought the trees had somehow got to him and were making him pay for the hardship he had caused my mother. Those trees were never out of our thoughts or lives.

It was a familiarity that veiled a depressing history. My parents had not been original discoverers - they had only responded to some colonialist's neat dream of acquisition. They came out to this country and settled in an environment that was already prepared for their security and cultural continuity.

The temple and the toddy shop were landmarks of this tradition. My father's red and bleary eyes revealed the discontent that overpowered him at the end of his life. Why had he given up? Didn't the temple and the toddy shop satisfy him? The first Englishman who thought of tall, swaying trees that produced the toddy and temple tucked away in a remote corner on the estate, must have seen pastoral existence without cynicism. My father's puffy cheeks and premature grey hair traced the history of cynicism which soured the very centre of that tropical paradise: nira, the manna from the skies and the god's chariot stored away in a dusty, dilapidated nook of the temple!

The toddy shop was always crowded, the precious, milky liquid drained by thirsty and oblivion-seeking throats even as the climber descended with foaming pots. Quarrels flared up over trifling trespasses: a goat had come to the cooking place and sucked dry the rice-water a tapper carried with him to work; a young man had eyed, lasciviously, a girl who had just come out from behind the coconut-leaf wall of puberty.

The women gathered behind the terrace, double-roomed houses, at the water tap and struggled with each other to have their pails and buckets filled. The water sparkled in their containers - foreign stars not shining for them - while they wrestled in words with one another. During the lulls, that could be called peace, they chatted and complained about their children's illnesses. Sometimes this talk didn't give relief either to the mother or the sufferer. Then it was that in the evenings the mother went to the temple and made a vow to the deity in residence that she would offer a special puja or that the child would carry a *kavadi* if the girl or boy was cured. Sometimes the girl recovered and the parents fulfilled the vow extravagantly. Sometimes the mother took the girl to the district hospital where she slept on the floor while the child was attended to in a cot, and then an air of slight towards the gods hung over the house.

---

kavadi - Small structure carried by devotees on Thaipusam day.

An energy, not their own, shuffled and manipulated them through life. The source was external, a national crisis or words radiating from the white administrator. They didn't explore; they supported and obeyed. Little plots of land sprang up for them from the white man's words. They were to lay out rows of vegetable patches - continuing the ruler's nature culture - and so become self-sufficient in food. A percentage of the yield was taken in lieu of the rent. "During the Japanese Occupation those plots of land kept us from starving," they said proudly and became lackadaisical about tending those very life-giving plots. "Too much to tap rubber trees in the mornings and dig the land in the afternoons," they said. So the land lapsed into idleness except for those owned by labourers who needed an extra income. These tenants planted banana, tapioca, sugar-cane and groundnuts and sold them to the Chinese man who came in his lorry and paid them prices that was not worth their sweat.

The men sometimes came down with diseases of the throat or lung. They coughed and spluttered for months and then, one morning, fell silent. Occasionally a woman carried her goitre as if it was a pouch of gold too precious to be left anywhere except at her neck. Women who sprayed chemicals to rid the rubber trees of their parasites, one or two of these women saw the afternoon glare advancing upon them too menacingly and so drank the weed-killer, breaking immediately the eternity of repetition.

The despair, unexplored, hung like a blood-tinged sky over them. What did my father see during his last days? And the children, my brothers and sisters, they had that glaze in their eyes that shone like the marble surface of exclusion. There was no light or colour or reflection. Nothing moved or formed itself behind those unseeing eyes.

Once in a while the older boys returned from fishing in a shallow river not just with scaly fishes but also with water-smoothed, odd shaped stones. They laid out their finds before the dull eyes of their elders and waited for magic-filled stories. But there were no torrents of words or sounds of surprise, only barren sighs and a turning away of heads.

That was the familiar landscape; the land beyond was hardly explored. Because this familiar environment filled them with so much suffering and futility, the land beyond this familiar pain was avoided as some territory of even greater pain.

So when Wali Farouk set himself up in imperious leadership, I kept my distance from him. I wasn't going to be led by the nose into seeing what he saw of the land. My father's disillusionment must have taken hold of me for I began to distrust Wali Farouk's words and comments. My father's words kept recurring in my mind as I trudged with the others: "We must leave the estate. We must go to the real land." That was what he said the many times we stood at the estate border and looked at the sprawling, hilly land beyond. "Must get to the centre," he said, "all by ourselves."

He meant, I think, not in the physical way. And Wali Farouk was giving too much attention to physical survival and respect for the ground beneath our feet. If you fell into another man's dream - your father's or a stranger's - you became displaced when you stopped dreaming. That wasn't going to happen to me. The little of the land I had seen until then bore the imprints of transferred history and culture. I wanted to see the land for what it was, unadulterated by any man's visions or fantasies.

Something happened that confirmed my views. One night, out of the five we stayed in the jungle, there was a faint moon up. The light had to filter through thick, intertwined branches and creepers. It was easy to mistake shadows for some living creature - a tiger, elephant or deer. Most of us discarded caution and treated anything dark as a shadow. Wali Farouk, on this particular night, sat up suddenly and listened, then crept forward for a closer investigation. How had those masses of black and grey come to be there so noiselessly? Their heaviness had, in the presence of intruders, changed into large wings of sensitivity. Wali Farouk crept back and hustled us silently out of the camp. No sooner had we gone a short distance from our tents then there came a light, thundering sound. Wali Farouk pushed us into safety from where we watched the horde we had mistaken for shadows, rumble through the camp. The strong tent cords came down or snapped like flimsy thread. Pegs came uprooted, pots were crushed underfoot like bottle caps. But the damage wasn't thorough; it was only a warning from the elephants to the trespassers.

I didn't, after that event, wander far from the camp and even if I did, my sense of direction always brought me back. On one occasion, having passed through the boundary lines I had marked out mentally, I found myself not in the forest but beyond in some intangible axis of activity. The silence was an intensity; the stillness was absolute immobility. But that combination of intensity and immobility seemed to produce a movement that didn't belong to this world.

I was rooted to a spot in the clearing over which trees arched and parasitic plants spanned. Their concrete, overhead entanglement gave way to a kind of pulse set deep within. Within what, at that moment, I couldn't make out. In fact, moments were of no account. I stood there arrested, wondering at the dislodging within my body and mind. If it was possible to become bodiless and mindless, I was that free-floating energy.

What was it that I had seen in my experience of the real land? I believed in those days that a man became native to the country only if he could identify with its landscape. What I saw in the jungle didn't invite any relationship; in fact, it only repulsed and rejected. The clearing where I had stood with its tall trees and creepers and undergrowth was too much itself. There had been no penetration. It had held me in a wide net, away from the axis of its inner meaning.

My father's dying days returned to me. There was always a black dream in his eyes; the film of drunkenness on them played up the murky depths. With all that drink in him, he was bloated up in the stomach. At one time he must have been a strong man for the shoulders still retained a roundedness. The slackened skin cried out against the emptiness within. My father had dreamed too much and achieved too little. This showed in the disproportion he carried about with him: this distended belly and the rarely used, thin limbs. There was little of him, when he died, to be buried or cremated. My mother had insisted on cremation as if the sight of the ashes would help her to expunge the memory of her life with him.

When I returned from that excursion, I began to see Lee Shin through new eyes. I didn't continue with *The Lee Shin Study*. Such an exercise had served its purpose. It only encouraged a passivity in me, a form of understanding that also encouraged passivity in others. During my absence, Lee Shin had taken another step into self-delusion. He had filled his room with furniture imported from China or Taiwan, which was revealing: it bore no relationship to the dull waking up every morning and taking into your consciousness the unyielding landscape behind the houses. Nor did it thaw the chill in your heart as you walked to the office buildings and, into work. Those tiny, beaded shoes he so repeatedly and fondly talked about had other memories for me.

My father and I used to go to town about once a month, he to satisfy a strange habit and I for a haircut. The barber shop was a crowded establishment and though I quickly got into the barber's chair, my father wasn't there to see his son shorn. He disappeared saying something about coming back soon. He didn't go far for I heard him in conversation with a man in one of the labyrinthine rooms. Then there was a gurgling sound and a sweet, sickly smell banished the bay rum pungency that hung over the barber's chair. I was soon finished and the barber himself took me to the middle section of the long shophouse, which also turned out to be a large kitchen for petty hawkers. The hawkers' handcarts and shoulder baskets were being loaded with all kinds, for me, at that time in life, delicacies. There were fried beehoon, koay teow, chi chong fun, maize cakes and an assortment of Chinese tit-bits which were eaten with chillie or kachang sauce.

These last, the tit-bits, were prepared under the supervision of a calm, patient Chinese woman. She was more than a woman, a grand dame, whose face bore, it appeared to me, the clear lines of royal descent. The young girls and the women who worked under her treated her with obsequious relish, listening to and carrying out her every order as if she was no less than the Dowager Empress.

When this personage saw me, she averted her face and nodded to one of the girls and, miraculously, there appeared before me a plate of those luscious cakes that were being loaded into the baskets. While I ate and waited for my father, I puzzled myself with a single question: why didn't this miracle-worker move about? Was it part of her powers and influence that she didn't have to? She looked as if she hated the very idea of movement. But whatever was prepared under her instructions tasted as if they came from her own toil and talent.

The sound of water drawn through a reed stopped and a heavy, pleasant silence followed. Then some planks creaked and my father emerged from a hidden recess but by that time I had discovered the reason for the dowager's immobility.

It all began with her head, on which the hair was drawn tight as scalp and gathered into a knot at the nape. This glossy skull-cap of hair - even my mother who used gingelly oil couldn't match her neatness and shine - was skewered into place with a stone-studded golden pin. Under this coiffure, her head barely moved and her body, shrunken inside, was supported in an upright majesty by an elaborately woven mandarin coat or jacket. Even the mere sight of it made me think of weight. As my eyes travelled downwards, I saw the final cause for her stationary command. On her feet were a pair of the tiniest but most beautiful shoes I had ever seen. They were so entrancing, I wondered why she wore them at all.

From those dimunitive footwear came her power and beauty but also her helplessness. On another visit I found her not seated on her high chair of authority but being helped by two young women, her hair undone, her face desperately restraining pain, to the tin-shed at the back where tenants relieved and cleaned themselves. Even without her shoes and feet bound only in mummy-rounds of cloth, she wobbled and shook like false foundation loosening for a fall. There was a smell of rotten flesh and sweat-soaked powder in the air.

The sight of Lee Shin's room and those shoes brought these memories and once again I found myself rsisting the siren call of the past. No, I wasn't going to be trapped by nostalgia or sentimentality. He could call it whatever he wanted, even purity, but I wouldn't let him bask in all that sweet swathes of decay around the mind. The more I listened to him the more I felt compelled to give up the observer's position and detachment.

While Lee Shin talked about antiques in a refined way and withdrew, disgustedly, from anything that smacked of the ordinary, he himself wasn't, to look at, someone extraordinary. He had fine, even teeth and they glistened as if with an unquenchable hunger for food, talk and a slice of life, but he was also the most frugal of men. His obsession with antiques, banners, scrolls and tiny shoes was his way of spreading the red cloth of splendour under his meagre meals. Always he carried with him the severe marks of economy. He wore the same trousers for weeks although he washed it every four days or so. His shirts were limp and the collars frayed. His shoes bore the bulge of his toes and the heels were planed down to a tilt by his swaddling walk.

His taste in women was deplorable. When he pointed to a conclave of photographs in the museum that was his room, I had difficulty in keeping down my disgust. Those photographs - all of his fiancee, Mei - revealed a woman seated, a woman standing and a woman thrusting her face at the camera. Were these poses the culmination of womanhood for Lee Shin? In the frame where she stood, she was dressed in a long, white gown that reached her ankles. She held a bunch of pink roses and seemed to rise into an empty sky just as the artificial column did into the studio backdrop. Seated, her pink skirt - taking up the colour of the flowers - was spread around her, almost hiding the plastic chair, and gave her an inflated, ethereal presence. The profile that strained to come out of the frame, pouted at the lips and the cheeks once again flowed with a faint pink. Perhaps the light in the room picked out the pinkness in every snapshot or the camera man, under Lee Shin's instructions, had woven in the pink aura into every frame of his work. Whatever the cause, I was struck by the unreality of the feminity these pictures wanted to impress upon the viewer.

A new mood took hold of us, that is, those of us who had graduated from the university in the sixties: a backlash to the freedom we celebrated. When the British left the country we put aside the revelling and the drifting; we stored away the sense of glory we had felt at having the land returned to us. We came out of the illusions of ownership, banished the yearning and nostalgia for a heaven on earth and, instead, over the years, built up our self-worth and our abilities.

This mood indirectly influenced and developed a different kind of interest in women. Needing some kind of expression for our new attitude, we turned towards them in search of support. We felt we were masters of the streets, stars in the coffeeshops, builders of hotel lobbies and studs on the beaches. We eyed women as if we had inherited proprietory rights over them.

There was pride in being crude, a sense of triumph in openly confronting them. What did it matter if some of them turned away in disgust? Perhaps we were in quest of our ideal woman when we met the Spotted Lady. Her real name was May and she came out of our dreams to us on a beach one day, at dusk. The Spotted Lady squatted between two mounds of sand, urinating. There was no time to turn away and we saw the whiteness of her buttocks shine at us, in the approaching darkness, with a sensuous invitation. She came towards us, soon afterwards, pulling up the bikini bottom, saying, "Never see woman make water before?"

She became for us, when we knew her intimately, the embodiment of our vague desires and ambitions. We lost our sense of place and time and began to see ourselves differently. We followed her, now changed into a clinging dress in her hotel room, to the seaside stalls. We were suddenly filled with a strange hunger. Lim, my closest varsity mate, had fallen in step with her but she stopped now and then to adjust her short, tight dress or bend down to empty her shoes of sand and as she did so, we brushed against her warm flesh without embarrassment or shyness.

Then we were at the stalls. We had never, transformed as we were, seen such stalls before in our lives. They were all brightly lighted and the smell of food was everywhere. Bowls steamed and plates were heaped high; chopsticks struck into the air and banished censure; spoons and forks gleamed and staved off inhibitions. A surge of people came up and pushed us to the last table in front of a well-stocked stall. We sat down on the stools and hung on to our places as if what we were going to eat was the last supper.

Perhaps it was. Food had never looked so inviting, so seductive. *Sotong* strips hung from hooks, gleaming like newly-skinned fruit bats. *Siput* and mussels were heaped into bowls, the red of the flesh showing through the steam. In glass cases, streaming from the shelves came golden strands of mee; translucent beehoon and glossy, thick koay teow; the cooks handled them as if they were delicate skeins of precious,

---

sotong - Squid.
siput - Sea snails.

molten gold. They shuffled, rolled and pinched the mee into the bowls and ladled hot curries over them. Fish balls crowned the spicy mound and onion stalks, sliced, were scattered around them.

"Start with the siput," the Spotted Lady said.

The drinks man came and beer was ordered and poured into glasses, the yellow liquid foaming and frothing. We gulped the beer down while waiting for the shell-fish to arrive and felt a velvety freshness swirl in our throats and wash away all our squeamishness and timidity. And when the siput came we cracked them open, spilling juice and blood on the table, and gobbled down dark-tinged, red flesh with feverish gluttony. The Spotted Lady nudged the men on either side of her, licking the shells and sucking the flesh out with her lips in a swift, almost horrifying movement. Nevertheless we laughed and followed her example, our skins prickling and sweating. We had revived and the feasting went on until a bloated sense of well-being overcame us.

The Spotted Lady led the way again - she must have covered this route many times - and we were at her hotel. We followed her up to her room, a little anxious. We needn't have been. We saw and were drawn into, not female ingenuity but feminine capability and desire at work. All those adolescent fantasies and emissions were nothing compared to what she put us through. Her hands, lips and mouth were everywhere so that the parts of our bodies we thought had never existed, came throbbingly alive. She would have two of us at the same time and though our youthful stamina flagged, she wouldn't stop until she had had her fill. At a point in the activities, her face took on a demoniac grin and she went at us with a fury that astonished us. In a few hours we knew our bodies and blood as we had never known them before. Then she lay back, not spent, but feeling regenerated and triumphant.

"That bastard," she said, hoarsely, "he teach me all this. I like though. Ah, that Scotsman. So cold outside, so hot inside."

She had met the Scotsman, she said, an engineer when he was contracted to build a bridge in her hometown in Perak. Used to come to her father's coffeeshop to drink beer. "The bloody Chinese," she said. "Anything white, they go for." So she was made to serve him - a girl who had just turned eighteen. Sometimes she sat with him and then he drank more beer and said her hair was just like he had imagined Asian lasses would have had. "Not the tattered dog's breakfast Scottish women sprouted," he had said.

Then he took her to show her the bridge and later the bungalow where he lived. That was where it had all started. He still ordered beer, crates this time, from her father's shop but chose to drink them in the bungalow and she had been ordered to wait on him.

"Now this," the Spotted Lady said. "He think I don't know. Send me back home for holiday. How to go back to family, ah? The small town call me whore, bitch even. These words. Always shouting these words. Whore! Whore! Bitch! Bitch! Give me some more. That what he wanted. He tired now. Can't give me what I want."

She was, like us, done with that kind of seduction and enchantment. She would free herself, and others, in order to be what each wanted to be. Lim was awakened again and she said, "Nothing of shyness. Where shame? We all want." And made of him, before our eyes, an energetic, sparkling young man again. He struggled against her, wanting and not wanting, trying to avoid the final dredging up she would demand of him. Her fingers touched spots on his body so that he became frenzied but also controlled and she swallowed him and he was swallowed by that musky whiteness we had glimpsed on the beach, in the dusk. Night followed night until we began to hunger for those voluptuous moments of tension and release always triggered off by a new inventiveness, an unexpected ingenuity.

The Spotted Lady - a bout of smallpox left her face pockmarked - remained with us in spirit. She helped us find the practical expression of our new attitude to life. She put us in contact with ourselves, renewed our vitality. Whenever our energies flagged we returned to May. That was her name. She said, "You know May as the month of May. Just ripe and full of juice." If she wasn't there, she found numerous understudies and trained them to carry out her duties. She was no mermaid or siren - these came from the old, exhausted imagination - but someone who vibrated with the desire to live intensely in this world. She taught us to accept women for what they were, not as idealized pink dolls, bloodless and desireless.

While I had spent my time thinking about May, the Spotted Lady, Lee Shin had withdrawn deeper into his isolation. I saw and heard him less. We hardly met at our working place; he seemed to have effaced himself into a deep silence and invisibility. That flute was silent and most nights the house was shuttered and dark.

The tall drills and derricks stood like bony fingers stabbing into the sky beyond the workshops, laboratories and office buildings. Perhaps the silence from the house up on the hill had got to me. My sight and hearing began to be affected. On some nights I heard strange sounds - somewhat like the thuds the bats had made on my wall - from Lee Shin's house. I saw wild, fleeing shapes tearing across his compound.

One morning, when he was reported missing from work, I went up to his house and knocked on the door. At first I heard nothing. Then there was a scraping of chairs and tables, as if Lee Shin was putting up a barricade against the door.

"It's me, Rajan!" I called.

After a long while - as if Lee Shin had used that time to make up his mind - he opened the door.

"You," he said, looking around suspiciously.

He gave me the impression that he had difficulty in recognizing me. I wondered if the furniture that filled his room had released their ghosts and phantoms to haunt him. He didn't look at me as if I was someone real.

"Came to find out why you aren't at work," I said.

"Come to trouble me like him?" he said.

"Who?"

"You know," he said. "That one wearing the strange hat. And insulting me all the time."

He was clearly referring to Wali Farouk, our guide, teacher and non-specialist. The misunderstanding between the two mounted to an unwarranted hostility. Wali Farouk had shown in no uncertain ways that he didn't want Lee Shin on that excursion into the interior. Lee Shin, in his turn, gave a flimsy excuse not to tread in Wali Farouk's shadow. What I didn't understand at that time was Lee Shin's paranoia. Wali Farouk was known for his harmless, practical jokes. That was his way of livening up the dull days on the settlement. He had travelled all over the country and came and fitted himself into the life of the settlement as if he had been there long before us.

"What did he do this time?"

"That man has gone too far," Lee Shin said. "Whispering all kinds of dirty things. Throwing stones on the walls. Dressing up like a woman. Saying I can't touch any woman."

Was Lee Shin speaking from within some illusion? As far as I knew, Wali Farouk was incapable of being obscene. Even if that side of him showed itself, it must have been Lee Shin who aroused the vulgarity in him. There were moments when I wanted to let fly four-letter words in Lee Shin's presence. His ignorance of women and preference for the so-called virtuous life could disgust anyone. Behind all that innocence there lay, I sensed, a deep prurience bred by suppression. That old, perverted process of sublimation was certainly producing hallucinations.

"May be he's right," I told Lee Shin, looking at my watch and noting that there was work waiting for me. "May be you're only imagining all these things."

"You too!" he said and banged the door in my face.

The matter didn't end there. I wish it had. The manager called me into his office later in the morning. He studied me for a while before broaching the subject.

"I notice you spend some time with Lee Shin," he said. "What I mean is the other officers can't get anywhere near him."

I nodded.

"Well," he continued, "something has to be done. Lee Shin is a good worker when his mind is in its place. Unfortunately, his mind isn't here at all. It would be a pity to dismiss him. May be a change of scene and activities might be good for him. Just do the trick to make him normal. Do you think you can arrange that? The Company will meet some of the expenses, of course."

There was no alternative but to accept and so, once again, I nodded. I didn't know what I was going to do but the Manager assured me that I would be given time to think of something. In those days very few people wanted to work in such remote areas and replacements were difficult to find. And so Lee Shin was grounded and he sat around in his house, brooding.

I set to thinking about how I could find the means to restore him to normality. I began to wonder if he wasn't deluding himself about his fiancee. Could she, like the destructive activities of Wali Farouk, exist? The photographs he had shown of her could well have been rigged up. He hardly got any letters from her and, unlike other men, he made no visits to her. It seemed, therefore, that he had to be taken roughly by the hand and shown the real world. I couldn't think of anyone more capable than the Spotted Lady for the job.

I don't know what the Manager said to him but Lee Shin put himself reluctantly in my hands.

"So you've the secret for a healthy life," he said, laughing cynically.

"I don't want to be involved," I said, "but I've no choice."

"Yes, must oblige one's superiors," he said. "What do you intend to do?"

"Take a holiday," I said. "For a week or so."

"With all expenses paid, of course," he said.

CHAPTER FIVE

I had not 'arrived' yet in those days to own a car. The motorcycle I had, being a second-hand one, however, gave me the service I needed. It took me to the small sea-side town, five or six miles from the settlement, for my meals and other necessities. It was a pleasure, therefore, to put away the rickety machine and take a taxi to Penang. Lee Shin and I occupied the back seat together with a third passenger, all the six hours to the island. He didn't say a word during the entire journey, which made me wonder why he had consented to come at all.

We booked into a modest hotel and after a nap, bath and change of clothes, were out on the streets of Penang. I recalled those times Lim and I had wandered around looking vaguely at ourselves and even more uncertainly at the women. Until we met May, the Spotted Lady. She would be there, as she had promised on the phone, and I knew there was no hurry. I wanted to savour the freedom I had lost tying myself to a job and an ambition.

As I look back now, from this pool of emptiness that surrounds me, I wonder if it wasn't the enclosed living we did on the settlement that forced me into a relationship with Lee Shin. If he could blame time and place for his unrooted existence, can't I do the same thing to explain my behaviour? There is the history of my family, of course, all the time in the background; there is my father's premature death. His death, it seems to me even now, was a going to meet and mingle with a greater void than the one he occupied while he lived.

But I must return to that evening in Penang. There was a flutter within me like the one I had experienced just after I left the university. The time and place seemed right. I found myself, even as I walked along with Lee Shin, entering the promenade of history, a legend that had been created for all men. Lee Shin's presence, in fact, accelerated that entry and sharpened the rediscovery. The short stretch of sea I had crossed, from the mainland to the island, that afternoon must have triggered off those expectations and the mood.

The popular view of Penang, as the pearl of the orient, was disgusting to me. Nothing, it appeared to me, was as evasive as the desire to believe in something finished; nothing as evasive as the desire to touch the glossy shine of the unreal. The sight and development of the island never stood, in my reckoning, as those alluring lights of a completed dream. It was incompleteness that had attracted those men from the West. Francis Light, when I put myself in his shoes, must have dreamt of a land which he himself could mould into shape. The planner, the designer brought his energies to work upon a human dream and so accomplished an entirety. That was how he must have seen it, I told myself. And how quickly he had connected land, enterprise and money, all in a single band of insight! Scattering all those coins through cannon shots had made men work and clear the land and so see what could be produced out of a jungle.

The buildings, streets and statues named after them were not mere monuments. They stood and spread themselves out as symbols of man's spirit not to submit to domestic traditions and fear of the unknown. Those men had struck out boldly though a few of them later buried themselves in what they had thought out and executed.

Lee Shin's tread beside mine became shadow walk, insubstantial. He hovered about me, lost without his specially set up room and his flute. I remembered how his flute had called out into the silence, seeking companionship and intimacy. Relenting, I spoke to him about my own family and friends. He listened with an intense expression on his face. We were seated in a bar drinking our beers, Lee Shin much more slowly than I did. It was late at night and the pub, The Crystal Palace, was filling up with people who hated to go back to their lonely rooms or boring families.

The Crystal Palace, full of lights, managed, at this late hour, to take on the look and atmosphere of a bazaar. The lights were so dim that the people couldn't be separated from their shadows. They traded here, conspiratorially, for the power that would banish fear and timidity. The band struck up and the dance platform began to fill with couples. I studied Lee Shin watching gravely, sceptically, the activities on the platform.

Suddenly he turned and nudged me. A woman in a black dress was doing the tango with her slightly shorter partner. As she flung back her shoulders and let her long hair whip her thighs, I thought she looked familiar. Lee Shin, I noticed, didn't take his eyes off the pair. Did the woman in black resemble his fiancee? She didn't have a pale skin at all; it was more a lusty, tanned complexion.

The time passed. There were only a few couples on the dance dais but the woman in black and her partner were still there. The dancing had slowed down so that the dancers appeared to be clinging to each other for movement and support. The lights added another dimension to the fantasy-like setting that was beginning to take shape on the low stage.

The woman in black held our attention as she wrapped herself languidly round her man. The other dancers played accompanying roles to the pair. Ever since the woman in black had come into The Crystal Palace, she had not given herself a moment of rest. As the night progressed, she minimized her movements and at a certain moment the pair appeared to be plastered to one another. The other dancers wove a web of sensuality around them. The web became still and seemed to trap the hardly moving pair in its sticky promise of warmth, strength and deceit.

Perhaps that late night scene had taken hold of Lee Shin for when I took him to meet May, the Spotted Lady, and her companion, his resistance seemed weakened. While this jaunt had been planned almost entirely for Lee Shin, I too wanted, once more, to be reawakened to the fundamental needs of existence. It was a relief to see her after all those years of not meeting but she also struck me as a changed person, not so much in character as in appearance.

She had become neater and more expressive. The dress she wore, almost resembling an executive suit, nearly put me off. Then it was that I realized, on closer inspection, that she was trying to fit into the present setting and tastes, with some modifications. While the whole outfit hugged her form, the jacket neckline was brought down sufficiently low to expose the roundedness of her breasts; when she moved up a step the slit at the back of her skirt showed more than just the thighs.

Her manner, while retaining her former vitality, was more compactly expressive. She did not lay herself out as she had done before but the little gestures she made carried the old sensuality and power. She took immediate charge of Lee Shin and I was handed over to Tina, her able but not talented disciple. After a few ritual dinners and drinks we went our separate ways.

Lee Shin and I hardly saw each other during those few days and before we knew it, we had to get back to the settlement. He was more talkative on the return trip. I only heard him inattentively as I surrendered myself to a warm, carressing fatigue that covered my body. It was only when we got back to the settlement and had been working for a few days that I noticed a complex change in his behaviour.

He moved about constantly from the house to the company offices, work cubicles and he even roamed the town. What began to bother me was this endless movement. At first I was gladdened by the thought that he had at last found his feet, body and the physical world. Whatever had gone on between him and the Spotted Lady had certainly liberated him. But why did he carry about him the air of someone entirely controlled by energy?

That was the most curious thing about him after his encounter with the Spotted Lady. I should have listened more attentively to his talk on our way back in the taxi. Then I would have known. He seemed to live purely within the physical and the practical. His clothes were washed more often and neatly pressed. He wore his shirt, trousers and tie as if they were flowers just plucked off the bushes and he liked their feel on his skin. Sometimes he did, in fact, stand close to some of these bushes with, it would seem, the purpose of entering the leaves and flowers. And then he grazed against them in a last, futile attempt at penetration.

There was a period when he came out of the self-absorption to seek me out and talk. He was even cordial. As he leaned against the railings of my verandah, in a kind of reversal of positions, I looked at him closely since our return from Penang. He appeared to have, silhouetted against the darkening sky, something of the child in him. That stance and smile irritated me at the time. It was like looking at someone who, having tried hard to be an adult, had relapsed into a kind of infantile paralysis. There was a glow on his cheeks that would have come from the flesh on a baby's face. He had begun to eat ravenously - of this later - and had put on some weight.

There was present, beneath the surface of his actions and talk, something I didn't recognize at that time. I seemed to have missed it, preoccupied as I was with my interpretation of his behaviour. I've seen it in myself, over the past few months: a frenzy for playing roles. The months, until my confinement here in this room, saw me being many things to many people. To my office workers, I was the good humoured boss. With my wife, I was dutiful to the point of being intolerable. Perhaps my children knew before I did what was happening to me. If you talk about mirrors, they were the reflections of what

I should have been. They laughed and jeered and scoffed at me as if my desire to humour them was merely a show; they danced round me, poked my ribs and took the words out of my mouth as if I was only a puppet.

I got the impression that Lee Shin was floating on the crest of a last wave, the very wave that would wash away the shores of his familiar world. But I didn't admit to myself, consciously, that his swaying this way and that, the gambolling off all over the place, the taking on and discarding of many masks and voices came from a deeper flush of release.

We went out to dinner, at his invitation, in a decent restaurant in the small town. Knowing that we were officers from the settlement, the proprietor himself came out to take our orders. Lee Shin didn't seem to see him or the honour done to us. Instead, he ordered a number of dishes without thinking about the taste or expense. When they came, he just wolved down the food. How repulsive, I thought, it was to watch the rice, meat, fish and vegetables meshed by the relentless grinding of his teeth? To watch the sweat stand out on his lips and forehead? Did he want to make himself deliberately disgusting?

When the waiter brought the Chinese tea Lee Shin liked, he gulped it down so hastily that he spilled some on his shirt.
He spoke all the while about this and that as if he didn't care whether I wanted to hear him or not. What surprised me was the utter distance between him and the words that poured from his mouth. I might as well have been a stranger for all the rapport that existed between us.

Then I didn't see or hear him for a few days. It was only when the general clerk informed me that I realized that he hadn't shown up for work that morning. I nodded at the clerk and headed for Lee Shin's house. On reaching it I knocked loudly on the door. There was no response. I called out his name several times. There was no reply.

When I tried the door I found that it could be opened to a slit. I rammed my shoulder against the door; it gave way and thudded against the wall. The bare furniture in the hall had been covered up with newspaper. The door to Lee Shin's room was ajar, which was unusual. He always closed and bolted it. I remembered the click of the bolt behind me as I came away from my rare visits to his room. I approached the door with misgivings.

The morning light penetrated the gloom and showed me a ghastly sight. The room, with all its antique furniture, was in a complete mess. It was as if Lee Shin had gone on a rampage and flung everything down on the floor. The calligraphed banners lay like snakes, mangled and shredded into spiteful death. The antique dresser, on which had stood his fiancee's photographs, was dislodged and the contents of the drawers scattered about.

And where was Lee Shin?

He was on the floor, beside the bed. Not a mere falling off. There had been some kind of a struggle. But with whom? Or what? I couldn't look at him for some time. The first glance had shown me that he had been dead for more than a few hours. Had I, being the nearest to him, heard some commotion during the night?

Was it possible for anyone to die in that posture? His legs were drawn up to his stomach; one hand clutched a wad of notes and the other seemed to have pawed at the floor. At his head were his fiancee's photographs almost spilling out through the crack in the frames. Instead of the babyish smile on the woman's face, there was a kind of leer - the stamp of some unfathomable victory.

Standing there motionless, I studied the circumstances under which Lee Shin had died. All kinds of pictures and images flashed, like cinematic frames, through my mind. Lee Shin had been caught off guard. The intruder had come upon him suddenly demanding whatever he possessed: money, furniture, dreams, ambitions. Lee Shin fought back, turning the room upside down so as to keep a protective distance between himself and the enemy.

But who was the enemy? There was hardly any crime in the place, nothing got stolen, no one was beaten up. Who had crept up on him without warning? Absurd as it might seem, I could only think of the young woman, his fiancee, in the photographs. Could pictures be fleshed out? Could dreams become realities? If he hadn't struggled with a real person, he couldn't have escaped the many ghosts and spirits that haunted him.

Yes, the young woman must have come out of the frames, having lived too long in his mind. She confronted him, suddenly, with the unreality of existence, plans and hopes. The next part was difficult to explain but I felt she must have demanded some sort of a settlement. He took out the money from the drawers and thrust the notes at her. She had protested, "No, not enough! Something more than money. Something real."

He fought back for she asked for nothing less than his life. He lost, of course. You couldn't fight back dreams; you could only control them. Lee Shin had never exercised restraint; he had given himself entirely to his dreams. They had twisted and discoloured him.

I had a proper look at him. He was an aborted foetus, man-like in completeness but in everything else not formed at all. His thoughts had had no coherence; his life had had no direction. The shadows and phantoms that inhabited him had taken over. The money he had hoarded couldn't satisfy the spirit and the will to live. The hopes he had harboured came out, as his fiancee had done, to demand that he give an account of himself.

Why did he have to lie down there on the floor like an unfinished task he had set for himself? Could man be more distorted? The hand that held the money seemed to clutch at desperation. The other hand, having pawed at the floor, lay like a sculptured piece of action that had reached its conclusion. His face was dark - as dark as mine - and the rest of his body blue-black. I couldn't accept this sudden change in colour, particularly the ashen lips which were snarled at some vengeful violence.

CHAPTER SIX

THE morning outside my room is bright, calm and unimprisoned. The house that I worked so hard to acquire seems like so much tiles, marble and bricks. A big house, it is too quiet and too cramped with the trophies of my achievements. I am hemmed in by all kinds of external laws; rules and regulations that govern success but not the well-being of a person. Why do I feel so left out of everything and, bereft?

The morning that Lee Shin died there had been the same sense of calm but was also touched and enriched by some kind of achievement. Looking at his grotesquely twisted body, I resolved I wouldn't let anything rob me of my life. Nothing would distort my body or my mind. But as I walked away from his death, I was also accompanied by a discontent I blamed on the heavy silence that hung over his passing. Why hadn't there been the sounds of triumph I ached so badly to hear?

The settlement lost some of its colour for me. There was no one else - I wondered even then why there was a need - to take Lee Shin's place in my life. Perhaps he had passed on some of his intensity to me so that I found the office chatter and laughter too superficial. Had I grown attached to Lee Shin without my knowing it? I filled the vacuum his death left in my life with work and a lot of reading, an activity I've now revived. I had never read so widely or intensely since my university days. Though for many days I forgot Lee Shin, there were some evenings when my eyes searched for the seated figure on his verandah. Then I turned abruptly away from the vacant darkness and rode into town for a beer or just the bright lights.

It was on such a night that I decided the settlement had served its purpose. It had given me financial security and more, a nest-egg with which to strike out on my own. The invisible gains were something else. How did I explain that to myself? As I sat in the empty house there in the settlement, my things packed in boxes, the real reason came to me.

It had something to do with Wali Farouk saving us, on that excursion into the interior, from the elephants and the woman in black Lee Shin and I had seen dancing in The Crystal Palace in Penang. Even now I can't work out the full implications but on that fateful night everything came to me in a flash.

Those elephants and the woman came together in some combination in the dark recesses of my mind. I saw them both as tramplers: they wouldn't stop at anything to get their way. They would reduce to crushed bottle-caps and flattened minds the objects and people that hindered them. I didn't want to be anywhere within the radius of such menace.

After I resigned my position and moved south to a larger town, I set myself up in the property business. The company I registered, named the Apex Co., dealt in all kinds of transactions but chiefly in the buying and selling of cars, houses and land. As the demand for land grew I found myself more and more involved in land deals.

It was a whole new world; there was none of the gloom that had hung over the settlement. Everywhere there was light and brightness and movement. The sunlight fell directly on the skin, not through the filtering sieve of leaves and creepers as on the settlement. It became clear to me, as the days passed, that I had finally freed myself from the phase in history that had trapped and killed my father and his generation. It was not a force, I realized, that was confined to a specific time and generation. It could come down even to my own times and enclose and smother as it did Lee Shin.

The Apex Co. had its offices in a shophouse fronting the main road of the town. The groundfloor was done up in style with its secretarial section and the manager's, airconditioned room which looked out, through a one-way glass panelling, on all the activities along part of the street. That strategic location not only allowed me access to the goings-on outside, but also to take stock, over the years, of the transformation that time brought. I recall now that I felt I was stationed next to a glass-walled laboratory of changes.

There was an awakening which I, isolated as I had been in the settlement, couldn't miss. There it had been a digging into the material resources the land could offer; here it was a thrusting deep into man's skills and abilities. The subdued, subservient manner of the people seen everywhere before independence was gone. There was now a breaking out from the self-willed habit of conservation. People simply came out, it appeared, to see themselves going about the town. At corners and in the coffeeshops men stood or sat talking, laughing and nudging each other as if they had emerged from the long sleep of suppressed life.

The glass wall window opened into insights. From behind it, I watched the skyline change and felt I too was being moved by that innovative force. More than that - I was one of its agents. I was going to influence individuals; I was going to influence the times. This I had already done, in a small way, by starting my business. There were a lot of land brokers in those days but they were a shuffling, self-effacing bunch. They carried their offices - battered briefcases and options on land grants - everywhere they went. They looked more like shabbily dressed petition writers found in front of court houses, wooing the illiterate farmer or estate labourer. I changed all that by opening a respectable office with long, cushioned benches for my clients. I was always to be found at my desk between nine and five and if I was out looking over a piece of property, my clerks and receptionist were there to attend to prospective buyers and sellers.

The strict regime I followed was guided by the desire to be the master of my own destiny. While that was the inner purpose, what people saw was the office and my regular presence there. They saw a man willing, in all kinds of weather and situations, to forge his way ahead. I came to be associated with reliability, perseverance and determination. My neighbours on either side, plump prosperous looking businessmen, sometimes called on me with worries about their businesses. Perhaps it was my manner or supreme self-confidence which affected them. Whatever it was, they soon went away feeling reassured and strengthened in their determination to succeed.

My office with its cushioned benches, was, just like the street, never deserted. There was always a kind of traffic: people moving in and out, files started and closed, letters typed and posted, mail received, people welcomed, fake clients told politely to leave. Just as the same kind of bustle found on that street but on a smaller scale. Beneath all these there was another kind of movement, that of identification, in terms of development and history, with that street.

We were like two strangers, united by some inner purpose, whom the people of that town could never have pictured in their minds until we began to make the scene. Both of us, the street and I, had had a brooding, dark past. Those days when I was down in the office before the secretarial staff arrived, I felt that we were always awakening to another, bright new day after the murkiness of a confused period in our lives.

The street with its adjacent cluster of squat buildings - the District Office, Court House, British Club and residences - was already undergoing change when I arrived. The close, humid air, reminding one of a hot greenhouse was being slowly replaced by a more open ambience. Some of the older buildings had already been knocked down and their foundations removed to make way for the town's Lake Garden. The District Office and the Court House were still to be brought down; there was an ongoing, heated discussion as to whether these buildings, so full of history and culture, should be destroyed at all. The whole town seethed with talk and there were many camps, attitudes and opinions.

Even my office became a ground for thrashing out the controversy and I was, reluctantly, drawn into the fray. Towards evening the receptionist would let the men into my room and order tea or coffee from a nearby coffeeshop. They were, like me, tenants or owners of shops in that block along the main street. The two men I remember vividly are Ramasamy and Kok. Ramasamy, the bookshop proprietor and much older than me was always there, smiling, ageless. His smooth-shaven face was neither bright nor dull; it shone with a kind of velvety assurance. He wore a streak of ash with a *pottu* in the middle, on his forehead. That red spot, ringed by sandalwood paste, came as a surprise to me since most of the time he wore a well-creased trousers and an immaculately ironed shirt. Sometimes he even put on a tie.

Kok was altogether different. In his mid-forties, he had inherited his rubber-dealer business from his father, who, in turn, had inherited it from his own father. Jimmy, as Kok liked to call himself, laughingly said, "Latex has always run in my family blood, you know." He spoke a peculiar brand of English that bordered on being half-British and half-Chinese. But in his clothes he was unpredictable. Sometimes he wore a decent pair of trousers and shirt; sometimes he shuffled about in the rubber-sheet laden shop in shorts and slippers. There were days when he dazzled us with his flare pants and a silky, long-sleeved shirt. There was something nebulous about him.

The receptionist, after seeing that we were quite comfortable, closed the main door and left for home. Whatever guardedness remained in us, thawed, and in Jimmy Kok's words we 'let fly'. That meant we could say anything

---

pottu - Red/black dot worn by women on their foreheads.

that came into our minds. He himself never sat on the cushioned bench in the receptionist area. He walked about the place as if to underline with his movements the importance of what he was saying. Ramasamy, on the other hand, sat immobile, only his mouth moving - another odd thing about him - as he munched on his sireh leaves and betel nut shavings.

While Jimmy Kok paced about, stopping now and then to stoop and gulp down his coffee, Ramasamy placed his free hand - the left one always held the cigarette tin into which he spat the sireh juice - now on one knee, now on the other as if in deep contemplation. This habit of his irritated me for it slowed down the talk and took the heat out of the argument. On that climatic day, however, he simply flowed with words. He had freed his mouth from the wad of sireh before speaking.

"We can't let it happen," he said. "Must not happen!"

Jimmy Kok stopped in his tracks and wagged a finger at Ramasamy.

"You Indians are so woolly-headed," he said. "What shouldn't happen, man?"

"Woolly-headed, keely-headed!" Ramasamy said. "The thing people are talking about. Breaking down those buildings."

"You're not saying why," Jimmy Kok said. "Emotional as usual."

"Must have feelings," Ramasamy said. "Don't you agree, Rajan?"

"Depends on the situation," I said.

"Right now, this one," Ramasamy said. "No other situation is looking us in the eye."

"Too much happening too fast," Jimmy Kok said.

"You're making money fast," I said.

"That's different," Jimmy Kok said. "Everyone makes money. That's the only thing to do. No use chasing after women."

Jimmy Kok often ended his conversations on this note of warning about women. He had tried, so he told me during the many coffee hours we had together, to marry the right kind of woman but he had always ended up spending money on a particular one without gaining anything from the relationship.

70

For some mysterious reason, the women concerned invariably left him for another man.

"We can't have the wrong kind of feelings," I said.

"Not that kind," Ramasamy said. "Not those silly palpitations of the heart. Come fast, go fast. The other kind."

"What other kind is there?" I said.

"Tell him, Jimmy," Ramasamy said, smiling, as if he was going to flash his trump card at me.

"When you just know," Jimmy Kok said. "Without bothering to think. That's the great feeling. Take my own case. My father wanted me to be many things. A doctor, lawyer, architect and so on. I aided and abetted him in his dreams. All that time, when I was in England or Australia studying, there was that feeling I was no good for these professions. Look at me now. I'm doing all right."

"Your great feeling, Jimmy," I said, laughing, "is to come into something without sweating for it."

He stopped in his pacing and looked at Ramasamy.

"You tell him, Rama. He thinks I've been a loafer and an idler. Always making the attempt," Jimmy Kok said.

"Yes, yes," Ramasamy said. "Always going to this country or that. To study. Not happy inside."

It puzzled me how these two men, with their sophisticated business sense, could talk like that. For a moment I thought of packing up and leaving them to their great feeling. Then I relented.

"The protest must be concrete," Jimmy Kok said. "The citizens of this town have to voice their opinions."

"Arrange for a meeting with the Town Council," Ramasamy said.

"They won't listen," I said. "The protest will gather dust in some file."

We were silent for a while, each thinking his own thoughts.

"We just can't think of this as a simple town affair. It must spread to other towns. Must become a national concern."

We put our heads together that time; worked with quiet excitement. Our minds ranged over signature campaigns, rallies in front of the District Office, lobbying of the Council chairman, protest leaflets and even demonstrations. We all agreed in the end that these would be sensational - exciting newspaper reports perhaps - but would bring no practical results.

"The newspapers! The newspapers!" Ramasamy almost shouted, falling out of his contemplative posture. "In front of my eyes and I didn't see it!"

"What's the strategy?" I said.

"Just write," Ramasamy said, calming down. "Get the reporters on the job."

"That won't be any good," Jimmy Kok said. "They always colour the situation to their liking."

"We could all write to the papers," I said. "Present different viewpoints. Keep up the controversy, week after week. The newspapers are duty bound to publish them."

"He has got a point there," Jimmy Kok said. "Flash something in the public's mind constantly and soon it's accepted as the reality."

"We've to be sophisticated about this," I said. "There must seem to be a difference of opinion. There must be a clash of views."

"Yes, ask for the impossible," Jimmy Kok said, "and you might get what you really expect."

"That's good strategy," Ramasamy said, laughing.

We passed the word around and soon recruited a number of men willing to make up the dissenting camps. But when the letters went out to the papers it became clear that they were not merely playing a game of strategy. Some of the opinions expressed, as far as I was concerned, seemed to come from a narrow-minded self-centredness. The groups acquired such distinct individuality that we found ourselves avoiding people and moving only within our own cliques.

I wrote my own response to the situation towards the end of the controversy. Ramasamy and Jimmy Kok felt betrayed by the position I took. They gave me no choice but to do what I did. Ramasamy and Jimmy Kok, after that meeting, assumed an air of proprietorship over me that was irritating, if not humiliating. Their behaviour reminded me, for a while, of Lee Shin. They, like him, believed they owned me instead of working together so as to discover a common ground for identity. As the controversy continued, it became clear to me that what they represented was unacceptable.

Ramasamy's pretensions to progressive thinking had deceived me. Whenever I passed his shop, he seemed to be holding a book in his hands. Sometimes he even ignored a customer as he flipped over the pages, absorbed and thoughtful. He also stocked, it appeared to me, books that no one in that town could have read except him. These were thick volumes, standing massively beside the occasional medical dictionary, that he took down and dusted sometimes. And he always managed to get, through some uncanny ways, the companion books that higher form students needed to pass their final examinations.

"The mind is like a garden," he said when I stopped to chat with him. "If not cultivated, it goes wild. Listen to the sayings I've in this rare book. 'A busy man is a busy mind. Timeless are misfortunes; timely is the effort of the man who overcomes them. Marriage isn't the union of two spirits; marriage is the entry of two into one spirit.' And the one I like best of all. 'The sun shines and the moon wanes even if man doesn't care.' So simple, so profound." I had come away from these chance encounters feeling uplifted.

What he wrote in the papers disappointed me. I remember a lengthy paragraph - everything else escapes me - which I put down here:

A man's life is not his life; a country's progress is not its own progress. The events that time brings shapes the destinies of both. And time flows like the river, moves like the sea. It can push against the banks and pull them down; it can wash against the shore and take away the land. But both the river and the sea can also pull away from the banks or the shore and leave us with more. These buildings the Council wants to pull down are the more that has been given to us. These structures that the British have left behind do not belong to them alone. They do not only reveal their domination and culture. They reveal us too. They reveal us as shaped by forces that have worked within the larger force - time.

And what did Jimmy Kok follow up with? What he wrote contradicted the way he presented himself to the world. I didn't see in his writing the pacing about, the slovenly, careless clothes, the choice to build within a sense of freedom. He didn't come through to me as an uncertain, searching man. What he said seemed to confirm what he secretly believed.

This is the only memorable part from his article that I can salvage:

The point I am trying to make is that there must be order. This can only be achieved by a study of those cultures that gave us order and system. We are not against progress in this country or have become members of that invisible group that 'obstructs the sense of belonging to a country.' We merely question the wisdom behind the words 'sense of belonging to the country.' This expression has been used to cover, ironically, almost everything from eating habits to the games that ought to be played in this country. I assert that everything that has happened in this country belongs to us: the past makes the present and the present makes the future. These buildings are records and reminders of the systems that have come down to us. In destroying them, we are destroying our past and, more importantly, our future.

They had become, as I noticed at that time, truly the voice of the public. They seemed to have forgotten that they owed a duty to themselves too. There was much self-congratulation and mutual admiration but hardly any original thought. This merging with the masses bothered me. It was as if they had run out of individual resourcefulness. Didn't a man have to put something of himself into the shaping of the country? I told myself I wasn't going to be so easily influenced by public opinion.

So one morning, just before the town woke up, I came to my office and leaving my briefcase there went out to view the buildings that had caused so much controversy. I wanted to be certain in my mind what they stood for before I made any comments. The sun had just risen when I reached the District Office. The building rose before me, a mass of bricks and tiles relieved by blocks of plank. They reminded me of the estate office building where my father went to collect his pay or be ticked off for misconduct. The District Office building too had been the source of money and administration, but on a larger scale.

When I was older, I heard the estate clerk say, on the occasions the salary was delayed because the DO had not okayed the pay-out order. Still later, when as a young man I passed any District Office, I saw men hanging around the entrance, dressed officiously and holding empty canvas bags imprinted with the letters HMS on them. There had been, I recall, in the District Office I once entered, a mammoth safe cemented into the brick wall. As I stood there that morning, I realized how much the District Office, together with its adjunct, the Court House, had ruled my life. There it had been that my birth certificate was issued, my father's citizenship papers obtained, copies of my own school certificates verified and stamped for application to a university; there couples had committed themselves, one to the other, in marriage and there too it was that death certificates were received for the final exit.

By the time I had gone all the way round the District Office, walking along the dirt-caked, darkened verandah, the sun had come up and brightened the place. I chuckled to myself as I remembered the assertion: 'The sun will never set on the British Empire.' Nor will it rise again, I told myself as I stood, finally, at the bronze plaque commemorating the official opening of the building.

'Opened by His Excellency, the High Commissioner to Malaya, Sir _____, OBE, on the fifth day of July, in the year 1948 A.D.' The words could be barely made out as fungus had eaten into the metal. And the sharp smell of erosion that came with exposure to the local air, was unavoidable. It was at this point that my spirit was moved to recognize what the District Office represented. Without going on to the Court House, I hurried to my office to set down the words that later became a full-fledged article on the demolition issue.

It appeared only a week or so after Ramasamy's and Jimmy Kok's in *The Malaysian Standard*:

> The underlying reason, and the main one, why people are so opposed to the demolition of the District Office and the Court House buildings is simple: they cannot bear to see what has given them a sense of security be brought to rubble in a few hours. The destruction of the familiar is a destruction of the comfortable. If we look deeply into the phenomenon, we will discover the imperative for why these buildings will have to go. How did these buildings come to be erected? What do they tell about the spirit of the people who built them?
>
> They came to this country even without hearing of it. In other words, they took a chance, made a leap. They leapt across the sea of the unknown to discover new territories for themselves. They left behind themselves the safe and the domestic to carve out a new land for themselves. There was no continuity, past or future. Once they got here, they looked into the resources available and built a familiar environment around themselves. They transplanted their language, culture, systems of order, justice and administration.
>
> That is what we have to do: make a great leap. Now that we have the land we have to build the systems that will support our hopes and ambitions. We must not allow ourselves to be trapped by the past, by the familiar. We must go forward into the great unknown.

The town was mixed in its reception of the article. Ramasamy and Jimmy Kok did not talk to me for weeks. Some of the Town Council members sought me out and congratulated me. They looked on me as a valuable source of sympathy and support for the planned modernization of the town. However, I still detected an aloofness in them that told me they had more up their sleeves than I could ever know. A lot of other people came into my office to shout abuse, ask for explanations or nod knowingly at what I had written in the papers.

Ramasamy and Jimmy Kok continued to keep their distance from me all the time I stayed in that town. The District Office and the Court House buildings were razed and the foundations for an up-to-date block of offices laid. Though Ramasamy and Jimmy Kok kept away from me, I didn't make the mistake of interfering too much in their affairs. I accepted them for what they were.

That brought me a sense of relief and entry into a new phase of life. While the town changed, I progressed deeper into my business. More and more land deals came my way for I was rigorous and honest in my evaluation of whatever came under my purview. I let nothing escape my attention. Both the seller and the buyer had to put up with standards not easily recognized in those days. I didn't value just the productivity of the land; I went in for a kind of aesthetics.

Those remaining years in the town were creative and prosperous. My land aesthetics grew. There was no need, I realized, to get too involved with the land. That only led to despair and futility. The other approach was the saner one: it led to a clean, knowledgeable way of living. Soon the land came to reside within me as some material that could be shaped into whatever it had use for. One only had to read into its resources correctly. There was land that I acquired and allocated for housing development. There was land that could be turned into factory sites. There were stretches I never touched and knew could only be used for the building of highways, which the authorities did as I had predicted. There was land, large and shapeless masses throughout the country that could never be approached at all. This kind of land I didn't even bother about, even in my dreams.

What went wrong? What happened to the confidence I built over the years? There is a blank now in my mind where once there used to be a wide, scenic canvas of the country. It surprised me, the land I mean, lending itself to so many uses none of which had anything to do with emotional turbulence. It stole upon me, suddenly, already laid out in well-surfaced roads, the jungles kept beyond the possibilities of intrusion.

At the peak of such self-confidence there appeared in my life a man, Sivasurian, to whom I hardly paid any attention. He was an inconspicuous, pleasant sort and I didn't mind his sitting about in the waiting room. He even slept there on some nights, asking permission well in advance. When I went to the office the following morning, the rubber-foam cushion looked as if it had not been slept on at all.

There was something about the man that attracted me to him. Usually I didn't care much for idleness and the appeal for charity. But in his case I seemed to have had no reservations. His having no particular occupation didn't offend me. And though he made no appeals, direct or indirect, for kindness, I gave him shelter and, sometimes, food for no apparent reason. No one had seen him before, neither Ramasamy nor Jimmy Kok and they had been in that town longer than me.

He was soft-spoken, docile and always polite. Looking at him, I found it difficult to place him, culturally. Outwardly he looked Indian, the blue, tattooed pottu on his forehead testifying to that, but in everything else he was an enigma.

"I come from a long way off, *thambi,*" he said, "and sometimes I don't know from where."

---

thambi - Brother.

78

That was the way he spoke and he always called me thambi, meaning 'brother'. At that time I took it merely as a polite form of address but since I started looking at the book he left behind for me, I've begun to have doubts. He had some disconcerting habits, not censorious or harmful. I felt a little disturbed whenever I listened or talked to him. The pottu between his brows stared at me like a third, probing eye.

He appeared and disappeared mysteriously. Looking back, I realize he was around during those times when I was on the edge of some crisis or upheaval. He was there when I wrote that article for the press; he was there when I met Zulkifli for the first time.

He was detached from and flowed into events all the time. That is the only way to put it. Sitting there in the reception hall, he looked as if he had no connections with the world beyond the tinted glass panes. Then, when I met him outside, say, in a coffeeshop with a plate of food before him, he would have picked up some companion and at such times he belonged nowhere else. What was his outstanding quality? As I recall, it was the calm intensity with which he talked or developed an intimacy. He seemed to be looking on or ahead even as he listened or spoke to you.

He talked, when he was in the mood, endlessly and quietly. And his words, hardly absorbed at that time, now appear to have registered themselves in my subconscious. How else can I remember the details of those numerous conversations? His voice has become a kind second voice inside me. Over the years I've heard its murmurs and discontent but I've remained oblivious to them. Now that my mind has been cleared of its personal bric-a-brac, the voice comes out much more clearly though I don't understand what it is saying.

As I read his book for the first time - reading keeps me in sanity, repelled as I am by the realities outside that I helped to shape - the voice becomes even stronger. The book unfolds a quiet flood of questions and wonder. His book is addressed to no one and, I feel, to everyone. It isn't what he says but how he says it that arouses my other, almost extinct feelings.

My wonder is how he could have written that book? And I go back in time to look at him again. He seems to be always there and his words, "I've come from a long way off" seem, in a new light, strangely true. Yes, he has travelled through a great distance of time and reached me. But with what?

CHAPTER SEVEN

A T about that time another man, Zulkifli, came into my life. Though around my age, he was already married and had two children. He didn't come to do land deals with me; he came to sit around somewhat like Sivasurian, in the reception hall and observe the goings-on. His interest in me puzzled me for a while but I could see that his self-assurance had received a knock or two.

"You've a lot of customers," Zulkifli said, one late afternoon when the office was almost empty.

"I work hard," I said.

"I can see that," he said. "But you only work for money?"

"What else is there to work for?"

"You don't know the real land," he said. "Otherwise you won't be selling lots of the land like this."

"People come to me with land," I said.

"People facing hard times," he said.

"And there are people who want to buy land," I said.

"But they don't use the land properly," he said. "I heard what the town people said about what you wrote in the papers."

"I only want to help," I said.

"That isn't helping," he said. "You must see the real land."

He looked at me for a while, then got up and left. There was something on his face that said he wanted some feeling about the land. Long after he left, I sat on in the office, vaguely disturbed. Sivasurian caught me in that mood when he walked in some time later. He put down the neat but small cardboard bag he always carried beside my desk and sat opposite me.

"I'm not disturbing you?" he said.

I shook my head. He took out his embroidered pouch and began to make a sireh wad for himself.

"You see, thambi," he said, munching on the sireh, "I don't know how I came to be here. I don't even know if I've the right to be here. Too many people talk about rights but don't see the other things. Many say that birth isn't a choice.
It just happens. What do you do after you're born? Shouldn't people give some thought to that?

"You've been kind to me. May be I should give something back. But I don't have anything except my life and that also isn't mine. (He had a rhythm to the narration that somehow roused feelings different to the ones found in my line of business. There was no knitting of the brows, the impasse, then followed by a breakthrough and finally a liberation. Sivasurian seemed to hold everything together so that one swelled with the recognition of some invisible uniting force.) What little there is, I will give. Because it was given to me and hoarding will only wear it away. Have you seen how a saw rusts if it isn't oiled or used?

"Almost everything I have has come to me by accident, not through design. I haven't chased after shelter, food, name, wealth or happiness. I'm not rich or unhappy; I don't have a permanent roof over my head. There is no one profession I follow all the time. Yet, there is some money in my pocket and food in my belly all the time. The affection and generosity people show me are my only wealth.

"I was born to parents who were driven away from me by poverty. Their faces are not in my mind or memories. Since then I've had many parents - people who became my father and mother because they looked after me. I've not regretted not having my set of parents. Whether I liked it or not, I became a child of the world. From the beginning my feelings were opened outwards, to people other than kin and kith. At that time, when I was a child, I didn't know all this. Now I know it was training to prepare me for the future. Thoughts centred around the self arrests you in time."

(He often dressed his thoughts in mystifying words and soon I got into the habit of not paying too much attention to them. How I wish I had been more attentive!)

"The places where I slept and the families that I lived with kept changing. Sometimes I slept out in the verandah with only a thin vesti to protect me from the cold. Sometimes I slept in a room crowded with tired and sweating bodies. There were days when I fed on rice soaked in water, munching on a green chillie for spice. There were days when there was always chicken curry on the plate.

"I was growing attached to the first estate where my parents had abandoned me when something happened. I was about eight or nine years old and the work of herding the cattle on that estate had fallen on me. It was a pleasant job; it took me all over the countryside. I wore a sharp, long knife at my waist for fighting back and also for cutting down fruits and wild sugar-cane. There was a bundle of rice and curry in a small canvas bag I carried slung across my shoulder. In my right hand I held a sturdy, well-seasoned rattan staff.

"The blue sky, the green and brown slopes and the clear, running water in the river made me feel I could have been anywhere. At midday the heat danced all around me and the trees and the ground seemed to break up and sway unsteadily. Just watching them gave me a pain in my head. The cows I herded could have been horses. They looked so different. They galloped about as if whipped by the heat. This didn't happen so often in the early days but became almost an everyday thing later on. When I returned to the estate in the evenings, I was too tired to speak to anyone. I found a corner and fell asleep.

" 'The loneliness has scrambled his mind,' the people said when they found me tongue-tied and reluctant to join in their activities. Perhaps they were right. I don't know. The only thing I knew was that the distance between them and me was rowing all the time. The evenings on the estate were covered by a cool dusk yet the people became, day by day, strangers to me. I moved about in a daze. Then I moved into dreams and soon the dreams became nightmares.

"When I went out with the cows and goats, I became dizzy. The worst was when the sun was overhead. Then the heat struck into my head like needles. And the dreams and nightmares of the night before returned to torment me. They were always the same. I would be going out towards the estate people and a sharp axe fell before me so that I couldn't advance. The people seemed not to see me. They followed the tail-end of some procession and I stood there watching, unable to join them.

"When the afternoon poured like an unbearable flow of heat on me, I sat down under a tree and let the cattle stray wherever they wanted. In the evening I brought them together and goaded them home. This went on for many days until one day having fallen asleep under that tree, I woke up somewhere else. In a shop, far from the estate. To this day I can't remember the name of that estate. The shop where I found myself so mysteriously faced the main road, a busy one. How did I get there?

"You see, thambi, I didn't remember anything of the place I had left behind. Only in the last few years have those things come back to me. I only remembered the sun like a sharp knife piercing into my mind. So when they - the shop people - asked my name, I said Sivasurian, meaning the lord of the sun. Why did I make that choice? It just came to me. Lord of the sun. He looks on everything and has no opinions. Nothing to say for or against. He just looks at those who don't hide anything. Those who hide soon have to come out to him. Without his warmth and light, they will die.

(Again, as I recall, another of his puzzling observations. I've been staying under this artificial fluorescent light for so long I feel I don't exist. No shadows play on the wall or on the floor

84

and if I stay too long under it, my body goes cold. My mind is often chilled so that any thought that comes has to be like a chisel breaking ice.)

"They gave me some work," Sivasurian said, "in the eating shop. It wasn't a clean or a big shop. Tables were pushed up against the blackened walls; tables took up the centre and corner spaces so that there was little room for anyone to walk about. Your place here is so well arranged and ordered anyone would feel comfortable. But I didn't think about comfort in those days. To tell you the truth, thambi, I had no time for thinking.

"The proprietor of the shop was a kind but strict man. He sat there at the cash-box like a god, almost like Ganesha, the remover of obstacles. He was a remover of obstacles. The day they found me, he didn't leave his niche behind the counter.

'Who's that boy?' he damanded.

'A lost, dazed fellow,' one of his workers said. 'Can't even stand properly.'

'Give him a tumbler of tea,' the god behind the counter said. 'That will put him on his feet.'

'What if his parents come looking for him?'

'If he gets better give him the washing to do,' the god said. 'Then we'll see.'

"That's how I came to be employed in that eating shop. As I had no parents, I had no trouble working in that shop. The man's workers could do with another pair of hands, so I stayed on.

"It was an education for me. From early morning till late at night, I was at the sink beside the kitchen. That small, porcelain tub was my world and I learned about the customers from the plates and cups they left behind for me to wash. There were fussy men, angry men and meek men. There was always something they had to themselves that was different from the characters of other men. As I washed, I pondered on this difference and found no explanation.

"I was learning in other ways too. Part of the shop, the section next to the kitchen was where the proprietor and his

85

family lived. The two rooms, private kitchen and latrine, couldn't be reached except through a hidden door. All the time I was there, I saw only glimpses of the man's wife. How a person could be so invisible amazed me. What amazed me even more was the wife's power over the proprietor. At certain times of the day he disappeared from the counter. These were at meal times, just after a few customers were left in the shop.

"Sometimes I heard voices in a quarrel; sometimes I heard the woman sobbing. There were times also when the man came out of his living quarters looking humiliated. Then we, the workers, were careful not to rouse his anger. If we forgot and stepped on his toes the mildest we got was a tongue lashing. There were days when he came into the shop shining like the sun. Then some of us got holidays, together with gifts of money.

"Even after a few months' stay with the shop people, I found nothing changed. If I had fallen from the sky, some years later, I would still have found them the same. They all looked like figures shaped out of clay and not yet dried. They kept looking at the clock but they didn't see time moving on. They were ruled by the clock as if it was a whip which would soon snap and they would all be free.

"I don't know how to say this, thambi. Language is such a useless instrument. It's only an instrument. What comes through it is sieved and filtered according to its capacity. As I continued to live among those workers and customers, I felt I was becoming like their clay - waiting for the right kind of sunlight to bake me into something solid.

"Let me say it in another way, thambi. As I said, the proprietor's wife didn't show herself but I heard her voice behind the hidden door. It was a magical voice beside the entrance, whispering, persuading, even forcing the human being to go forward. In this case the human being was her own son. He was about six or seven years old and had just started school.

" 'Go, go out there!' she was saying. 'Sit at the counter. Your father sits there all the time. And see how much money we get! With only a little we buy all your toys. Go out there, son. The people are there. You can't be afraid of them. I'm only a woman. Never mind about me. But you're important. One day you might become a pilot. Be an important person in the government. The government looks after everybody. Don't you want to look after your mother?'

"The voice kept on talking and persuading, behind the door. If I didn't hear it for a few days, I got worried and uncomfortable. The words were like my clothes. Without them I felt naked and weak. Then one day I fell sick. May be it was all that work. May be it was the closed up place with its smoke and dirt that made me sick. The proprietor ordered one of the workers to take me to the hospital. The District Hospital. Different from what they are today.

"Perhaps the new place and all those sick people made me think and see differently. Fortunately, the voice behind the door wasn't there to influence me. After the days of fever passed, I was kept on in the hospital ward. Different and yet not so different from the eating shop. Here the people were being eaten up by all kinds of diseases. Some of them were not even diseases of the body. They were not diseases of the mind. At certain times of the day, the patients behaved in a strange way. Those patients who could walk and look after themselves, suddenly became helpless. They just stood near the large windows - almost like doors - and looking outside, they began to shiver. There was something outside the ward that frightened them.

"The eating shop didn't have people shivering about in fright. The shivering was all inside them, which they tried to hide by keeping busy or talking or reading the same newspaper many times. Their eyes and faces were vacant. When I returned to the shop, I was a changed person. The boss and even the helpers noticed it: the little fire I had inside me before was lost.

"You might ask me how I could think about such things when I wasn't even twelve years old. That was also what puzzled me. How do these thoughts come to me? I wondered. The more I moved among those people the more I felt different from them. At first this made me very unhappy. There were nights I couldn't sleep even though I had worked the whole day. Then one day I decided I would wait for the day of understanding.

"That decision changed everything for me. From that day I was freed from the burden of worry. I entered the joy of living. Again the men around me saw the change in my behaviour. I let them think whatever they wanted. The voice behind the door continued to whisper; the hum of the customers' eating and talking didn't abate. The proprietor's son came out to the counter with his books and kept up the chant of learning.

"Years later, thambi, I began to collect my thoughts and put them in a book. You must have the book. There is something about you that says you'll need it one day. Please forgive me for presuming so much."

Though Sivasurian talked that evening and on many other days, these are what remained in my mind. Zulkifli too, figured prominently in my life at that time. He kept pestering me to go on a trip with him to see the real land. Sivasurian noticed that I was getting impatient with the man.

"You see, thambi," he said, "we never know until later what's happening to us. Something has gone on inside men's minds to change their whole view of life and the world. They've even changed the world into what was never meant to be. What I'm saying, thambi, is that the sun isn't itself."

(I had become so used to his strange way of putting things that I merely nodded to him to go on.)

"I'm not myself. You're not yourself. We're always travelling on the road we choose for ourselves but not on the one chosen for us. That's why we're always travelling back to find out where we got lost. You've to go back so that you'll know what you are."

"You're not listening to me, thambi," he said. "Anyone can see that. Never mind. Live in the present so that you can go back to the past one day."

As far as I was concerned, the past was dead. I didn't want to return to something that was dead. Zulkifli kept on bothering me about that trip into the interior of the land.

"You've to come and see for yourself," he said.

"See what?"

"The country to which you belong," he said.

"Wali Farouk tried to show me at one time," I said.

"Who's Wali Farouk?" he said.

"Never mind," I said.

"I'm not Wali Farouk," he said.

Why did I go on that trip with Zulkifli? Was it out of curiosity or was it to prove to myself that nothing could influence me?

The barrenness of this room, in which I've chosen to exile myself, doesn't disturb or frighten me any more. I've grown accustomed to the uncluttered existence the lack of furnishing has imposed on me. The fluorescent tube burns night and day, abolishing any shadow that might have fallen across my life. For a few days now I haven't been returning to the past. Instead, I've let it find a place for itself in my life. This is thinking like Sivasurian, whose voice often comes to me from out there.

My wife keeps the business going at the firm. So she tells me. I feel neither jealousy nor impotence. When she talks to me in the evenings after she returns - a disguised report on the progress or lack of it in the business, which she hopes will bring me out - I turn my back on her and look out of the window. A strange thing happens to me when I do this. I want to tear up the roads to see what is beyond the foundations;

I want to tear down the houses to see what the land looked like before it was built upon. But I restrain myself.

"Is there anything you want to say?" my wife asks, having finished and I don't even shake my head. There has been a remarkable change in my wife since I shut myself up in this room. Where did this new person hide herself while she cleaned the house, looked after the boys and cooked the meals? Sometimes when I look closely, I only see a stranger in her. Is it possible to suppress yourself so completely that you come to accept what you are not?

When we married, we shared a common dream. That was what I felt sitting there on the marrriage dais enveloped by the mysterious chant of the priest and well-wishes of those who attended the function. The young girl who sat beside me through the ceremony had not come out of her silence to say anything that contradicted my views on life. She had merely passed from the marriage ritual into the ritual of home-making.

Over the years I did notice some changes: a resistance to moving from one town to another, a suffused glow of satisfaction over the property and money we acquired, a constant need to be thought of highly by the people with whom we mixed or who lived around us. She had the habit of going through the ledgers I brought home and occasionally picked out a miss-entry or a fault in the balancing. She could anticipate the rise or fall in the value of certain kinds of property but this knowledge she communicated to me indirectly, almost shyly.

There were the usual domestic quarrels, none of them devastating. There were days when we said hardly anything to each other that mattered. I had come to accept her - or so I thought - as she was and she had accepted me as I was. But these last few months her voice has taken on an edge that seems to probe into everything.

I can't help but think that this entirely new Vasanthi must have grown all the time without my noticing the signs. (When

I met her the first time and was told her name, I could only think of a lily surrounded by calm, unmoving water.) There were minor alterations - cosmetic changes, I called them - that I remember: the discarding of the sari for looser skirts and blouses; then she began to wear pants and T-shirts; her language was infiltrated by expressions from the newspapers and magazines; her face finally began to accept the veneer of make-up. The early days of marriage saw her using only the saffron stick and only on Fridays. Otherwise she remained unadorned and surrendered to her natural, youthful suppleness, scents and odours of the body and lustre of the skin.

Many years later I recognized, proudly, that this was not the small town girl who had had only a secondary school education. At last my influence was beginning to work on her. In those days, it seemed important to me that I affect people one way or the other.

But when I remember her private room, I can't understand her at all. When I first walked into that room, I thought it revealed Vasanthi's past and imprisonment. There were days, I recalled, when she disappeared for a couple of hours without leaving the house. I had always assumed that she either busied herself in the kitchen or pottered about in the large garden. What did this room offer her that the rest of the house didn't?

The simplicity of it all struck me as an offence to my tastes. But I held that feeling down, thinking after all she must have some purpose in doing up the room that way. My view was that she wanted some kind of comparison to all the luxury she found in the rest of the house. Perhaps she wanted to use it as a reminder of the poverty from which she had come.

One evening Sivasurian came to say goodbye to me. He handed me a hard-cover exercise book.

"I'm going away," he said. "And a small gift for you. You've been kind to me."

"Where will you go?" I said.

"I don't know," he said. "When I wake up in the morning, I'll know." Then he looked at me as if to read my mind. "When you're ready, you'll have to go the way you came."

That wasn't the last I heard from him but physically he went out of my life. I missed him in the evenings when the office was closed and I was by myself. But not for long. Zulkifli began to show up more frequently. For some reason or other, he was bent on provoking me. What I record here is a compression of the many days of heated conversations we had.

"I don't understand people like you," he said. "You come as people with ideas but you only dishonour the land."

"What dishonour?" I said.

"You divide the land and sell the lots like pieces of cloth," he said. "A middleman, you say. I know what you are. Somebody without a soul."

"A person doing business can't have a soul." I said.

"Then choose some other job," he said.

"Why do your people give me their land to sell?"

"The times have changed," he said. "You must have money for everything now. Everything has to be bought."

"Why are you complaining?" I said. "I'm not selling my own land. I've no land of my own."

"You'll have it if you really understand this country," he said.

"I already understand it," I said. "It's like any other country in the world."

"Then why don't you go to any of these other countries?"

"Why should I?" I said. "I'm doing well here. I work hard, so I live well."

"Then nothing is hard for you," he said. "You must see the tiger."

"What tiger?" I said.

"Are you afraid?"

"You want me to go tiger hunting?" I said.

A wistfulness came into his face and I saw that his aggression was merely a disguise for some other concern. As his face softened my own anger fell away.

"We've to know what this country is, together," he said softly, uncertainly. "You must discover its spirit as my people did."

"And how do we do that?" I said, curious but sceptical.

"We've to go on a trip to tigerland," he said.

"Tigerland?"

"Don't you know that the tiger lived in this country long before we came?" he said. "We must look at the country through its eyes."

"Have you done this yourself?"

"No, my forefathers went through that experience," he said. "I want to experience what they saw. You must come with me. Then, may be you'll believe."

"I want to shoot a tiger," I said, deciding I must have a purpose if I was going on that trip.

"You can try," he said with his old self-assurance, "but you won't succeed. Not with this tiger."

We agreed on a day, about two weeks from then, and he went away. After he left, I wondered if I had done the right thing by agreeing to go. But the doubt vanished as I succumbed to an old dream of mine. There was a part of me that had remained irrational. In the days to come I gave myself up to this irrationality. I saw myself striding through the jungle vanquishing everything that came in my way.

The nights before we went were filled with dreams. Was it because I had loosened my guard against Zulkifli that they came? There was this particular one that I can't ever forget. It comes so vividly to me that I seem to be watching and even participating in an unstoppable process.

The mists clear: a land comes into view. Out of the furziness emerge the boiling, unformed strata of the earth. The colours, all mixed, swim in an endless effluvium: brown tinged with black, white swirling with red, red swelling with green. The green bubbles and disappears. The flux sets but there is an under-current of subdued upheaval. On the outside shapes begin to appear, hardening into existence. The earth steams

*and settles; the burgeoning inside breeds and screams. Seeds pop
and push roots through the ground; trunks groan and heave
themselves through the resinous soil. Grass swarm over the forming
slopes; creepers web themselves under the blossoming foliage.
Pungent, musky fruits slither down the darkening branches; below
there is an uncoiling of hisses and growls and screeches. Between the
mushrooming trunks there appear flexing muscles; between furry
and lean bodies there appear ripping claws. Between these
interstices, gasping his way through, comes a naked man, his long
hair wet and sticky as if with birth.*

The dream remained with me as I went to meet Zulkifli and
accompany him into the jungle. The excursion even seemed to
be an extension of that dream. For how else could the
extraordinariness of the physical details be explained? The
trees didn't appear to be trees; the leaves were anything but the
veined catchers of sunlight. The ground we walked on, though
covered with bushes and brambles, didn't have the grainy
resistance my body yearned for. By nightfall, on the first day,
time had ceased to matter.

We barely slept that night. Zulkifli began and kept up a long
conversation, much of which is lost to me now. What I do
recall is that his voice rose and fell and steadied itself, rich with
the memory of his ancestors. I resented this in him for I
couldn't think of anything beyond my father, whose life had
been a waste. He did tell me about my grandfather in India but
my memory retained no images. Out of this resentment was
born a strange ambition: to outdo Zulkifli in everything he
could do. And I decided not to give in to his desire to reveal
his private vision to me. I would remain my own man.

"We must find the tree stump my father mentioned,"
Zulkifli said the next morning. "My grandfather told him.
There's always a tree stump somewhere that man must pass."

"Why?"

94

"A sign," Zulkifli said. "Sign of men who have gone before. Sign for men who come after. But must be found."

His face had taken on a haunted look so that I felt I was there merely to be a mirror for his words. He barely noticed my presence filled as he was with the necessity to discover a way through to his ancestral memory. We seemed to be going round in circles. Then he stopped.

"No, I'm thinking too much of direction," he said. "My mind is working too much."

"Why must we get to that tree stump?" I said. "Why can't we use another way?"

"That tree stump is the door to the tiger's world," he said. "When we get there we stop being men."

"What do you mean?"

"You'll find out," he said.

He was like a man possessed and there was nothing for me to do but to follow him. We scurried this way and that; we cut diametrically across the route we had taken. We criss-crossed our own trails until we were lost and then he said, "We've found it!" And there it was, the sawed off tree trunk, like an ancient monument. Yes, it did look like a sign but not in the way he understood it. It stared at me like an abandoned, faulty compass, left there to warn man against trespassing in alien territories.

"Once we cross over, we change," Zulkifli said.

In spite of all my determination, I was a little frightened. Already way out of my normal, business world existence, I felt alienated. What will I be, I thought, when I stepped over? Zulkifli seemed like a man with a warrior-like ambition: to seek out the invisible enemy whose features he knew. I felt for the gun I had borrowed from Jimmy Kok. I had never used a gun in my life but its presence there, at my hip, gave me some confidence. There would be nothing, I decided, he could show me that would frighten me.

Had his words begun to work in a subtle way on me? When we stepped past that tree stump, a resisting stillness came up at us. The mind became quiet and expectant. It emptied itself of all its previous convictions and became, strangely, blank. This frightened me and I struggled with myself to recall a familiar idea, a reassuring thought but none came. I looked at Zulkifli and saw that he too, was going through a similar dilemma. But instead of resisting, he was surrendering himself to the blankness that destroyed.

"Must go through it," he said, trying to reassure me. "My forefathers did the same. Have to free ourselves from thoughts given to us by the past. Otherwise we can't move forward."

"I've no past," I said.

"Everyone has," he said, "including the one he wants to throw away. There mustn't be any resistance."

He didn't waste any more time on explanations; he moved on. I kept up with him but it was an effort to move my limbs. My legs seemed to strike against invisible currents of repulsion. Here where action seemed to matter, it was also being obstructed. After a few hours - a guess in that timeless zone - we made no progress and came to a helpless halt. We stared at each other, then lay down to rest and fell almost immediately into a deep sleep.

It was not so much a sleep as an awakening. You dreamed but the dream made no sense. You dreamed but you were not alone. You felt there was a watcher watching you dream and seeing you struggle to make sense of an incomprehensible thing. What I became aware of, when I woke up, was of a presence attempting to interfere with my thoughts and feelings. Had Zulkifli been there, inside that dream, vigilantly observing me?

In the duration of sleep or lapse into some kind of primordial forgetfulness, something had happened to us. When we became conscious, we were strangely open to each other. He didn't say anything about his forefathers and I didn't even think of preferences and desires. We hardly said anything: we just went into motion. From the present, I see that from this part on the excursion certainly took something of an unrealistic air.

Everything until then has the concreteness of the familiar but what follows is a nightmare of being trapped in the abstract. Both of us were overcome by something beyond us. This could be felt even in the way we walked. Our bodies seemed to respond to a rhythm we had never known before. Our bodies were no more in our control.

Freed from our influence on them, they came into their own expressions of motion. I didn't feel as if I was walking; it was more like my legs were leading me to the hidden core of its own birth-place. Zulkifli too looked as if he was being led. The hands and legs, swung, and flung themselves out, following some arc of their own progress. We didn't move so much as float through the thick undergrowth, creepers and the interstices of tree trunks. The ground came up at us in intermittent mosaics of colours and shapes so that we almost felt giddy. Our motion had a unity that couldn't be destroyed by ambition or self-centredness.

Time ceased to matter as we were led into the interior. I could hardly recall the town where I had my office. The dusty labyrinth of streets, walled in by buildings, seemed to have lost all its history. Every little gesture I had made in walking those streets became foreign to me. I seemed to have entered a bubble that shut out my sense of the past. Zulkifli and I walked as we had never walked before.

When darkness was added to the semi-darkness, it was as if the first day of creation had not come to an end. Our legs ached to go on but needed a pause to retain the freshness in them. So we lay half-awake and half-asleep in some corner of awareness. Or did I, alone, feel that way? And the dream that came, did I have it alone too?

The dream was strange: it stands out, even now, vividly. I am not myself any more: I am not a man. I am a chameleon. I see the world through a pair of eyes that never close. These apertures that are always open invite more and more of the world into the consciousness. The rough skin that covers my body tightens and slackens over a quintessential globule of life. That globule itself is filled with a network of nerves radiating in every direction to capture and make its own everything that comes in its way. What is outside those eyes, the skin, the nerves and what is inside are all one. From my perch up on a tall tree, I see everything. The ground below is covered with leaves of varying shades and colours; my claws let go of the firm grip on the tree trunk. I am hurtling now through the air and my skin pulsates with the changing patterns of colours and shapes. I am the flower I brush against, the bark I scrape past and, finally, hitting those matted leaves below I become the veins through which run centuries of blood.

Then we have got up and are moving again, not caring whether it is morning or night. From dream-time I enter personal time. Though we still walk in unison, I seem unable to repeat the effortless co-ordination of the time before. Something has begun to intrude. Something moves within me as a kind of impersonal ambition. Like an amoeba, I want to gobble up everything that comes my way, whether I can contain them or not.

Progress becomes a tension enjoyable for its own sake. I am determined not to let Zulkifli get ahead of me. But he goes on, almost blissfully ignorant of the stirrings within me. The air plasters itself like a thin, tensile membrane against my body, almost placental. I move with confidence and pride, as one who has newly discovered the strength in his limbs. Walking is work but work for which I have the capacity. Zulkifli's attention to getting to the inner circle, as he informs me, matches my own concentration. We seem to be held together by an invisible line that tugs us towards our destination.

"We've another crossing to make," he says, breaking a long silence. "The last one."

"When do we sight the tiger?"

"When we're ready," he says.

"I'm ready," I say.

"We must prepare ourselves for the tiger to find us," he says.

"I've my gun," I say.

"This is a tiger you can't kill," he says. "You've to see it first."

"I'll be the first to see it," I say.

For suddenly I am fired by the ambition to get past his protectiveness. How can he protect it when he can't even see it? I think. I have also begun to tire of the excursion. We have lost count of the days; the absence of time puts a great strain on my mind. So I move on ahead of him. Zulkifli shows no surprise or even envy. He merely follows, keeping me well within reach.

We go on in this way until - I can't say after how long - we come to a stop. Is it merely night or deep-centre night? All around us there is an immense silence. It isn't like the earlier silence which we heard because we had only just left civilization behind. This silence has a primeval impenetrability about it. Have we come nearer to the tiger? In the dim light - the batteries of our torchlights are getting weaker - I see Zulkifli is weary and inscrutable. His face gleams with a bronze-like impenetrability.

That is what we come up against in out next moment of wakefulness: impenetrability. We come into a clearing and are, suddenly, enclosed by watchfulness. The silence of the era before has now become all eyes. We can't take a step without being scrutinized for dignity and magnificence. We can't stand still without being assessed for our stature. We can't breathe without being aware that life is a gift. I am determined to hold on to this life, no matter what.

"The tiger is watching us," Zulkifli says. "But we are not ready to see it yet."

"We've to outwatch it," I say, feeling for my gun.

"No one can outwatch it," he says in a voice rich with heritage. "It has been here longer than us. Longer than man.

How much wiser it will be! More than an animal. More than anything we know."

As he speaks, he appears to be transformed. There is no more the haunted look he had when he started out. Or is it the filtered light that creates this impression? There is something abstract and inhuman about him. It is as if he has ceased to be himself and has become merely a voice. The tiger's voice? But I dismiss the thought as nonsense. How can a man know the tiger's nature?

"We've to leave everything behind," he says. "We've to be nothing to know the unknowable."

He begins to frighten me. I am going to hold to what I have at the moment. His words anger me. Why do I have to submit to his fantastical talk? I try to move but make no progress.

"The gun has to be left behind," he says. "I'm leaving the *parang* here. From now on we carry no weapons. They are useless."

Is it a miracle when after I dump the gun in a cachement of leaves my movements become more fluid? Some of the resistance to our advance seems to withdraw itself. As we go deeper and deeper some of my fatigue falls away. But I can't escape the vigilant eye. It is there on my head or back or legs. It is there in the front, ahead of us, beside us but all the time disconcertingly near.

"Any time now," Zulkifli says at my side. "But we've to take on the character of the tiger first. We must see through its eyes. Feel through its body. We must become the tiger."

"I'll kill it first," I say.

"With what?" he says.

"By surprising it," I say.

"Nothing can surprise it," he says. "We don't have the intelligence."

"You seem to know everything about it," I say.

---

parang - Long knife used usually by Malays.

"Through the instinct that has travelled to me through the blood of my ancestors," he says.

"Are you saying I can't have such an instinct?"

"You don't have ancestors here," he says.

"I can go directly to the tiger," I say, remembering the chameleon of my dreams.

A fresh wave of determination surges through me. Yes, I will sight and surprise the tiger. But once again this self-willed movement towards a goal is met by resistance. We have to push ourselves through an almost solid wall of resistance. Do I have to enter his rituals in order to enter the presence of the tiger?

"You must be without purpose to come into his presence," Zulkifli says as if reading my thoughts.

"Then I won't," I say.

"You've come this far," he says. "You must surrender your self to be the other self."

The letting go of purpose didn't happen at all. But Zulkifli was not to be opposed. He went into a ritual on my behalf. All I remember of it is the incessant chanting that came from his lips. Though the words poured from him, I only remember their sound. It was, if I can put it in this way, out of this world. So much so that it even affected my sight. The jungle became, suddenly, a seething mass of colours that glowed as if in a subterranean landscape. They fell all over my body in bands that were at first warm but later became almost intolerably hot. They didn't actually burn my skin but I could feel it peeling and leaving me in a vulnerable nakedness. Was that when I turned and ran? Or much, much later when my personality threatened to dissolve into nothingness? All the time the chant poured from Zulkifli's throat like an ageless invitation to disown whatever I was and to merge with the tiger. I didn't wait for that to happen.

CHAPTER EIGHT

PERHAPS I knew as I wandered all over the country, presumably in pursuit of wealth and stability, that there was something else to life besides money and success. How else can I account for the those intense periods of insatiable reading? This was a secret part of my existence before I married. I could shut myself away during the weekends and public holidays - numerous in this country - and do nothing else but read. In this I was fortunate that I had moved, during my university days, with friends who studied literature. I used to snatch some thick volume or other they had with them and return it a few days later. Many of the titles they mentioned or discussed remained in my mind long after I left university and I searched for them, tracing them to second-hand bookshops and the meagre collections in the odd public library. This pastime of mine was completely alien to my nature. Perhaps all that reading provided a contrasting view or views of life to the one I led.

There were moments when I needed reassurance, somewhat like my wife going into that private room of hers to re-immerse herself in the life and values from which she had come. I had to do it the other way - the world I came from always accompanied me - to view from a distance all those other worlds that didn't bear any resemblance to mine. The exercise gave more solidity and validity to the world I had created for myself. Was there any other reason that took me to fiction?

In the last few months I've got my wife to bring me books so that I could while away the time. Or is it because I want to discover a different sense of time? Isn't time, after all, the chief problem in a man's life? If you're attached to time, you're bonded to a machine that gives you no chance to breathe. In the time that I've been in this room, I've also been free. That's a strange thing to say but it is true. The clock traps you within its division of hours; the walls of a room, on the other hand, release you from confinement. Am I thinking and expressing myself like Sivasurian? Like Zulkifli? I've been reading Sivasurian's book. He writes in his book:

Not A Story, Not A Chronicle

Even though what I write here is about myself, it is also, looking from another side, not about myself. Before I forget - forgetfulness is the food which fed me with the life I know - I didn't even think, at one time, I would hold a pen and write into a bundle of pages. I didn't, at any one time, have a writing language. I only had a speaking language and that too different from the language people talked.

When I first heard the English tongue, it was from the mouth of a boy getting ready to go to school. Perhaps I had a good teacher in that boy. The innocent teach more fully than the grown-up. I had to sit, with my legs crossed, before him and play that I was his pupil. That was during the in-between hours in the eating shop. Those hours when business was not going and the proprietor's wife wanted to sleep. But, as I found out later, even the language the innocent teach becomes corrupted as one grows up. (I hear that the boy has grown into a famous lawyer. What a waste of energy!) So my language doesn't always obey my thoughts. It always is jumping here and prancing there. I'll try to use it in such a way that its showing-off can be controlled.

I've always been a wanderer; that's why, I think, my parents were removed from me very early in life. A wanderer cannot carry too much baggage with him, not even his next meal for it might spoil before it is eaten. He has to be light in his body, mind and the other thing people put near the heart. Soul? Atman? Brahman? (Words stand for things; they are not the things themselves. How can they hold within themselves invisible qualities?)

People look at me and wonder: Does he worry about not having a family, a home? They even ask me the question face-to-face. I've no answer. There has always been a home for me wherever I go. When I go and sit in the verandah of a house after miles of travelling, no one chases me away. If I don't look at what they own, at their women like other men do, they soon offer me a glass of water. I never tell them sad stories for I've no such stories. I only say, 'If you can let me lie in a corner of the verandah, I'll be happy.' If they have an empty room, they let me sleep there. They give me something to eat. And always the food tastes good because it is given freely. I do some work for them the next day but usually they don't want anything in return.

In such a manner, I've travelled all over the country, through the years, through my life. But the years have brought changes to the people and places I've known. I can only talk about the differences, not saying which is better - the old life or the new one. I look around and see men and women going through a lot of suffering. Why is there so much suffering? Why is there so much pain? There is pain only at birth, for the woman; pain at death, for the person who dies. There is nothing to pay for being born and nothing to pay for having to die.

And between these two happenings there is a country to give your life a place and a time. Any country. I was born into a country without making a choice. There must be a cause for this happening - a cause outside the understanding of man. Man knows many things but understands very little. He knows how a car runs and feeds it with petrol. But when it stops and can't move again he runs for help to the man who understands. I always wonder why man has stopped being man. When man is not himself, he can't run to anyone. He has to go back the way he came to understand what he is. But has he the courage to go back over his own steps?

104

The Old Time

I remember when the times, made by man, was bad, the people who settled in this country were in doubt of themselves and the land. Man-printed money was like a river that had dried up. Everywhere I saw people trying to push themselves up from the floor of poverty. They cheated and said false words. A woman, in front of my eyes, hid a fistful of rice from the swollen belly of a starving child. The people who had come from India, cursing its poverty, now saw in their hunger-filled dreams a motherland flowing with milk and honey. They had a picture of a land which, in their absence, had grown into the tree of plenty. So they cursed this land, its heat, its rains, its not giving them work to earn the money for their food.

And the people who ruled the country too saw them as a burden that must be removed. So the song of the motherland was sung and dry faces made wet with tears. Desperation was piled upon desperation until there was no reason left. And soon they, the discontented, took up the cry, 'Let us go home! Let us go home! Our mother there will feed us, clothe us, give back to us our dignity.'

The little work they had, they stopped doing. When you looked at their eyes you only saw the walls of their dreams. They collected their pots and pans, pillows and mats and waited for the day the government would give them tickets to get into a ship. There were few ships and those who could get places packed themselves like sardines in a can. There were some who couldn't get places and jumped into the sea and drowned.

And war was approaching in the white man's land and the Japanese were also becoming war-like. The rush to return to India became wild. They didn't only want food and dignity but also safety. Wherever I went there was only this talk: 'Will there be more ships? This small land can be swallowed up by those powerful countries. Can't our bones be buried in the soil that gave them flesh?'

At last these voices were heard no more. The land was ours. A fresh wind blew through everything. Men, women and children looked at themselves as if they were born again. Their eyes burned with fires of their own, fires not polluted by ambition, dissatisfaction or longing. They didn't know of anywhere else; they didn't belong to anywhere else. They were in the land that had been chosen for them.

I stayed near a *kampung* not far from the sea that separated Penang from the mainland. It was from there that I saw the people take their no-understanding away with them. I stayed with Murugiah, the carpenter, who had a house on a plot of land between the kampung and the small town. Murugiah had never talked about going back to India. When these others left, he let out a sigh and said, 'Now we can do the work we're born to do. Now we can stay where we're born to stay.'

When everything else becomes barren there is always the earth that yields. The people who stayed knew this and a gladness came into their hearts and strength into their bodies. They worked with quickened hopes. I didn't want to wander about for a time so I worked with them.

There was always sharing. I went, sometimes, to the kampung to visit Sulaiman if I didn't see him at the river bank. He was always on the steps of the verandah, satisfied with what his hands had done for the day. He too had worked on the land and gone to the river to get some fish. 'They're hiding from us, Siva,' he said. 'I think they know we'll kill even the young when we're hungry.' But he said this with laughter in his eyes. There was always laughter in every word that came from his mouth. I gave him some *brinjals* and maize; he gave me a comb of bananas and some groundnuts. These things became our kind of greeting and understanding. He sometimes came to Murugiah's house and we sat under the tall, many-branched tree. We sat and talked as man with man, not as people made differentby their own kinds of worship and living.

Not only the two of us. There were meeting grounds where more of us gathered. One was the river bank, a few yards from

brinjals—Eggplant.
kampung- Village.

Sulaiman's house. In the mornings and afternoons, the river was a place for washing and bathing. In the evenings the people from the kampung and the houses near Murugiah's gathered here. The children played late games; the men and women talked.

'We're always river people,' Sulaiman said. 'Without the river there is no life.'

'We're sea people,' Murugiah said. 'Without the sea we won't be here.'

'The river flows into the sea,' Sulaiman said, laughing. 'So we can't remain by ourselves. We must mingle.'

River-people. Sea-people. Such good words. Words that kept us together. Both the peoples also met under Murugiah's tree, this time the town-people coming to join us. These two places, the river-ground and the tree-ground, became important in our lives.

There was that time when already having to tighten the cloth around our bellies, we also had to face other problems. That was one time when the smiles went from our faces. We were sitting on the beating stones, tree trunk benches and just looking at the river or smoking when Sulaiman came to us, worry on his face.

'My daughter can't be found anywhere,' he said.

We all knew her, a girl just turning into a woman. Though Sulaiman didn't say anything else, we sent word to the people in the estates, the town and to neighbours nearer to us. None of them had seen her.

Families which had daughters looked at them with new eyes. They were not just girls who had to be fed, clothed, taught household work and then be married off. They were lives that could not be put out of the memory.

We gathered at the river bank or at the tree-ground. We were more of a community now. We had only one ambition: to find that girl. When the police, newspapers and our own search-men failed, we went to the *bomoh*. This bomoh had only one leg but his reputation had already travelled to many states. He spoke in riddles and Sulaiman returned with these words,

---

bomoh - Malay shaman.

'If Rosnah can find her mind, then she would be found.' An elderly Indian woman seeing the despair on Sulaiman's face, said, 'We must go to someone who speaks more plainly.'

She took Sulaiman to an Indian *mantra* man; this man was an ascetic and read ashes. He had a tray of holy ash in which he burned camphor. He spoke thus: 'We're in your beholding. We've come from ashes and we will return to ashes. But before you claim us, you must clear the obstacles that stop us from returning to ashes.'

Then he took the girl's birth date and wrote it down in the ashes and made some calculations. He chanted and burned more camphor, then began to breathe in a heavy way. Then though he was in a trance, he began to shake his head and say, 'You've consulted others before me? Why do you come to me? They have spoken the truth: find her mind and you will find her body.'

No one talked about hope or mentioned sorrow after the mantra man's words reached them. Work went on. People still talked to one another. Sulaiman said to me, 'To have lived life for better or worse is better than never to know what life can lead to.' Something had made us all deep inside ourselves. Sulaiman never talked that way.

Everyone joined in the search for Rosnah but not Ah Chong. He and Sulaiman had been good friends. Ah Chong could never have had a daughter if Sulaiman had not helped him. His marriage had been barren for some years. At the time I speak of, he already had three children: a girl and two boys. Sulaiman had helped him have the first child, the girl. He took Ah Chong and his wife to several men who knew country medicine. At last one of them made Ah Chong's seed grow inside his wife's womb. After the girl was born, Ah Chong turned away from Sulaiman saying it was his own blood that had brought the child into the world. They had not spoken to each other from that time.

---

mantra - Magic verse.

108

He was always in his sundry shop. If he left it to visit people, it was always with something in his mind. If he talked politely to us, it was because he wanted us to buy from his shop. He never gave anything away. 'Why should I give anything free?' he said, without smiling. 'My life isn't free. It was never given to me. I had to buy it with hard work. Get up at six o'clock and don't go to sleep until late at night.'

He was right. He never rested. When the lorry came to unload things for his shop, he helped to carry them like a coolie. He mended torn sacks so he could sell them back. He swept the shop himself. There was always in his eyes the look that picks out only one thing for consideration. But when he came to us one day, a month after Sulaiman's daughter had disappeared, there was a kind of shadow in his eyes.

We were seated on rattan chairs on the tree-ground in front of Murugiah's house. He stood for a long time listening to us.

'This isn't right! This isn't right!' he said, suddenly breaking into our talk. 'She can't disappear just like that. She is a human being.'

'It isn't your worry, Ah Chong,' Sulaiman said.

'What I did wasn't right,' Ah Chong said. 'It was long ago. You must forget that, Sulaiman.'

'What can we do, Ah Chong?' Sulaiman said, surprised to see the change in Ah Chong.

'The life must be replaced,' Ah Chong said.

'My wife is too old for that, Ah Chong,' Sulaiman said.

'No, not in that way,' Ah Chong said.

'What other way is there?' Sulaiman said.

Ah Chong looked away. When his face was returned to our gaze, we saw on it a hardness as well as a softness. He put away the stiff Ah Chong we all knew.

'Only now I see how you've all been looking for that girl. All this while I was thinking it can't happen to me.'

'Has your daughter also disappeared?' Sulaiman said.

'No, but can also happen to her,' Ah Chong said.

'Something has gone wrong inside your head,' Sulaiman said.

'Everything has become right,' Ah Chong said, laughing, and so he made us laugh too.

It wasn't human beings laughing; it was just laughter like rain falling on their foolishness. Ah Chong didn't have to say much; we understood. His words came released from the purity of his heart.

'We mustn't give up,' he said.

'We've tried everything,' Sulaiman said.

'Not everyone has tried. I've done nothing,' Ah Chong said. 'Now it's my turn.'

He became part of our sorrow and part of our search. It was not as if we were searching for a lost girl; it was as if we were searching for something lost in ourselves.

'I won't give up,' Ah Chong said. 'The day I give up I'll give my own daughter into your family.'

'The feeling is good enough, Ah Chong,' Sulaiman said.

'Not good enough,' Ah Chong said. 'We've to act on our feelings.'

He was true to his word. Though he stood behind his counter every day, it wasn't in the old way. There was something moving behind him. The machinery of some world we didn't know about, was working away behind him. We could even hear the sound but the shape of the machine we couldn't tell. It was like waking up in the middle of the night, when everybody else is sleeping, and finding yourself in a strange world, real and not to be ignored.

'Nothing yet,' he said when he saw us, 'but it will come.'

After about three months he looked tired and defeated. Sulaiman was treating his daughter's disappearance as one of life's misfortunes. One day Ah Chong came to us, looking sad.

'Pak Man,' he said. 'It's time I kept my promise. It's time for my daughter to go to your family.'

We looked at each other and saw there were no strangers among us. It was as if we had known each other long before our separate births. We felt there was no need to give or to take. Taking and giving were of this world; our common blood had its own universe.

110

'There's no need for this, Ah Chong,' Sulaiman said. 'Being together in this is enough.'

But Ah Chong was not to be consoled and went away even more determined to find Sulaiman's daughter. To make the story short, it must be said that Ah Chong managed to find the girl. She was living in the south of the country. She had missed her family but was told by a relative that a tragedy had struck them. She had followed this man, who called himself a relative, to a new home. Fortunately, she looked after herself well so that she wasn't abused. The so-called relative, as Sulaiman found out, was only an adventurer who carried away young girls for immoral purposes.

When the girl returned, there was great rejoicing. Everyone, for miles around, came to the *kenduri* given with the money and provisions donated by every quarter. Ah Chong was the chief donator. I've never seen such a gathering before or since. It was, for me, the last memorable occasion of the old time. There was so much togetherness, trust and innocence. We didn't behave like single men or women but more like a people with a common heart and mind. Whoever reads this will think I don't belong to this world. He may be right.

What's there in this world to belong to?

And so I come to the place that is now called the world.

A New Time

It was after the war that I returned to Murugiah's house and compound. The war had brought many changes but what I saw when I reached the small town, I couldn't believe.

There was a smell in the air that wasn't pleasant. The war had done much damage but the physical ruins had been more or less removed or repaired. The smell came from deep inside. It showed itself in the neglect of the trees, plants and animals that my path crossed from the railway station to Murugiah's house.

---

kenduri - Feast.

111

When I got down from the train, the afternoon sun looked like the pale unhealthiness on a sick person's face. The track I followed was too cindery and passed the river where we had met so often. What a change had come to it! Long before I could see near the bank the firm river bed underneath the clear water. Now the water was muddy. All kinds of things had been built into the river: something like a scaffold rose out of the middle to make me think that people were dipped, hung from its bars, in the river. Did the Japanese do that? Did they show to man another difference between life and death? And there was a low, concrete box with tiny holes in its sides, built against the bank. It looked like a man's squashed head, the eyes like slits that would see nothing.

The last time I had been in that place, the river had been important to us. On most evenings, after the women and children had bathed and gone home, the men gathered there on the open space beside the river. That was where Sulaiman had come with news of his daughter's disappearance; that was where we had discussed the ways to find her. The river had joined us together, run like a hidden current through all our hearts. During those dark, quiet evenings it was another voice behind all our voices. When we came to its bank, angry and hot, it cooled us down and soothed us. When we came happy and jubilant it cradled our lighted hearts. Now all that was left was a murkiness and as I found out some days later, very few people came to its banks.

Beyond the banks more houses had been added to the kampung. The new houses were bigger and had larger compounds. I looked for Sulaiman's house but couldn't find it. I went on to Murugiah's place. And there I found another strange thing: a barbed wire fence had been put up all around the compound. And what had happened to the thick-branched tree, which had been another meeting place for us? It had been cut down. The stump, I could see, was just beginning to rot.

I had always called it the man-tree because it was built like a man's waist and the branches above rounded off like shoulders. The other reason why I called it the man-tree was

112

because it was shy of wearing flowers. It wasn't like the flame-of-the-forest which was proud of showing off its flowers. The *angsana* shamelessly dropped its flowers all over the ground. But this tree hid its bunch of flowers up at the top like a bride unwilling to unveil her beauty. Another thing the tree did: it tried to turn away our attention from its flowers with the winged fruit it cast down. Just as we said, 'Ah, at last we can see its flowers!' what should come spinning down from the top but the winged fruit. The fruit spun and turned and whirled down with such a gentle sound that we forgot everything else. The tree couldn't hide its true nature. The wings of its fruit were the petals of the flowers it was trying to conceal. It didn't have the guile found in the human world.

Murugiah had put on age and death was always in his mind. Two of his older sons had died at the hands of the Japanese on the Burmese Death Railway. Out of the thousands who went to build those tracks, only a few returned. I heard stories that told of all the men in a family - father and sons - dying while constructing that hated railway. It was no surprise to hear that Murugiah wished for death.

'Do you know what's happening around us?'
he said. 'Worse than the death railway. That's a kind of madness that happens only in centuries. Here we're building madness for centuries.'

Sometimes what you see you don't want to believe. That was why I journeyed back to the small town. The rest of the country, it seemed to me, had entered into behaviour that went away from the spirit of sharing. I couldn't understand what was happening all over the country.

There were gatherings everywhere. Not in celebration but in some other mood. The Japanese had surrendered; the British had returned. The war was gone but what it had brought, remained. I had travelled about during the Japanese Occupation freely. I had nothing to lose: no family or relatives of any kind. If the Japanese soldiers made me bow before them,

---

angsana - Malaysian tree with yellow flowers.

113

I bowed. If the body bent in humiliation, the spirit inside still remained upright. If they made me work, I worked. So moving down the country in this way, I saw a lot of happenings not found in peace time. But now I saw that there was no difference between war time and peace time.

Instead of waving guns and swords, they fluttered banners with slogans written on them. Instead of submitting to a foreign invader, they made enemies among themselves. The hiding of themselves, in fear, away from the public's notice, was gone. Now the people were to be seen everywhere but not joined together by some common feeling.

I stayed a few weeks with Murugiah and saw what had become of the people I once admired. At last, after some days of hunting, I discovered Sulaiman. He had not gone far away; he was only busy going here and there among the kampungs not far from the town.

He had moved farther back so that his house now stood on a larger piece of land. He was building the house, room by room because after the war there was little money for anything. He greeted me warmly but also with surprise. There was something about his face I didn't understand immediately. It was only after I had seen and greeted a few more men that I recognized what I had seen in Sulaiman's face. There was sadness in it and also an anger like smouldering fire.

He didn't look at me when he spoke. His eyes looked at something behind my head. When our eyes met accidentally, he quickly looked away. During my previous stay with them, this had not happened. We had always looked into each other as into a pool and saw everything there. There had been nothing to hide.

"Where were you living during the war?" he said.

"Here and there," I said.

"You've not changed at all," he said. "Terrible things happened here. Terrible things are happening."

"What terrible things?"

"You've to see for yourself," he said.

We didn't have more time to talk. He had to go to another kampung, as he said, to wake up the people. I came away feeling even more lost. Sulaiman showed all the friendliness I expected but something was missing. He didn't mention his daughter or Ah Chong.

Suddenly invisible walls had come up all over the place. Did the war do that? The fear of the Japanese, I knew, had joined the people together. There was something between the Chinese and the Japanese. A happening in some other country, some other history which made them unnatural enemies. So the Chinese were made to suffer the most. They had to make all kinds of money donations to the Japanese; they were called the running dogs of the white men. In Ipoh, I remember, many of them had their heads cut off. These heads were then stuck on bamboo poles and shown in public places as a warning to all traitors. How their women suffered! Young girls had to have their hair cropped and wore boys' clothes to escape the attentions of the Japanese soldiers.

Many Chinese families went away into the countryside and lived in rooms built under the rooms of houses. And the Malays helped many of them to escape Japanese detection. The price was their own lives! What was it I saw during those four years of Japanese occupation of the country? A common look, a common feeling, a common desire; face - Malay, Chinese, Indian - filled with disgust and fear, hearts filled with hatred for the enemy and a yearning for freedom.

What did I find when I returned to the small town and its surroundings? People who wanted to make history. Fortunately for me, I don't have a history. No past. No desire to give value to a past. No ambition to make an undying story of events in my life. For what wants to live must die. But men think they can go on living and whatever they build must not die.

The Japanese wanted to build but they only built destruction. They sowed the seed of hate and violence, the seeds of a false superiority. Therefore it was a time for people to shine. They lighted all kinds of lamps to show up their personalities. It was a time when a man tried to stand out in the crowd. And each man wanted a country of people behind him.

Before there was only one country. Now there were many countries inside that one country. This became clear when I went to see Ah Chong. He wasn't there standing behind his counter. He was in a room, deep inside the shop. His sons asked me many questions before they let me see him. And then I had to wait a long time before he came.

While waiting, I looked around myself. It wasn't because I had nothing to do. It was because the place had changed so much. During that other time, the things in the shop lay about everywhere. Sometimes even Ah Chong didn't know where to find something a customer wanted. Sacks of rice were piled on top of each other; cardboard boxes were stacked even higher. Between them were small packets of sugar or salt people needed. Those sacks, boxes and packets didn't have to worry about a home. They could just be left to lie wherever they could be found.

But this time, after the war, standing there in the shop, I had a different feeling. I might have been in a railway warehouse. Everything was stuck with labels and put in the right place. Sugar packets were unmixed with salt packages. Rice sacks had their own neat place; flour packs were arranged next to them. All the small things needed by households were at hand, easily seen. There was too much order and convenience. It made me think of people who were packed and ready to run when necessary. It also reminded me of people who wanted to save as much of their property as possible in case of fire, flood or other troubles.

When Ah Chong came at last, he looked a changed man. The hard face wasn't there, nor the soft face. His eyes didn't look into just his own world; they seemed also to guard against other worlds that might try to push down his own world. He didn't smile when he looked at me; he was like a man in a hurry and had no time for people. He was like a man who worried whether people would take away his possessions.

116

"Why do you come here?" he said. "This place isn't good any more."

"Better than other places," I said.

"You've just come," he said, shaking his head. "You haven't seen many happenings."

"The war?"

"After the war," he said. "Now the armies have sweeter tongues than your friends. Go away to some other town."

"It's the same everywhere."

"Then stay and fight for your staying," he said.

His words were strange. As I went back to Murugiah's house, I thought how strange it was that men could become violent so suddenly. Had the war fed them with a taste for violence? We had all seen all kinds of atrocious doings. Men had soap water pumped into them and the same soap water pumped out by a soldier jumping on the stomach. Men having their nails pulled out; men beaten until their flesh hung down like shreds of old clothes. Men beheaded. Why didn't these spectacles horrify them?

May be violence had changed its face and become something else. It didn't show itself so much as the desire to harm another person in the body. It went even deeper. I saw it sometimes in the faces of the people who had been my friends and companions. The people I had known had all become so transformed I couldn't recognize them any more.

It was a nightmare land I slowly entered as I stayed on in that small town. Murugiah allowed me to stay in his house with a welcome that was frightening. He made sure I was in the house most of the time. He fed me well; he gave me a comfortable bed. This wasn't hospitality. It was an aggressive desire to have me to himself. But I got away as often as I could.

What I saw during that second stay with Murugiah remains still like a nightmare in my mind. I had never seen people become peoples. Yes, I know this is a strange way of saying it. But, to me, words have not the power to be things. People were things; their feelings were things; their ambitions were things. These were too real, if sometimes hidden beneath the surface.

A man's looks became vulnerable; the clothes he wore became important. The property he owned and the car he drove became powerful. But the most important thing was that he make himself grow in the eyes of the people. This growing in the eyes of other people became such a passion that everything else was forgotten.

The soil of such growth was crowds or gatherings. There were tea parties, feasts and public speaking on platforms. They became festivals for those men who wanted to make something big of themselves. These men talked, scolded, sang, criticized and even danced. They behaved like any other actor on the stage. The crowds grew excited as they would when watching a stage show. As I stood there, among the audience, I felt like them: I wanted more and more of the emotion the speaker could stir in me. But when I came away the emotion just died. May be I wasn't like the other spectators who went every day to these performances. And the performance lived beyond the stage, through the many conversations about what the performer had said and done, in coffeeshops and houses and families.

I saw Sulaiman go up on that stage; I saw Ah Chong go up on another stage...

Sivasurian's writing doesn't come to an end there. I suddenly realize I've to go on a journey. I recall his words, "You've to go back the way you came so you can know where you are." I don't know where I am but I can sense that the road I've travelled so far is paved with blindness. What's it exactly that I haven't seen? I seemed to have gone on some stage myself and insisted, in my own way, what I thought life and country should have been. So, now, as I see it, another kind of travelling lies before me. I've to return to that region where I can meet Zulkifli and try to look at things through a different lens.

CHAPTER NINE

WHEN I packed my simple bag for travel my wife was surprised but also relieved. Was she glad because I was at last stirring from the room or because she could at last be herself, even if it was only for a short while?

"Where are you going?" she said.

"To bring back some people I had left out of my life," I said.

"The place?"

"Up north," I said.

"For how long?"

"I don't know," I said.

She opened her mouth to say something else, then stopped herself. And so I've been on the road for some time now. No, I haven't been going directly to my destination, which is the kampung where I still hope Zulkifli is living, up in the north of·the country. After all those months of staying in my room, I found the first few days in the outside world a torture to my sight and to my body. I could hardly move with any sense of balance. It was like watching my own birth: the limbs ached with lesions and the head throbbed with a hundred, bewildering impressions.

The sight of the contractor giving instructions to his workers, from beside a dusty, parked car, disgusts me. Is it because I was myself in that man's position not too long ago? At another place, along the newly-built road leading into a town, I see men cutting down trees. Already small, wooden stakes have been driven into the ground and string stretched out in a tight line between them. These marked out areas, which will soon be paved with rough, cement blocks rouse an unexpected anger inside me. All these I observe from my seat in the bus going up to the north. I've taken to travelling as an ordinary man for, then, like Sivasurian, I might see more.

I break off journey, sometimes, in a small town, away from the highway. I choose an old-fashioned hotel with rooms partitioned off with plywood sheets and serviced by a communal bathroom. The dust and the noise come in from the streets outside but I don't mind them. In fact, I like the cold water, drawn from the fungus-bottomed tubs, cutting into my fatigued flesh. The grains of sand or dust that get into the crevices of my body give me the sense of being in contact with something real.

I'm looking outside these days, without any attempt to colour what I see. Though I feel vulnerable, I'm not afraid. It's an unseeing I'm going through, that is, removing all the layers of personal prejudice I gave to everything. Mani, the goat, that was slaughtered on that Deepavali eve, keeps coming back to me. What is it about his eyes that still fascinates me?

The towns I've stopped at, so far, are barely touched by the modern rebuilding spirit. The buildings I've seen seem to be filled with a history of their own. Time hasn't - if this is possible - destroyed their personalities. They stand, these shops and houses, witnesses to the sufferings and trauma their occupants underwent.

The travel continued, with stops here and there, and I'm at last in the town where my firm, Apex Co., had its origins. I don't look back on that part of my life with any enthusiasm. The drive I had at that time seems to have gone out of me. The town itself has changed beyond recognition. Some of the moves I initiated have become assimilated into a larger complex of expansion. I see little of myself in the town. Perhaps that's a good thing too.

When I dropped in on Jimmy Kok and Ramasamy, they didn't know me at all and took a bit of reminding before they recognized me. Jimmy Kok has become paunchy and is coarser in the face, which is heightened by the secretiveness in his eyes. Ramasamy simply rattles on, indifferent to what the others have to say. Their businesses have prospered and you can see the pride with which they accept their positions.

As I walk around the town - I stay in the newly-built hotel - I find it hard to reconcile myself to the idea that I once lived here. My office building is now occupied by an air-conditioned restaurant. The court house and the district office buildings have hardly left a trace of their existence. A whole history has been eclipsed. It's unfortunate that I had a hand in such a process. But looking back - yes, I contradict myself here - I see that history always meant something more than just places and events. History, as I now realize, is an accumulation of the individuality of man's and peoples' actions. Without these there can be no recognition of ourselves in the times that we lived. I've lost that anchorage in my life and only vaguely sense where I've to turn to for a more meaningful centre. Perhaps this zigzagged trekking back to Zulkifli might help me find that centre.

Pak Zul - that's how people address him now - hardly had any difficulty in recognizing me. I seemed to detect the reverse in him: an intense familiarity with my features or with the features of my kind. His eyes glowed with suspicion and hostility, then assumed the warmth of hospitality. His wife, Kak Jamilah, did not hide her resentment and indifference towards me. All the time that I stayed in her house, which was only for a night and a day, she kept away from me. She put the dinner and the lunch on the table and withdrew.

"Something happened in our family," Zul said, the following morning. "I'll speak of it later."

After the afternoon meal he indicated that I should pack my bag and follow him. I accompanied him to a hillock, half a kilometre away from his house. Built on its slope was a small hut on stilts, almost hidden from view by a clump of trees. The kampung road, for progress has come here as elsewhere, runs past the hut - rubberized and darkly assertive - a few yards away.

Zul has put me up in the hut without, at first, telling me its history. The hut is sufficiently equipped for a simple, solitary existence. Beyond the small hut is a basic kitchen with a charcoal or firewood stove. Against one wall is a rough table where meals can be eaten. Plates, cups, a kettle and a kuali were still where the previous occupant had left them. About three steps connect the kitchen and the hall, on one side of which is a single room. A small window opens onto the tree-surrounded solitude of the place. The shutters are, for some strange reason, nailed tightly shut along plank pieces laid diagonally across the frame. This puzzled me at that time but I didn't ask Zul for an explanation. I wanted him to thaw out in his own way and in his own time.

The day he brought me here - some time has passed - we sat in the verandah watching the sun set. When it was night and mosquitoes began to buzz around us, he went into the hut and returned with a box of chemical coils.

"I hope they still burn," he said, extracting a dusty looking coil. "Bought a long time ago."

He had to scrape a few match-sticks before the coil glowed and filled the air with its acrid smoke.

We sat in the dark for a while longer, in silence. Then he cleared his throat and spoke as if with a hidden purpose. With age his voice had taken on a gravelly, convincing tone.

"You went away without saying anything to me," he said.

"Business took me away," I said.

"Why did you return?" he said. "We're not selling land. There isn't enough land for our own planting."

"I didn't come back to buy or to sell," I said. "Business doesn't interest me now."

"Have a lot of money in the bank?"

"I don't even think about that," I said.

"You don't have to think about anything," he said, an accusing tone coming into his voice. "I didn't think I would build this hut. But I had to."

"Tell me," I said. "May be I'll understand."

"You ran away from understanding, remember?" he said.

"I've returned," I said.

"May be you'll like this story," he said, "even if you don't understand. A long time stands between us. You never really saw my family, my children. I came always to your office room. And we went on that trip. Then you went away. And my children grew up. They began to read about ideas, listen to ideas and even try out ideas. Like you. My eldest son, Mat, he was always reading, watching television. One day he packed his bag and left for Kuala Lumpur. Just like that.

"He was there for more than a year. Wrote to us sometimes. Going to some institute. Working in some company. Then nothing but silence. Then without any message or letter he returned to us. He had long hair and had grown a beard. His mother nearly fainted. His brothers and sisters were too afraid to go near him.

"Mak Milah went into the kitchen and stayed there a long time. I stood in the verandah, my heart beating fast. I asked myself, 'Is this my son or a stranger?'

"Though his neighbours and former friends came to greet him, he didn't look at them or say a word.

"After he had bathed, he sat in the doorway, his wet hair curled like snakes around his neck. He took the tea his brother, Jamil, offered him and, whistling, drank it. He wouldn't notice anyone.

"A week passed without a single word coming from his mouth. He went to the kitchen and ate when we were not there. He made a bed for himself in a corner of the children's room. Soon they came to us. 'He fights with enemies we can't see,' they said.

"Suddenly, in the middle of the second week, he hugged his mother and cried for a long time. Mak Milah thought he was her son again. That evening he broke some cups and plates, throwing them against the kitchen wall. 'None of you understand!' he shouted and ran into his room.

"Every day, for a week, we didn't know how he would behave. Sometimes he sat with his head in his hands. Sometimes he stood without moving, his hands on his waist as if he was holding a weapon. Then he would talk for a long time with some invisible friend.

"When he went away to the city he didn't smoke. But now, on some mornings, he never stopped smoking.

"He lived out of one bag. The others were tightly shut and no one could go near them. All the clothes his mother washed were folded and put in that one, open bag.

"The nights were embarrassing and without sleep for us. He shouted, screamed and banged on the walls. Our neighbours looked at us in a certain way. I told Mak Milah that we had to send him away.

" 'He's of our blood,' she said.

"In our culture no man loses his mind. Something may trouble him but he would soon return to his senses. I consulted the elders in this place and I built this hut for him.

"Mat seemed pleased. He wandered around the newly-built hut. He smiled at us. He kept himself busy while we dug a well for his needs. It was unnecessary, we thought to bring the water pipes to the hut. We expected him to stay there only for a short while. When the water came into the well, he scrubbed and washed the floors of the hut. We could visit him but he wouldn't let us into the only room in this hut.

"Even before he went to the city, he was fond of playing the harmonica. He had brought one back from the city. From it floated strange tunes in the evenings. When the nights were still we could hear them even from our house. Sometimes there was a strange fury in the music. On such nights I couldn't sleep until morning.

"I looked into the hut the next morning. He was curled up there, in the hall, sleeping. The window and the door were open. I found an extra sarung and covered him up.

"In the afternoon, after such nights, a far-away look came into his eyes. He sat there on the steps, shivering, even when the day was hot.

"The harmonica music was good to hear sometimes; at other times it wasn't so good. The following morning he was either silent and withdrawn or violent and noisy. He cut marks on the kitchen table. He threw stones and soil on the walls of the hut. Many times he hurt himself. We had to clean his cuts and put medicine on them.

"All this time he didn't talk to me face-to-face. When I visited him, he went on doing whatever he was doing. I was just another thing in the hall. If the lamp's wick grew dim for lack of oil, I filled the small tank. I had stocked the kitchen with a kettle, pot, cups, plates, coffee, sugar and milk. He bought some other things for himself.

"When I made coffee for him, he drank it quickly even though the tongue could be burnt.

"Then one night he began to talk to me. He only wanted me to listen. Words came out like a river in flood: there was destruction even of the simplest thoughts and of the world as I knew it. His face was distorted; his hands made aggressive gestures. I got a strong picture of the life he had led in the city.

"When I went there to look for him during those months of silence, I learned a lot of things. People didn't calmly survive as we do here. Even those squatter houses I saw possessed something more than dirt, squalor and ugliness. They possessed spirit, showed man at his toughest. Man was indifferent to the present; he planned and worked for the future. Here there is a tide of events towards death. There is only one thought in our heads: acceptance.

"Those tall buildings there seemed to show how man could fly through the air while his feet were on the ground. How amazing everything seemed to me! But my son had a different view. He saw darkness where I saw only light. He talked about long tunnels that went through the very buildings I had seen. He talked about invisible strings that controlled painted and neatly dressed people. It was necessary to flow, he said. To sweep obtacles away. Progress was another name for loneliness, for coldness between people. Those tall buildings were, for him, sharp razors that tried to cut to shreds the soft, blue sky. The planes that flew over them were monsters of disaster. They took man away from man though they reached foreign countries and arrived at new cities.

"It was difficult to follow his thoughts but his voice forced you to listen. Those puppets in the city cut you down without mercy, he said. They trampled all over you. They built large houses on your broken bones. Their cars drove over your ashes.

'No, Mat, no!' I said, but he wouldn't stop talking.

"They care more for the bodies of cars, he said than for the bodies of men.

"Suddenly he stopped talking.

"Mat left his moorings behind: friends, neighbours, relatives and family.

"We didn't have to wait long for the worst to happen. Mat sometimes roamed the kampung. He wasn't violent or used abusive language. Sometimes he picked up things along the way. Flowers from a house or a cardboard box that had been thrown away. If anyone saw him doing it, he asked for permission.

"Though he didn't talk to me, he treated his mother with respect when she visited him. He didn't smoke when she was there. And always he begged for her pardon. Mak Milah always returned with wet eyes.

"The kampung people shared my troubles. They were always on the lookout for new ways to bring back my son's mind. Nothing brought results. There was only one thing to do: send him to a hospital. We disliked that. Only God can cure the ills of the mind and spirit.

126

"Time didn't bring peace to my son. Most of the days he pretended to be a soldier, acting under special orders. He patrolled the hut and stood ground over it. He threw suspicious looks on all who passed its steps.

"I should have paid attention to the knife cuts on the table in the kitchen. The way they were made showed frustration and anger. I missed all the other signs too. The grass on the slope had been pulled up in patches. Some plants beside the hut were neatly slashed, their branches made sharp and pointed.

"Mak Milah, when she visited him on the eve of the fateful day, found him calm and almost normal. It was she who cried now and Mat who consoled. He told her that the light of reason had at last touched him. He talked of a kenduri for his return into kampung life.

"The day the tragedy occurred, a deep quietness lay over the kampung. Even the children, who usually played noisy games, were hushed. The women made no conversation while they worked. The river in the distance could be heard faintly slapping against its banks. The sound receded as the afternoon advanced. Then, suddenly, the evening was upon us, too quickly, and full of early darkness. The children, who had remained subdued, broke into sudden clamour.

"It was above that noise that we heard the first screams. The children fled to their families. The moment of silence that followed seemed like an eternity. Then from all over the kampung came the sound of chaos.

"My name was shouted. Screams and cries filled the air. Men and women ran past my house.

" 'Your son! Mat!'

"The first wave of men who had fled returned holding long, thick sticks. They gathered at the steps of my house.

" 'Your son is wild, Pak Zul!' they called.

"If he had killed, I decided at that moment that I would kill him. Running into the kitchen, I came back with a knife but the men knocked it out of my hand.

" 'A stick is enough,' one of them said.

"The *penghulu* hurried towards us.

" 'Send for the police,' he said.

"A young man ran towards the kampung shop which had a phone. We went cautiously in the direction of the hut but before we could reach it we sighted Mat. He had just come out from Pak Amin's house and he stood in front of its steps, holding a curved, grass-cutting knife. The blade was red with blood. I had never seen that look on Mat's face. His eyes bulged and his cheeks were puffed. Groans came from behind him, from the house.

" 'Don't go near him!' the penghulu warned me.

"The other men stood in a half-circle waiting for Mat's next action.

" 'We've to get into that house,' the penghulu said. 'People might be dying.'

" 'Let me talk to him,' I said.

" 'He recognizes no one,' the penghulu said.

"Before he finished talking, Mat rushed at us. The men scattered and then formed another half-circle behind him. The penghulu rushed past them and into the house.

" 'God! God!' he cried out.

"I followed the penghulu, not waiting to see how the men would take away the knife from Mat.

"What I saw inside the house is something I'll never forget. I rushed out again looking desperately for something to throw at Mat. I picked up a few bricks.

"Mat slashed savagely at the sticks the men held out in defence. I threw the bricks at Mat.

" 'Don't provoke him!' one of the men called. 'We're trying to make him tired.'

"Mat struck at the sticks, making small chips fly. He struck and struck in blind fury.

---

penghulu - Malay headman of village.

128

"Some policemen came running towards us, guns in their hands.

"Mat struck with greater strength and the attack became too furious for the men. Then as one of the policemen prepared to shoot, Mat's knife cut deep into a stick and the man plucked it out of Mat's grip. The other men threw themselves on Mat.

"An ambulance arrived and took away three injured men; another was already dead.

"The police took away Mat. I saw Mat only once after that day. He was in a hospital. They had shaved his head and face and filled his veins with medicine so that he looked like a child again. He didn't recognize me."

Zul stopped talking and I waited for his voice to come out from the darkness again. And it came after a long while, changed, full of accusation, which didn't shock me.

"He is living and not living," Zul said. "We can accept the results but we still have to look for the cause. You ran away that time. From the tiger. I've become old and wiser. When I look back I see you and others like you as the cause. We lived well, may be too peacefully, before you all came with your ideas and energies. Ideas that can even destroy the tiger, the oldest symbol of our civilization. You gave up everything to come to this land. We offered you what we had. But you all became greedy and wouldn't share. Saw no other world but the world of progress and money. And we had to make the sacrifices. This time I want you to experience what my son went through."

"I can try, Zul," I said.

"He saw the tiger," Zul said. "I made him see the tiger. Yet, when he went to the city, everything was destroyed."

He paused for a while, then went into the hut, looked for the lamp, found and lighted it, and called me inside.

"I want to show you something," he said and led me into the shuttered room. "Look at the walls carefully. Each wall has a story to tell. And behind these stories you'll find the cause for my son's illness. Stay here for a few days. Go through the feelings my son went through. Then you'll understand."

He left me in the hut for the night and the following days. He brought food and my bag the following day but he wouldn't talk to me. I took a brief look at the walls of the room. They were plastered with all kinds of pictures. I thought of just leaving the hut and going away but that would be breaching the rules of hospitality. So I've stayed out in the hall working myself up to go into that room for a kind of confrontation.

At last I went into the room, this evening, and put myself in a state of mind to enter Mat's mind. His attention has progressed from wall to wall but some obstacle or development has made him leave the fourth wall empty. The head-wall, the one that carries signs of his having rested his head there, is plastered mainly with newspaper and magazine pictures of pop stars, both local and international. Then his interest focuses on actors, stars of thriller films, held in desperate, masculine poses: bare-bodied men, glistening, locked in a death struggle; the monstrously distorted leg of a kungfu fighter packing a powerful kick; the intense concentration of a face, a gun held to its temple.

Further down are press photographs of well-known artistes and film stars framed by happy smiles after their marriage announcements; of similar couples at marriage dinners; of others taking off for their honeymoons or caught by a candid camera enjoying their marital intimacy. These images of connubial love are gradually replaced by actresses or other women modelling their bodies for the camera. An assortment of these pictures progress from the fully clothed to the revealingly attired.

Then the mood changes: the pictures are now solely of nude women got from the under-the-counter magazines, not quite pornographic and not quite innocent. Then from banned, foreign magazines, frontals, both male and female, following upon which are frank, sex materials. He seems to have chosen the most disgusting acts of copulation, the most revolting forms of coupling. The number and variety of these activities suggest a desire for a kind of exorcism.

I passed over these to the next wall, which reveals a preoccupation with death. There is, surprisingly, John F. Kennedy taking a stroll down a deserted path, just before his assassination. Jackie's grief-stricken portrait, her children clinging to her in another, are placed on either side of the lone Kennedy. As the eye moves down and up another column, the groupings of the grief-stricken are replaced by starker shots of death. A man is sprawled by the roadside, his body mangled by an accident. Still more bodies are scattered on the floor, on the bed, across an armchair - the victims of gruesome murder.

Fields mutilated by bombs, bodies and limbs strewn all over. Collapsed buildings, in rubble, allowing legs and hands and heads to reach out beneath, in a last struggle towards life. A faded, large picture of bodies piled upon bodies - probably a mass burial - and the print so spotted and disintegrated it seems to catch the very process of decay and the return of the flesh to dust. Smaller mounds of bodies, the bellies bloated, faces swollen, a child held protectively to the breast by the mother. Corpses lying, discarded like garbage, maggots arrested in their rapacious greed only by the finite frame of the picture.

Cemetaries, memorials, tombs, crematoriums are like epitaphs to these views of brutal killings. They present, occupying the last column, romantic notions of life after death. The stark headstones, the elaborate tombstones, seem such poor attempts at immortalizing man. And the anger I had not felt for a long time, came, so that the transition to the next phase of Mat's interest was easy.

The third wall is an armoury of all kinds of weapons. But the interest comes to rest on the *kris.* Their range and make are so varied, intricate and beautiful that being impaled by any of

---

kris - Malayan traditional knife/blade.

these would be heroic death. After all the abstract images of death, the handles and curved blades are real and potent.

I've come out from the room and remain in the dingy hall, waiting for Zul to appear. Will I have a confession to make when he comes? Can I make him understand the vulnerability I feel now? This is what I instinctively - I dare use the word now - must have come for: to feel ripped up and shown what I can be. That time when I went tiger-hunting with Zul, I wasn't ready to go the whole road. I had been young and impetuous. I had thought too much of myself. I assured myself I was an individual set distinctly apart from the others. But I realize now that this can't ever be so. I don't mean that I should rush off in the other direction: identify, merge, completely with the others. Actually, I don't know what I mean. Mat's columns of pictures disturb me. What disturbs me even more are the accusations that Zul flings at me through his glances, words and attitude.

It has gone past the hour when Zul usually comes with the food. But I'll wait. I'm surprised at the lack of impatience in me. Time doesn't seem to bother me at all. I know I'll have to go from Zul's kampung soon but that's neither here nor there. I sit out here in the verandah, writing. The small kerosene lamp burns beside me and a mosquito coil glows at my feet. The kampung road is still filled with activity, life. The laughter of young girls comes floating to me. There is something about the sound that seems foreign to me. Is it because I haven't laughed for a long time? No, it's only partly that. That melody of shyness, freshness and energy suggest something else, of which I'm not certain at the moment.

Somebody is coming up the slope; it isn't Zul. It's his younger son, Jamil. He has a tiffin-carrier in his hand; he looks shyly at me. He puts the tiffin-carrier on the middle step and nodding his head vaguely in my direction, goes away without a word. So Zul isn't coming tonight.

I didn't really sleep the whole of last night, lying there half-awake, going over in my mind why Zul had taken on an accusative attitude towards me. This morning the matter still remains confused. My bag is packed and I'm just waiting for the final confrontation. Zul came almost as if he had read my mind - I'm writing this back in my room, in my house - and he came around noon with some food.

"Eat this," he said.

He watched with the friendliness one extends to a stranger: a friendliness that was focused upon a moment in one's life and didn't go beyond. I felt uncomfortable but since I wanted to hear what he had to say, I went through the enforced ritual of accepting his hospitality.

"He ate like that too," Zul said, "quickly."

"I've taken too much of your hospitality," I said. "I've to leave."

"But you can't leave," he said, "even if you walk away from here. There isn't any more place which is safe. Not after you saw those pictures. This kampung isn't safe any more. Any one can turn on us. Our neighbours, relatives, friends, even our children. I tell you this because my son behaved in a harmful way. Not because he was born that way. He was made to behave in that way. As at one time you almost changed me. Tried to turn me away from my own nature. Why am I speaking to you like this? Because the others of your kind have no faces. You can change and so change them also. Remember, you must moult completely. Not just have your skin made artificially into something else. Like my son's."

He spoke so clearly that I wanted to protest but I was still trapped within my own confusion. So I didn't say anything. Instead, I stood up and looking straight at him, offered him my hand. He took it without any warmth, only with a gesture that comes from ingrained habit. I'm glad I was cryptic in my words and gestures. Now I know certainty has a way of throwing limitations around life.

So I've returned to staying in my room after I left Pak Zul - I've to accept his latest standing - and go through a simple routine every day. It isn't an exciting life but for the moment I want the quietness needed to release the hidden energies within me. Mat's preoccupations take up, as do Lee Shin's, a lot of my attention. But time I have, too much of it, to be filled with the reality I missed.

I don't yet want to go back to family life, not just yet. I sit with my wife and sons sometimes at dinner time so as to let them be aware of my presence. But most of the day I'm by myself. I seem to be digging into those interstices of my mind and events which I had overlooked before. I don't force my mind into any direction; I merely examine and turn around whatever comes into it with a wondering thoroughness.

Mornings pass easily enough. I've breakfast in my room and go through the papers my wife has brought up. The afternoons are tedious and soul wearing. Everything comes to a standstill where I'm concerned. Hardly any thought crosses my mind and my feelings barely stir. I keep the air-conditioner on and doze off. Then I wake up suddenly as if my heart has missed a beat and has to be shocked back into working condition. I feel disoriented, as if my mind has never existed and has to tread its way through a new consciousness.

After my recent visit to Pak Zul's house and family, I do seem to enter a new kind of awareness, where none of the guilt he tried to foist on me, exists. Though I haven't seen Mat, he comes to me clearly in that semi-conscious state in the afternoons.

Mat resembles some of the young men, really boys, who leave the kampung and small towns for the city in search of the glamorous and successful life. Some of them, in fact, worked for me as couriers or office boys. During working hours they are as responsible as they can be to their jobs. But after working hours you can see them loitering around in the lobbies of shopping complexes, looking at young women and slapping each other as they laugh at their private jokes. I never thought about their private lives as I drove past their groups on my way to my club or house. But impressions, in spite of my keeping them down, still remain in my mind.

They sit at the pavement or roadside during the lunch hour, eating cheap food while watching Mercedeses and BMWs enter the basement parking lots of hotels or restaurants. It amused me at that time to study their faces, often in derision, to see what was registered there. A kind of playfulness was there, which I took for lack of ambition and drive. They would sit and watch rather than go towards specific goals, I thought at that time. But behind all that playfulness, I now see an innocent wonder. It's as if they were saying to themselves: 'Look, that car the man is driving! Isn't it wonderful he can drive such a machine? Man can make such a machine! But so expensive, lah!' And they laugh but are well aware of the beauty that the power of money can buy.

You saw them, and their kind, waiting at the bus-stops along the highway not far from the factories where they worked, in the evenings. Their red, blue or yellow uniforms didn't say much except that the wearers were supposed to be gay and thankful for their lots in their lives. Where did they disappear, the majority of them, after their working hours? Into dingy rooms, as I became aware by accident when I went to look for my courier one evening, camping it out with room-mates. Clothes hang all over the window sills on raffia or nylon strings. Sometimes there is a kerosene stove in a corner or simply an electric coil and a large, enamel mug.

Pushed out into the sidewalks and into cheap, dim rooms what could they think about? Only register the images of life they see around themselves. Their dreams of success fall back into an inaccessible recess. Buildings are constantly rising around and above their dreams of a good life, as do the prices of clothes, food and bus fares. Then there is the other kind of hemming in: stronger and more enterprising men's will towards ascendency. Almost invisible, it is nevertheless there.

They can kick at stolid furniture, scrawl graffiti on latrine walls and sully the monolithic faces of bank buildings but they can't obliterate the impalpable force that puts them in their places.

But is Pak Zul right in blaming people like me? I haven't gone the whole way. An illusion gave me an immediate sense of purpose. The structures of our minds we see so clearly may, after all, be the first impressions of a truer consciousness. Lee Shin's illusions became so real that they killed him. Mine are beginning to slowly disperse like incompletely formed storm clouds and are incapable of coming down upon the earth, destructively. Sometimes we don't even know we are brooding and collecting such destructive energies. As Sivasurian says in his book, words don't have the power to express the true nature of thought and experience. I'm experience. I'm exhausted now and therefore re-enter that state of inertia in which I'm helpless.

Some days have passed. Thoughts torment me: they pull me in so many directions. But my body is still intact, healthy. I wish I could go to someone, talk to him and be reassured. I wish I could sit in some temple, on the wide, clean floors and look upon the shrines for answers. There are questions in my mind that it evades or hasn't the knowledge to answer. The knowledge I gathered about myself from those early childhood days wither at the advance of these questions. Or is it because I consciously threw that background I was born into, overboard? I recall now that I ran away from my parents' - especially my father's - background and history. I remember, ironically now, expunging my memory of them. Yet when I use memory now there seems to be nothing in it. Only a blank. Is this a trick of the mind or a fact?

This is perhaps what Pak Zul indirectly made me recognize when he sent me to view his son's picture panels. This is why, after I had viewed them, I felt vulnerable, defenceless. That, like him, I had nothing left in me to rely on. That, like him, I had assumed when I ventured out into the world that I had a

system of belief to support me. A system of belief, not inherited, but discovered by myself. Nevertheless, that outer world had unleashed its forces on us in the form of excess: for him through forces outside him, for me through forces residing within me. But the effect on us was the same: we could not accept what we had become.

Again my mind doesn't give me the ground I need to tread on. It has become, curiously, a dead field. First my memory and then my mind seem to have become useless. What else remains for me with which to view myself, life and the world? This feeling of inadequacy accompanies me in everything I do, which is almost nothing. I lie now, most of the time, in my room, waiting. Those afternoon hours perhaps hold the key; those hours during which I'm neither dead nor alive but floating in an in-between state.

The border between the real and the unreal becomes fuzzy. Some afternoons I shiver out of my nap grasping the bedside table. I struggle out of a breathless state for I seem to have descended into some regions where ordinary living becomes unnecessary. These regions come up against me in flashes, stand etched out clearly, draw me into them as if to swallow me. That's when I push and fight and wake up.

I go for a walk in the evenings, after a bath but I don't feel refreshed. The late sun lies on the streets, walls and people like fragments of discarded cigarette foils, tinselly. More than a distance comes between me and the people who used to greet me so familiarly in this housing estate of exclusive bungalows. They seem to be wrapped up in swathes of remoteness. The nights in my room have the warm mustiness of leaves smouldering into ashes.

A sort of non-mindscape comes to exist during my semi-conscious states in the afternoons. I am a participant and yet an observer in that country, a country unlike any I've known. The borders of my consciousness are still not sufficiently destroyed for me to know the heart of that country. So I lie here on my bed, waiting, not thinking. I've given up resistance. It was resistance that had prevented me from entering the depths of tiger-land that Zulkifli had promised me. It has taken me so many years to stop running that I don't mind waiting for as long as is necessary.

The flashes become more prolonged states of light inter-woven with bands of darkness. Slowly the darkness lifts as if it has been there too long as an intervening shroud. And I see again the land that Zulkifli and I trekked into to sight the tiger. Without anyone to guide and impose on me, I am travelling with an agility of my own. There is no more an eye, neither Zulkifli's nor the tiger's, watching. I've suddenly become the eye itself. A lidless eye so that nothing can be blinked away; so that nothing can be distorted. The thick mass of the jungle surrounds me; a silence sings in my ears. But I am buoyant, being young - that's how I appear in this afternoon vision - and strong. My lithe body moves with an energy of its own. No woman can bring out the virility in you as this jungle can and I've covered distances without feeling a single muscle tire. There is no finishing in a single spasm, only a constant striding out towards no particular end. That in itself is exhilarating.

Everything smells fresh and in that freshness the body's sweat too is unsullied. Branches, bushes and brambles brush against the legs and hands and soft explosions go off inside the blood. Tiny cachets of smells and odours crack and spill their potencies into the thick air under the canopy of the tall trees. I become aware of an ancient effervescence that has defied time and remained here among the tree trunks and the fallen leaves, the original smell of the earth. The body, further invigorated, almost swings through the thickening trunks and creepers, towards a never formed centre.

Behind the netting of trees, foliage and creepers, clouds become visible in that timeless mist of formlessness. My tread quickens as if to reach the source that produced these shapes but the mist thickens and the clouds disperse and reform in some kind of a *makemeoutasyoucan.* I am not thinking at all but just moving, the body almost humming with motion. I lie down and rest with the chase still running through my limbs. And get up almost immediately without the need for rest at all.

The body is fearless but more and more the mind is confronted by the colours and the inhabitants of the jungle. A python snaps its jaws at me, a coiled mass of muscle, from a low branch. I escape just in time but its cavernous gullet I glimpsed looks to me like a slippery slide into certain doom. The light dips or I am beginning to enter gloom and objects are difficult to make out. A massive hood detaches itself from the smoky hues and I am narrowly missed by the cobra's hissing strike. Then I am drawn into a deep silence that spawns sudden crackles, hoots, whistles; sudden swishes underfoot, startling whizzing past my ears. I seem to be trapped in a net of sharp and piercing sounds, so tangible I beat against them with my hands. Then once again, all is silent.

The silence is unbroken even though I've pushed through the gloom and come into a bright clearing. This sudden brightness touches my brain; it wants more and more of this clarity. For the first time since entering the jungle, the body begins to flag. It hesitates, waits for commands and directions. Though filled with energy it wants some practical plan to follow, fulfil.

The mind, so long merely recording, now becomes active. It too finds what it has traversed is without pattern; it begins to look for meaning. It fears it may not be able to find any. More cautious and guarded it looks back on what it has passed and shapes out a pattern of meaning. The vastness of the ground it has travelled and the vagueness of what it has seen are all baffling. 'You can't have room for everything,' it thinks. It wills the body to move on, observing certain rites of caution and recognition. For a time it is happy.

The clearing is far behind me now. The ground, as much as the setting, has changed. It is harder now for me to take even the simplest steps. Is it because my mind is plagued by so many doubts? Creepers, matted into an almost impenetrable mosaic, confront me. I become aggressive and ruthless. I unsheath the parang - a gift it would seem from Zulkifli - I've carried at my waist. I slash my way through that labyrinth of creepers, thorny bushes and wall of other resilient plants. They seem to spring up again, in new patches and with the sap of resistance more potent in them.

I advance in jerks and halts; my parang is flashing all the time. My body begins to fatigue but some of the thin, cane-like branches that escape the parang, swish back and strike me on the face, hands and legs. I move relentlessly, bearing the tingling welts on my skin. It seems to me I am being unmercifully immersed in the pain of experience and doubt.

However much territory I cover, I am not really advancing. I seem to have come full circle to where I started. I almost become demented but I am even more frightened. The fear doesn't leave as I forge slowly forward. My mind begins to hope; it begins to wish for an end to all the labour and turmoil. An imaginary country comes to reside in it, a country more recognizable and manageable. For a while both mind and body make some progress.

The fear strikes again, making the familiar even more unrecognizable. I look ahead of me and see the thick impossibility of penetrating, and despair. This feeling is worse than fear for it destroys everything, including hope. I can't let that happen for hope is the lighted clearing I've put at the end of my labours, both physical and mental.

I sit against a tree trunk as against a bulwark. The tree, I recognize, props me up. I feel safe. That gives me an idea, a kind of spiritual discovery. Why can't I let whatever I can't understand be contained in an object? But objects, like the tree trunk, are fixed and immovable whereas my mind is all

motion, even if falsely so, and ever changing. There has to be something, perhaps a living creature, that can match my mind and even outdo it in agility and versatility. 'The tiger!' I cry out to myself.

Why the tiger? Because it is the swiftest animal my mind can think of. I've also caught glimpses of it in the thickets and bushes - so I think - as stripes and colours. I've seen a fearful glaring, a vast brooding in its eyes and in its muscles the quivering of an unconquerable power. My mind is satisfied; it has, at last, discovered for itself a spiritual goal. When I stand up, hope is translated into a practical quest: the trailing of and discovering all those qualities I've imagined in the actual tiger. It is comforting.

I become even more ruthless for I don't honour any other life as much as I do the tiger. I slash more furiously at whatever lies in my way: *belukar,* creepers, bushes. I take delight in going after small animals and plunging my parang into their defenceless bodies. Then, not satisfied, I lop off the stem of a straight plant and sharpen it to a point. I want to see blood spilled and must go after bigger animals. I want to offer a sacrifice to the tiger. All those that are small must pay homage to the big and powerful one.

I've been going for some time, careful and alert. The mind is revived now that it has to overcome unforeseen dangers, so I tell myself. Everything is noted down, stored for future use. Then one night - in this country of the mind anything can happen, even day converted into night at will - I sight a wild boar. Its tusks gleam under the moonlight that has filtered through the overhead foliage. They are like two curved daggers, sharpened and pointed, I feel, through centuries of use. I creep up on the boar but it turns and charges at me. I sidestep out of its hurtling path just in time. But now, we're bonded: we pursue each other. My mind's cunning knows no

---

belukar - Thick undergrowth.

bounds and I soon catch the boar snuffing with its tusks into the undergrowth for food. My spear skewers it to its death through the anus. I decapitate it and spill its blood in a circle on a selected patch of holy ground. I've made my sacrifice and my spirit is light. I know the tiger won't harm me for I've left the boar's carcass in the centre of that holy circle. I am now part of the tiger and it contains everything that needs to be known. There is now only the desire to come into its presence.

Though I haven't come face to face with the tiger, I somehow feel I know all its features. It is only a matter of time before I actually sight it. My progress through the jungle is accelerated and I've the feeling that I'm being watched. I also know that though the eyes are terrifying, they are not without kindness.

Everything becomes transformed. Whatever I see now has something of the tiger in it. A flower bud is the tiger's claw; a shaggy fruit is its thick coat. The green of the trees is the green reflected in its eyes. A fledgeling tree is its sinuous foot; an anthill is its muscled haunch. But more than all these I feel the very silence of the jungle is the tiger's brooding, inaccessible nature. So obsessed am I with its nature that I forget my own personality. This, I realize, is the ultimate sacrifice needed to gain access to the tiger's presence: the giving up of the self.

How is this to be done? I brood as I trudge past trees or cut through undergrowth, and the answer doesn't come until I see the colourless, transparent skin left behind by a snake. By moulting! By leaving behind everything that I am. The thought leaves me quite breathless. I'll be freed from the burden of being responsible for myself. As I already know, the mind can't contain everything. It is logical, therefore, to surrender my self to something more encompassing and powerful.

All at once I feel light. There is no more necessity to understand not only myself but also all those shapes, objects and the network of creepers that seem to be always changing. There is no more need to worry about the force behind the changes. There is only the need to be subservient and to accept. In this way, I discover that the qualities of the tiger are not out there but lie dormant within me. No wonder it has taken me so long to discover its presence!

With this recognition, I find myself burning to be set free. It is almost a physical sensation; it is as if the skin is peeling and my flesh merging with the flesh of another, the other. But something within me is beginning to protest. It pipes up like the voice of my childhood when innocent and therefore made bold, I accepted nothing, submitted to nothing. There is now a tussle between wanting to be merged with the tiger and the need to be really free. All the while I am advancing upon the presence of the tiger and the burning sensation continues to spread, from the legs upwards to the mind. The flames threaten to engulf the mind and what lies within and beyond it. I turn away from this vastness in fear; I rush towards the tiger's presence and the familiar authority I've created. But something else intervenes: the flesh melting away into something unrecognizable. I turn back. The idea that nothing of me will ever remain appalls me. Do I dare re-enter the frightening confusion the self always creates?

The vision vanishes, killed by these doubts. I lie there on the bed feeling, in almost months, the trickle of a vitality returning to my body and mind. It is the afternoon heat or the vision that has made me sweat: my body and the bed-clothes were wet. I take a bath and feel the water wash away the fatigue and the lethargy that seem to have lain on my skin for some time. Refreshed, and my mind pleasantly settled, I go out of the house to a nearby shop, for a drink. I now feel the need to get out of my room for a while. I go for a walk.

I've returned from the walk and have been sitting in the room, thinking. What does that vision mean? I recognize that it is some kind of a purgation. That trip with Zulkifli into the interior of the jungle seems to have gone underground, into my subconscious. And because I didn't complete the actual journey it has resurfaced as a kind of vision seeking completion. With its completion I see the true ramifications of that search for the tiger. I see now how I found a tiger for myself: in my attitude to my profession, the country and life. Unable to handle the abstract complexity of my existence in this country I designed, at least tried to, an imaginary country. It gradually became an outlook on the world and life, as concrete as the tiger, so that I forgot the subtle territory I must constantly cover, attentive and sensitive, in order to gain some insight into that vast country commonly called life. I know I am rationalizing, trying as far as possible not to be deceived by the fabrications of the mind. At the moment I am relieved I don't hold on to any authority, in whatever sense, and merely allow the stream of experience to reveal all the various shades of existence and meaning. Sivasurian is right. Words are so set and inflexible that what is felt deep inside a man can hardly be expressed through them.

My only wish now is that I never try ever again to impose my will or beliefs on others. And in return, I hope others will do the same. Zulkifli, I know, meant well when he tried to show me the spirit of the tiger but I've found out what the tiger means. (May I never become arrogant in such knowledge.) And Mat's obsessions with death and killing has, I think, to do with the desire to do away with all kinds of authority. I may be wrong, of course. There may be more deep-seated reasons for his behaviour. But from where I stand, as one who has survived the chaos of the mind, I feel doubt is necessary before clarity can be grasped. Too much clarity is what leads to authoritative behaviour and when matters become too complex, the personality breaks down. Mat's insistence upon and the translation into violence of his frustrations is the darker expression of the authority principle. There can be too much of a good thing - how wonderful it is to get down to earth! - and too much analysis may destroy the very essence of understanding.

CHAPTER TEN

L IFE is not all analysis. Just when I thought I had reached some sense of peace and clarity, I find odd things happening. Perhaps I was too hasty in coming to conclusions that restored a kind of mental vigour. Strange interferences - that's all I can call them at the moment - are coming into my sleep. Just when I thought my sleep would be undisturbed, there come these interferences. Is it because I've freed my mind from all kinds of suppressions and repressions that this is happening?

Now that the mind has no sieve-like barrier erected around it all kinds of images and occurrences pass easily into its territory. Mani, the goat of my childhood, is one frequent visitor. Later on Lee Shin comes with his flute and bewildered eyes. And at a distance, his once-upon-a-time fiancee, Mei, looks at me with bitter, vengeful eyes. There is nothing of the pink gloss of the photographs on her cheeks, which now glow with blood-red vitality. And there is Wali Farouk in whose laughter I discover a trace of the sinister.

As the days pass, these figures, though pegged down in my own past, come to be citizens of another reality and another time. What I enter nightly may, in one sense, be called nightmares. But in another sense, this drama that is played out in my sleep - sometimes I feel I'm not sleeping at all, only living on another plane - has the completeness of a reality I deliberately shut out in the past.

We are living in a settlement, like so many others, which inevitably grows into the landscape and breadth of a country.

The sun shines there as in the real world. There are dust, wind, rain and the milling of people in the shopping complexes, street fights, traffic jams, but it is a silent world, inviting contemplation and understanding. Somewhere in the background there is someone who manages the settlement, if not the entire country of settlements. Each settlement has its representative and all these men meet for a few weeks in the capital, every year, to deliberate over matters affecting the country. It is then that the leader of the country makes his calm and thoughtful appearance. During the rest of the year there are no signs that he communicates with the representatives but we do know that he is in constant touch with them through means accessible only to him. The people sometimes gossip about circulars, private lines and even, in this age of technology, about fax - pronouncing it 'pax' - machines. We, the ordinary citizens, are somehow aware of the leader's presence all the time.

Somehow word gets to him of the actvities of the man-in-the-street. Any man suspected even of thinking of subverting the leader's leadership is taken away and has things done to him. When the man returns, he is so docile even Mani the goat has more spirit. But quite often things don't get that far. There are check systems already operating at lower, ordinary levels.

These watch-dog institutions are not that obvious to the ordinary eye. They work through existing customs and rituals practised by the various communities. Though we all speak one language - the national language - we also use our parents' tongues. Sometimes when the different communities meet at a common function, it almost turns into a tower of babel. We somehow take exception to the common language and lapse into our mother dialects. Is it because we don't want the others to know what we really feel and think?

The rites and rituals I refer to are centred around sacrifice. There are numerous festivals in this country of the mind that give importance to sacrifice. And these sacrifices - they can

146

also be thought of as offerings - are of various kinds and orders: flowers, fruits, vegetables and a variety of cooked food; animals of various species. These offerings are sometimes made for personal or family reasons; sometimes for social, cultural and political reasons. What stands out is the emphasis on everyone practising or participating in one or the other ritual.

The offerings of fruits and cooked food is made all the time: to the departed, to deities and gods, to powerful men. These are found at graveyards, temples, and at stones - ancestral tablets usually - beside bends in the road. The most colourful and abundant offerings are made to men holding high positions and these are usually representatives with a string of titles before and after their names. Marquees are erected days in advance and the best caterer hired. A band is also hired and cultural dances performed. This is the glamorous side of the sacrifices. Behind it all, it is we, the ordinary citizens, who have to make a donation that goes not only to pay for the occasion but also for the expenses incurred by the representative when he goes on his campaign trail, nearer election time.

The sacrifices that weld us together in obedience to the ruling regime come in subtler forms. These are the cultural sacrifices: the slaughtering of a buffalo, goat or pig. My mind now dwells on the killing of Mani the goat or one that bears resemblances to him. He has been tethered, not as in the Deepavali ritual, to a stake near the slaughter shed but to a tree around which tents have been put up. Mani hasn't been tied down at all until this moment. He has been roaming all over the settlement, free to wander at will. He isn't like the other goats, cowed. Sometimes the devil gets under his skin and he kicks down flower pots or pulls down a clothes line. He is almost human in the way he looks at you; almost human in the way he protects his freedom. He doesn't allow anyone to put the rope round his neck.

Someone has reported his activities to the higher-ups in the administration and a directive comes for his capture and imprisonment until his execution. The directive also names a number of people whose presence at the ritual is compulsory. I'm one of them. All those mentioned in the list look around themselves with suspicion. I too do the same. Can Ramasamy, Jimmy Kok or Wali Farouk be the informer? Lee Shin is too much withdrawn to have the artfulness for such a deed. Wali Farouk, Ramasamy and Jimmy Kok immediately assume an air of uninvolvement. They are even extra-friendly to the ones singled out to attend the slaughter of the goat. By now, I've watched a few, voluntarily, and come to understand it is more a ritual of dismemberment than an ordinary killing.

Gold-edged invitation cards go out to the dignitaries of the settlement; among them are Wali Farouk, Ramasamy and Jimmy Kok. It is understood among the populace that such an honour usually precedes a more formal promotion. These three have been active, of course, in their own ways of spreading and upholding the administration's policies. But there is also detectable between them, not quite open, suspicion and hostility. It is as if they are competing with each other for better financial rewards and positions.

Somehow, before the directive arrives, Mani has premonitions his days are numbered. He shuns human company and takes to living with other goats and even dogs. The dogs try to shoo him away with their snarling and baring of teeth but Mani stays on adamantly. The dogs, safe in their being needed to guard property, feel above Mani's plight but one or two cast pitying looks in his direction and allow him to stay in their midst.

Why has Mani been selected, besides his trifling, destructive acts, from all the other goats bred for the customary festival sacrifices? Why be singled out for this special rite? His eyes, I think, are the cause. They are not quite animal nor quite human. They are neither quite smoky nor quite dark. They have an indeterminate quality. Mani may look at you but his behaviour and he has been kicked and shoved out of the way for it but he persists in acting in this disgusting manner.

On one occasion he really goes the whole road. I don't know what gets into him. He somehow creeps up on an important gathering. It is the opening of a multi-purpose complex in the settlement. Almost all the dignitaries and representatives are there. All those who hold some responsible position in the settlement are given seats. They are all seated, rather placidly, and are ready to hear the addresses as obedient citizens. We, the ordinary people, are standing at the back craning our necks to see what is happening on the improvised but colourfully decorated stage. Long banners with the national flower printed at intervals and three stripes of red, yellow and green running across - representing the main three communities - are draped round the podium and also hung, fluttering, overhead.

The representative and several rows of dignitaries are there on the stage. It is late afternoon, hot and stifling, but fans are whirring from strategic places on the stage. The spectators are seated, facing the podium, and are waving programmes to cool themselves. Time is being deliberately allowed to pass while the dignitaries desultorily consult the representative on some issues each might have to face in his own district.

Then, as we shuffle about impatiently, a sound expressing our discontent splutters above the important and dignified voices on the stage. We look at each other, wondering who has had the courage to show his feelings so openly but almost everyone else has the same, puzzled expression on his face. The sound is not heard for some time, then it comes again, derisively, to stop the conversation on the stage. The representative rises to his feet, clearly irritated, and goes up to the microphone.

Once launched, the representative rambles on about how the administration has only the welfare of the people at heart. He cites various projects that have been completed, all in the interests of the people. The people, he is referring to, shift restlessly on their chairs and feet. It is when he begins to talk

149

about how the multi-purpose complex represents everything that a society dreams of that we hear a raucous explosion, like a fart. The representative stops talking but the culprit isn't to be found. Security guards walk among the people, trying to identify the mischief-maker. The speaker continues with his praise of the administration's far-sightedness when we hear a bray, followed by the sound of someone urinating. The representative doesn't stop; he only hurries on and brings his address to a conclusion. Just as he takes the scissors, presented on a silver platter, and prepares to cut the ribbons the air suddenly fills with the stink of a goat's pellet-dung. But Mani is faster than the security guards and, having made his comments on the occasion, bounds away. He doesn't show himself for a few days. But he must have been in the administration's black book since then.

Now the time has come when he will be the centre of a ritual. He has been in captivity for some time already but his rebellious nature is not curbed at all. It only expresses itself in a different way. He has taken to fasting and will not accept food from anyone, not even his favourite banana peels. Whoever tries to cajole him is bitten on the hand. But the tactic he prefers to use is turning away his head whenever anyone approaches him. His arrogance is boundless. He lies there among the tents ignoring the presence of all human beings and this offends them like nothing else does.

The ritual is a complex one. Those compelled to attend can't escape participation. A sunny day is chosen for some reason and the execution - that's what I call it - is carried out in the morning. The morning of Mani's killing is there at last. The representative arrives in his white Mercedes accompanied by the man who will do the job. The man has mingled among us the previous day and asked a lot of questions about Mani, which were unwillingly answered. He has weighed Mani and felt him all over as if to determine all the nerve points on which he will concentrate the following day.

The representative is given a high chair from which he will watch the proceedings. He is already in position. The official in charge of the killing - perhaps dismemberer would be a better name - emerges from the changing tent in white trousers and bushcoat, the instruments of a slaughter tied up in a canvas bag. About a dozen of us, the compulsory participants, are beckoned towards him. We stand around him, listening to his instructions. Mani isn't far away but he doesn't seem to be listening.

The briefing the officer gives us carries the underlying code of the first part of the ritual. It is exclusively for us, the men. I am a little dazed by the rapid flow of words and the airlessness the crowding causes. The meaning of the official's terms escape me. My companions too seem to be going through a similar experience. All we understand is that we have been selected to be a human shield between the slaughter and the spectators, at least during its initial stages.

He unwraps his gear and lays them out in the order in which he will use them, on a slab of broad marble he has brought with him. There is the long, slaughtering knife, ending in a blunted curve. Beside it he puts a shorter blade, sharper, pointed and more incisive. Then comes a pair of pliers - not an ordinary one - with smaller instruments tucked away into the handle slots but which jut out to show that they can pull out, mangle, brand and even punch holes. Then a vicious looking metal with a handle we usually think of as a bearing scraper: it can twist into the belly, gouge eyes and prise open locked jaws. All are made of stainless steel and collectively shine with the menace of a vast, slaughtering machine.

The official signals that Mani be brought and we, the dozen or so helpers, hasten to do so. Mani, however, has put on an air of cold unconcern and we have some difficulty in hauling him towards the officer. He doesn't actually put on a struggle but his body is stiff with resistance. Meanwhile, the officer is busy bringing his instruments to a hair-thin sharpness and shows no interest in our tussle with Mani. Then we are there, panting, before him.

The officer feels him over and his hands linger at the neck, tracing the course of the jugular vein. He tests the strength and size of the throat and back-bone before he wipes his fingers on a white towel tucked into his waist. He unfolds a white sheet and spreads it over Mani's body so that Mani is covered from the neck to the haunches.

"This won't take long," the officer says but just at that moment Mani throws off the cloth and scampers away. He doesn't go far for the officer has stationed some of his men at the fringe of the sacrificial ground and they turn Mani back. Mani stands once more in the centre and looks at us, not at the officer, with all the contempt an animal can muster. His eyes have become completely foreign: they are not animal or human. They seem to shine with a light of their own. This is the first time I've seen them at such close quarters and I am mystified by what I see. The light is using Mani's eyes as a medium to reveal itself.

Where have I seen that light in my waking and sleeping hours? Though I rack my memory, I see nothing in my own past associated with it. The light only pulls me towards some inexplicable awareness I had in my childhood. A landscape and a boy, lost perhaps, return through that awareness to me. It is a frightful scene because drenched with loneliness but also a loneliness that has nothing to do with being human. It is a confrontation, which, seen through earth-bound eyes is dismissed as ethereal. But now - with the years in between destroyed - it is more than real.

There is a laterite road before me: a carpet stretching into an infinite tapestry of textures. A wind blows but it doesn't touch me; it might as well be a hurricane approaching but veering away from my body. I stand there, on that red expanse of infinity, chiselled into definition. I am not just a boy holding a canvas bag in my hand. I am part of an incomprehensible flow which will soon be lost to human eyes. The currents are coming from a mystical source but uncorrupted by the habits my family and society have instilled in me, I see the light. It is the light of pure living. It is there shining all around and into me. There is no ego, no self-interest, no loyalty to all the people I've known; only the desire to contain that light within me and take it out to the world. For it is the light of intelligence, not the darkness of the limited mind. For it is the vitality that keeps discovering; not the lack of stamina that keeps a man enslaved to a family, a culture and a country. It is the light of total responsibility to life.

The moment of recognition is swiftly replaced by the events happening around me. I see that Mani is still standing in the middle of the slaughter ground. He makes no further attempt to escape. The scorn on his lips is gone; instead there is now another unfathomable expression in his eyes. Am I seeing things or is Mani looking only at me? There is a rapport between the two of us. The light in his eyes is now only a single band of brightness, which could be mistaken for the reflection of the metal blade the officer is holding.

The officer gestures that we should form a circle round Mani. The crowd behind us is getting impatient but the officer goes about his job methodically and absorbedly. Nothing, I see, can break into his concentration.

"Hold his legs," he says quietly and four of us grab at one each and hold Mani down. I've been pushed towards the back by a bolder participant and end up near Mani's still tail. The officer sits on a low stool his assistant has brought him, not at Mani's head but nearer his haunches.

"Watch this carefully," the officer says. "He has to be taught a lesson."

As he talks he massages Mani all over his back and belly. His hands are adept and soon reach Mani's loins. The officer pulls up the white cloth and folds it over Mani's shoulders and eyes.

"See for yourselves," the officer orders us.

We bend down and see Mani in erection. Can the officer do anything at will?

"I didn't do anything," he says. "Even before my hand went there, he was like that. Makes the lesson easier."

All this while Mani hardly moves. He has become completely still after the white cloth covers his eyes and ears. The officer pulls out the curved knife, which at the point is sharp on both sides. He makes the incision slowly and precisely, as if used to such work. The thin, deep cut travels from the penis sheath to the scrotum, which hangs like two large, fused grapes, and returns to the other side of the sheath without the officer changing his position. With a tug, he pulls off, as it were a cape, what he has cut. The penis is still in erection with the testicles supporting it. The officer's work is so clean - there is hardly any bleeding - that we see the penis and the testicles in their naked and pristine glory.

Mani's silence and stillness infuriates the officer and with a circular movement of his hand, he takes the genital clean off Mani. Still Mani is unconcerned and indifferent to pain.

"The bastard can't play his male tricks any more," the officer says and lays the genitals on the marble slab. Even in its severed state, the penis rises like an undisturbed, powerful phallus. The officer uncovers Mani's head and neck and drawing the sword-like blade saws downwards, slowly, but again neatly until he reaches Mani's throat. But Mani is beyond the reach of the officer's anger or skill. The officer discards his calm professionalism and savagely hacks at Mani's throat. The strong breathing that comes from Mani, interrupted, turns, first into sharp whistles and, later, into a deep, booming growl. It seems to contain in it all the shades and varieties of human speech.

The officer moves back and we, the participants, follow suit. Mani's head has fallen to the ground but the throat seems to clear itself of the blood and continues to emit unearthly sounds. The officer turns away and signals to his assistant.

154

We are released but the officer, who has been haranguing the crowd, makes a signal and the people rush forward. They are like a thousand flies, buzzing, voracious. In no time at all Mani is skinned and dismembered. I see the people take away this or that piece of Mani, looking in the officer's direction with devotional gratitude.

After the bloody ceremony, I feel I am being followed. Sometimes it is Ramasamy, sometimes Wali Farouk. Even Jimmy Kok looks at me as if he knows all my movements. And Zulkifli is always there: smiling, beckoning, censuring. I try not to be impolite or polite; I try to be myself. But the choice is taken out of my hands.

"Why are you like this?" Ramasamy says. "You're one of us and yet your're not one of us."

"Can't a man be just himself?"

"When you were born did your mother leave you naked?" he asks and when I don't answer he says, "She wrapped you up in the clothes of our culture. See how it has fed you and strengthened you. Gave you mind and spirit."

"I can find them by myself," I say and he laughs.

"You've to fight everything our culture gave us," he says.

"I will."

"You'll be dead before you find anything," he says and goes away.

But he doesn't leave me alone; he gets at me in an indirect way.

Wherever I go people greet me sarcastically, the ones he calls 'our kind of people'. They say, 'When are you going to the temple? Better not go. It's holier because you don't go.' They say, 'What does your wife wear around her neck? Not the *thali*, surely? A string of gold coins! That's what she wears.'

When I am sitting in some Indian restaurant, they crowd round me with leering faces and say, 'What are you eating?

---

thali - Sacred thread worn round the neck by Indian women as
  sign of being married.

Rice and curry? Where does the taste come from? From women whose Indian arms sweated to grind the spices.' They get nasty. 'From thighs that were girded up while they mashed the cummin, coriander and poppy seeds. Money can't buy those arms and thighs.'

When I go to a friend's funeral, they heat broad drums over the fire, swill toddy and chant at me: 'Who will beat the drums for you when you die? Who will sing your praises? Who will tell the world the story of your life? Which wife will beat her breasts for you? Which woman will tear off her thali for you? Whose children will carry the pot of burning camphor and sandalwood sticks? Who will remember you after you're dead?'

Sometimes Jimmy Kok comes up to me in a coffeeshop. He has married at last and behind the business man's mask, I see ripples of contentment.

"You say things too openly," he says. "You must hide your real self. Otherwise you'll be in danger."

"If I'm not myself I'll be in danger." I say.

"See what I mean?" he says. "There are eyes and ears everywhere."

"Why are they everywhere?" I ask.

"We live by rules here," he says. "They can't be broken. New ones can't be made until everyone agrees."

"If everyone agrees how will the new be found?"

"This is an old story," Jimmy Kok says. "There can be no new rules."

"So sacrifices must be made?"

"We've been friends for a long time," he says. "This is the only way I can help you. By giving you advice. Play the game."

"If the game is bad?"

"Don't say I didn't warn you," he says and walks away, disgusted.

Zulkifli appears now. He seems to have overcome his sorrow for his son. But this victory has only given him a different kind of strength. There is nothing uncertain in the way he moves or talks.

"Can't you think of any other way?" he says. "We lose our sons as long as we lose faith in what we've inherited."

"I've inherited nothing," I say.

"You looked the other way," he says. "You come from a very old tradition. Men bred by that tradition came to this country a long time ago. They left us customs and habits we still practise. Consideration for others. Courtesy."

"But these habits build up walls. They prevent us from knowing each other, knowing ourselves," I say.

"It was politeness that allowed me to receive you in my house," he says.

"It was politeness that refused to let you listen to what happened to me," I say.

He looks at me sadly and shakes his head and disappears. I am now barren of support. Everywhere I hear the whispers of conspiracy. Am I becoming demented? But I remember Mani and the light in his eyes. Also I remember his dismembered genitals. A fear takes hold of me. I can't sleep any more. I lie awake, waiting.

Sure enough it comes, the thing I've been waiting for. It isn't so much a thing as a happening. The whispers of conspiracy take on the shape of reality. It becomes so real that the sight of it puts the hot coals of terror into my being. The light I've been keeping in sight moves back into the distance as if it is an enormous, infinite eye, to watch what happens to my being.

At first I don't recognize the shape. Then, when it becomes more visible I almost cry out in terror. It is a vast, intricate shining structure mostly made from fluid steel. Fluid because it in turn is a net, a dome and the very cells of a collective mind. As I train my eyes on one of these cells, I see it convert itself into Ramasamy's face, which soon dilates into a large dome. Another of these cells expands into the Jimmy Kok dome, as does another into the Wali Farouk-Zulkifli dome. Soon the domes form a network of unidentified domes within a larger, parent dome. It is this dome that slowly begins to descend upon me, like a press.

As it comes closer, I see it teeming with all kinds of images but chiefly of the officer. Then, in a moment, the press-like dome becomes a gleaming machine. It stops about two feet above my body and I feel it scrutinizing me. Then, barely audible, I hear a voice. The voice that suffuses my entire being is the leader's:

"We've been keeping you under observation, as we do all those who don't conform. You're a deviant and a nuisance to the society we've so carefully built. You're not a threat. You're not a menace. You make statements that are senseless. They're not even subversive. If they were subversive you would only glorify the leadership. You try to undermine in a subtle way, so subtle that no one understands you. We're doing society a favour by getting rid of you. You're useless even to yourself.

"We've to get at the root of your uselessness. That this machine will soon do. You can't escape its efficiency or power. You can only submit. When it has done its work, you'll be one of us. So, before I go, I say be thankful that we worry about you and take care of you. Goodbye."

As soon as the leader's voice ceases, the machine descends further so that I'm enveloped in a womb-like sheath. All kinds of instruments probe my body; I feel suction-like pads on my head, face, chest, thighs and feet. Then the machine pauses as if it has found the source of my non-conformity. There is a sharp pain as a clamp is rivetted to my temples; a sharper pain when a casing is fitted to my testicles and penis. I struggle, lash out, push and scream and scream.

My wife rushed into the room.

"Wake up! Wake up!" my wife said. "Anything the matter?"

"Nothing," I said, sitting up in bed.

CHAPTER ELEVEN

A FTER that nightmarish experience I went through - in sleep or semi-consciousness? - I've been thinking about Lee Shin. He appeared, I recollect, in that nightmare. And I've been looking at the letter that Mei, his fiancee, sent me so long ago. I've kept it like a talisman, unopened, for a long time now. The envelope has yellowed over the years and the paper is brittle. I took out the scrawled sheets inside and read.

Mr. Rajan,

I'll come direct to the point. If you're not guilty why don't you answer? Lee Shin wrote many letters to me about you. I think you will remember that he got many letters from me too. Almost two times every week. Then I stopped replying to his letters because I don't know what to say. His letters were strange. He had strange thoughts.

Who made him so strange? He had a clear head until he met you. He had dreams, of course. He explained all that to me. I think I understood. But later it was difficult to follow his thoughts. He wrote like he was frightened. Frightened like someone who is confused. He was a very educated man - not like me. When he came to stay in my house, he was always reading. And when we all were sleeping, he sat in the hall, drinking Chinese tea and thinking.

He didn't like the way we were living. Said we were too modern. By the way, that was why we were not ready to marry. He wanted me to change, be more Chinese. I agreed to try. Every time he came to visit, I behaved like a real Chinese girl, wearing cheongsam and serving him tea and all that. I tried very hard to be what he wanted.

Lee Shin was stubborn. You must know he quarrelled with his father. About the same thing. He said his father was thinking business all the time. Money all the time. Joining Chinese Associations only to show other people. Not because he was really Chinese. Going to the temple also for show. His father asked Lee Shin to leave his house. That was why he went to the settlement to work.

Also to save money for our wedding. I knew Lee Shin would change. That was why I let him think I was following his way of thinking. He wanted a real Chinese wedding with the lion dance and everything.

But what happened? He was slowly coming to think like I was thinking. Then something happened. Stopped writing to me. When he started again, talked about 'pollution'. That's his word. He talked about 'how a person can't be himself.' He say something about the 'privilege of individuality is the greatest possession in the world.'

Mr. Rajan, can you explain these things to me? What really brought Lee Shin's death? I must know because I can't get him out of my mind.

Foo Mei Lin

PS: Why did he call me *May* in the last letters? Did he meet a woman with that name?

I tried to think of Mei as she would be today. She couldn't be less than forty. Had she got over her grief? Did she find another man as good as Lee Shin, to marry? What could I have said to you that time, Mei? (I'm talking to all the Meis whose men had been or would be taken from them.) A lot of hot air would have come out from me.

Yes, Mei, I was guilty. But what was the nature of that guilt? I had, at that time, the arrogance of purpose. That prevented me from seeing fully what Lee Shin was up to. I saw only what I wanted to see. I remember now Lee Shin telling me why he had chosen to work in the settlement. There had been too big a difference between his father's and his own attitudes to living in this country. I was, in a way, holding brief for his absent father. I discouraged him from experimenting with ways of living here. This was a variation to his father's attitude. I see that clearly now.

At that time Lee Shin's behaviour appeared to be perverse. What was he trying to do? Was he trying to be a Chinese in a foreign land? You can only be a Chinese in China. So I thought at that time. Now his attitude has become a little clearer. There was no China, as of old, for the culture to grow. So he took it into his head to transplant that culture here.

Even this isn't quite the correct view of Lee Shin's aspirations. His thoughts towards the end, as you say, were strange. This was, as I see it now, because he was a purist. The odd thing about him was that he didn't go around preaching what he believed in. He just wanted to be left alone. I went around pushing down peoples' throats what I thought I had discovered about life. He, on the other hand, tried to practise by himself what he had found.

What had he found? He had found the daily business of living meaningless. Work was something to be done efficiently and correctly. When he worked, he was not to be distracted. The others, I noticed, found all kinds of excuses not to finish their allocated tasks on time. Lee Shin was a tireless worker when he was in the mood. But he thought life wasn't just work. Or the earning of money. His frugality had nothing to do with miserliness. It had to do with independence. Independence from the materialistic.

He loved things but not for their own sakes. He loved them for the mental and emotional space they brought with them.

Though his room was crowded with things, it wasn't cluttered up with just anything. His furniture, crockery, flute, banners, calligraphy and decorated dragons all marked out this sense of space for him. Come to think of it, he was trying to convert a country foreign by creating cultural landscapes and landmarks in which he could be at home. His house in the settlement was nothing else but this.

What he hadn't bargained for was interference. I know now that I was always obstructing him in subtle and not so subtle ways. But the strange thing is that he seemed to need me. I was like his alter ego without whom he couldn't develop self-assurance. Perhaps I overdid the role of reflector and censor. I began to lead him towards a certain direction. I'll come to that later.

Wali Farouk, the maverick, expedition leader, almost the oldest inhabitant of the settlement, was always playing pranks on Lee Shin. That is what the rest of the staff and I thought Wali Farouk's antics were. But were they activities planned out of an innocent sense of fun?

He doesn't represent - as Zulkifli does - the oldest inhabitant of the country. He wasn't in that line of descent. Looking back now, I realize his behaviour was always a little exaggerated. His appearance at the settlement had been mysterious but only because he cast an air of secrecy over his background and his past.

"Where do you come from?" someone asked.

"Oh, from everywhere," he said. "I know this country like the palm of my hand."

If you looked at his hands you realized that the callouses there had not been raised by his ventures into the jungle. They had come to be permanent little knots around the edges of his palms perhaps through holding the *changkul* or pick-axe. He was wobbly on his legs too and panted when carrying boxes containing machine parts into the store-room. He gave off the

---

changkul - Spade.

air of being a very physical person but the hidden signs were of someone who had been recently doing domestic or sedate work. He sometimes made tea for us and it was good.

"You must have been a tea-stall owner in your past life," we said, teasing him.

"I've many past lives," he said.

But towards Lee Shin, he was unrelenting. He used whatever opportunity arose to degrade and humiliate him. Wali Farouk, I recall, collected our soiled clothes and took them to the laundry in the small town. Though he never did this service for Lee Shin, he stood, on laundry days, at the steps of Lee Shin's house and went into a one-man show.

Wali Farouk walked with a stoop as if shouldering a burden and clacked, with his right hand, an imaginary, small clapper. An onlooker had no problem in making out that he was imitating the Chinese door-to-door clothes merchant seen around the country up to the fifties.

"Clothes! Clothes!" Wali Farouk cried. "Bring out your clothes! Bring out your clothes!"

Then he put down his heavy bundle and wiped his face with a handkerchief; he hawked and cleared his throat.

"Bring me all kinds of clothes!" he cried again. "I accept all kinds of clothes! Bring me the sarung, baju, kebaya, trousers, shorts, T-shirt, towels. Bring me the vesti, sari. But don't bring me the mandarin coat. Not the mandarin coat!"

In mock revulsion, Wali Farouk moved a step or two away from Lee Shin's house. I had seen Lee Shin wear the full Chinese suit, made of lighter cloth, on some warm evenings as he sat out there in the verandah.

"Not the Chinese coat or trousers!" Wali Farouk shouted. "Not the Chinese coat or trousers! I've seen Mr. Lee Shin wear them. He wears them for days. No, no dhobi will accept them."

Then he lifted the bundle of clothes he had collected from the other houses in the settlement and scooted down the slope, roaring with laughter. From my house, I joined in the laughter, though less audibly.

With his antics, Wali Farouk made Lee Shin so ridiculous that his colleagues began to avoid him. That was when his flute rasped out those heart-rending dirges. I, of course, took a perverted interest in his behaviour and so kept close to him and his doings. But there was very little to see and, therefore, to record as he withdrew completely into himself. This was the reaction that Wali Farouk had been waiting for. In his own way, Wali Farouk was a psychologist. He knew when to tighten the screws and when to lay off. He now left the fringes and took the assaults right to the centre of Lee Shin's situation.

Lee Shin was going through a period of great confusion. He barely recognized people or even saw them. He sometimes passed me on his way to the office but he didn't see me. He himself had become thin and light, almost an apparition. From the expression on his pale face, it was clear that a struggle was going on between the real and the unreal. All the spirits his flute and furniture raised must have been his constant companions. He stayed inside his room for long periods, playing on the flute. On the rare occasions he spoke to me, he mentioned you, Mei. He put so much passion into your name, I could see you in flesh and blood. (I did know you in a strange sort of way, Mei.)

Being aware that Lee Shin was more a citizen of the other world than this one, Wali Farouk launched some of his most damaging practical jokes.

After raining stones on Lee Shin's roof, tapping his window shutters like an army of bats and appearing as a ghost-like figure in a white sheet, he struck on an idea only a personal sense of vengeance could have hatched. He must have sneaked into Lee Shin's room, in his absence, to get a view of you, Mei, in the photographs. With his cajoling ways, he got one of the Chinese girls in town to impersonate you. In the faint moonlight, she almost looked like you.

But there the resemblances ended. I remember Lee Shin being upset when confronted by the suggestive spectacle Wali

Farouk made the girl put on for him. I didn't know the full details until Lee Shin and I returned from that trip to Penang. Wali Farouk told me, interrupted by gales of laughter, the sordid act your near look-alike had put on. But by then I was already guilty of complicity and could only be pleased with the fact that someone else had preceded me. Wali Farouk's intentions were not mine, I must say at this point.

Lee Shin being in the state that he was, completely fell for the act. He somehow believed you had appeared in some magical manner to provoke him out of his depression. Wali Farouk's hireling did everything short of stripping herself completely naked. It was only after the show was over that Wali Farouk and his companions began abusing you to Lee Shin. The insults didn't seem to touch him; he seemed to have entered another state of consciousness altogether.

If I had been sensitive at all, I should have remembered a story he reluctantly told me about an Indian girl - she flouted herself shamelessly - during his undergraduate days. I should have sensed that he viewed women in a certain way. He had already made that clear in the way he had you, Mei, photographed. None of these thoughts entered my mind at that time. Wali Farouk's trick on Lee Shin was just another send-up in an otherwise dull settlement life.

When he finally agreed to accompany me to Penang, he must have known what he was in for. Why did he come then? As you said, he can be very stubborn. That's where he met May or the Spotted Lady, as we called her. At that other time she was a great and moving spirit for us, the new generation. Now I know for certain that she was merely a woman selling her body. No doubt she did it skilfully but it was criminal on our part to have raised her to the level of a goddess of love and sophistication. Lust, as I've found out, is a romantic illness of the flesh.

Youth could be forgiven for such lust. But I wasn't a youth any more and was more misguided than them. What I saw lacking in Lee Shin was a lusty keenness for life. I merely intended to shock him into realizing that fantasies and dreams weren't enough to sustain him. I didn't realize, of course, that by indirectly insisting on my approach to life, I was putting his values in the realms of fantasy.

This was what quickened the crisis in Lee Shin. He stepped out of his own world in order to learn the ways of ours. The experience was not only degrading but also destructive. I think he couldn't accept the idea women weren't always genteel and could even be brutal. That was what May had become - brutal. She was suave, slick and shrewd. She was also greedy. Her simple sensuality was gone. She didn't eat for the sake of enjoying it; she only enjoyed the spending of money on food. This seemed to arouse a sense of power in her. It was a hefty bill that Lee Shin and I paid that night we took May and her companion out to dinner. And the shopping that followed was a reflection of the power she wielded. We footed the expenditure, taken in by the glamorous vision of living she built up through her incessant chatter. I shudder to think what she must have done when she had Lee Shin to herself in her room. She must have devoured him piece by piece as she made him pay the price for every little sexual favour she thrust upon him.

She hardly resembled you - going by the photographs in Lee Shin's room - in appearance. But to Lee Shin there must have been a blurring of appearances so that in the end he couldn't distinguish one woman from another. For this change within his psyche, I accept responsibility. I wonder if Wali Farouk will do as much.

You were the centre of his life. The weeks he didn't receive a letter from you, he was very depressed. Your letters were like a life-line that kept him afloat in the sea of indecision.

Though Lee Shin is dead, he has lived within me for a long time. I don't think I can completely exorcise him from my thoughts. Nor do I want to. At one time, I thought of the past as dead history. I don't think so now. The past is needed to make the present alive. But there must be no slavish or desperate clinging to the past.

One must be ready to let go even the most prized personal ideas and beliefs in order to come by an even more substantial grain of truth. The self, shaped by family, society, education and all that nourishes the ego, must be firmly put aside. One must escape from the prison of self-imposed or imposed upon order so that a new openness to life can be discovered.

I've made my apologies to the spirit of Lee Shin for he stands out in my mind now as a rare being. I put myself constantly in his position as he faced his death - I don't worry about how it came: I only see his death as a departure into waste. My senses and mind don't see another life, only a life that has been wasted and I become boldly conservative. I want to conserve what has been abused, distorted and destroyed. I can't say exactly what it is I want to conserve. Perhaps it is the light I saw in Mani's eyes or the light in ourselves.

CHAPTER TWELVE

THAT touch, when my wife roused me from my dreams, nightmares, visions or whatever, lingered in my mind. Had she changed? I wondered. After a few days passed, I visited her private room to reassure myself. The austere cot and sari-lined walls, the corner graced only by her and her family's photographs and the boy statue with his innocent face, didn't revolt me any more. Does the boy's cherubic face hold the key to understanding Vasanthi? I thought. I felt I had to understand her. After fifteen years of marriage, I hardly knew her. The marriage itself had been a grand affair. The feasting and drinking went on for about three days. Then, strangely, the moment I was alone with her, I felt uncomfortable.

A few years younger than me, she put up with all the dinners and outings I arranged during the first few weeks of our married life. Santhi, as I came to call her, sparkled and shone in her quiet way. We had talked before marriage of the life ahead, the few times I took her out for a spin in my latest car or for a meal. She had had to look after a bed-ridden older sister during most of her later youth and, consequently, her education had suffered. By the time her sister died, she was past school-going age. Most of her schoolmates were into nursing or secretarial courses. Feeling left out, she attended to domestic chores and hoped for an early marriage. It was this situation that attracted me to her, besides her looks and docility. Marrying her made me feel like a grand chess master who could plan his moves far ahead so that everything would be taken care of. I was, therefore, unprepared for the resistance I met from her after a few months of married life.

The sparkle and the shine faded away, to be replaced by a stolid devotion to household and wifely duties. She withdrew into silence and talked only when it was unavoidable. She cooked and placed the food on the table; she swept and kept the house neat and tidy. She didn't directly oppose me; it was the way she carried out my biddings that suggested reluctance. In spite of her unwillingness, she attended to the last, meticulous detail in everything that had to be done at the dinners I hosted for my friends and clients. My guests complimented me on having found a helpful, gracious and understanding wife.

At that time, I put down her behaviour to her inability to adapt to the new situation and surroundings. She had been used to a regimented family life, as could be found in most Indian homes. The rituals of breakfast, lunch and dinner were observed with strict punctuality and formality. The father presided, the mother and daughters served. In between meals there was the interminable household work to be done. And so the hours and days passed. There were no departures from this routine except for festivals, weddings and funerals. This kind of life must have been reassuring to her: there was always something to do and the results seen immediately. The washed clothes dried in the sun by late afternoon; night fell and there was the radio to listen to.

When she entered marriage all this changed. I left the house in the mornings and only sometimes went back for lunch. Dinner was never eaten at a set time; I was usually out with some client or other. The only time we met was in bed and that was usually a brief affair. I set aside time, of course, during our first months so as to break her into the new life and to reassure her but soon other responsibilities called me away from her. It was also bad for word to get around that I was tied to my wife's sari border. I had to keep up appearances in the outside world, which never overlooked any breach in social etiquette.

In that town, up north where we we_e married, we didn't own a house yet. I was then just an up-and-coming businessman. The rented house had only two rooms, one of which served as my study. It was really an office in the house, with filing cabinets, shelves and an executive desk. When I brought home work, it was in this room I stayed up late, poring over documents and title deeds.

If there had been more rooms, Santhi would have conver_ed one into a hideaway. As it was, she threw walls around herself with her silence. If my work hadn't taken me away from her, I would have broken down those walls. She simply had too much time on her hands and so was able to surround herself with those barriers. These were the thoughts that ran through my mind at that time, and, much later.

Now I know those thoughts were quite false. She carried that room everywhere with her once she got to understand my character. Since my return I've been looking at her in a new light. How different she appears to be! Every movement or gesture she makes is alien to her personality. But those gestures and movements are the products of submission. She has made submission the instrument of her protest.

I submitted too - to my idea of progress and success. How can she, knowing what she is doing, submit? I didn't stand outside my idea and look at it in order to know its value. The idea and I were one. Now the energy behind that is spent. But Santhi goes on.

This has been disturbing me since I got back. How can we start again? How can we release ourselves from the gestures that have imprisoned us?

I haven't been staying in the room, upstairs, all the time. I've been wandering about the house. The two boys keep their distance though they fetch the newspaper or get me a glass of water. Though thirteen and eleven, they seem too grown-up for their age. Did Santhi warn them against me? If she had, I wouldn't blame her.

The family gathers at meal times; the four of us are all there at the dinner table. There is hardly any conversation except for the boys asking their mother for money to buy a book or to have transport arranged for an extra-curricular activity in school. Santhi looks at me to say as if that I should be in charge of such matters. I look down at my plate and go on eating. I've grown awkward under her stares. The boys hardly direct their questions or requests to me.

The sky outside is as deceptive as on the day I first become aware of my condition. It is blue and unmoving, clouds stationed fluffily here and there. In the afternoon the sky darkens and the clouds burst and there is a downpour. The air is cleared and it feels cooler. Inside the house we continue doing what we've been doing the whole morning. I fall into a day-time dream.

"You've said nothing since you returned," Santhi said the other day.

"I've come back," I said, hardly looking at her.

"You left us without warning," she said.

"You saw me pack and go," I said.

She had been, for some time, suppressing these questions. Once they were out, she seemed to feel indignant. She went back to the kitchen to prepare the afternoon meal before the boys returned from school.

I sat there in the richly-stuffed armchair, inviting dreams. I've become a dreamer since I returned. No, not in the escapist sense. All I want to see is life unfold itself in its entirety.

The dreams come carrying images I've never seen before. They make me aware of the women I've known and of the women I've never known. There are days when I seem to be lying inside a large, white womb dreaming of the life to be. All it needs is for me to see Santhi, accidentally, at the stove bent over a pot and then the picture of a woman from long ago flashes into my mind.

"I want to do a home-coming puja," my wife said the other day.

"It isn't necessary," I said.

"Necessary for me and the children," she said. "As a kind of thanks-giving."

"There's nothing to be thankful for," I said. "Remember, I went away only for a short while."

"But you've come back now," she said, echoing me. "And you've your senses about you."

"I had my senses with me all the time," I said. "The wrong kind. Don't waste time or money on any ceremony."

"You never objected before," she said, not unkindly.

"I do now," I said.

"Why?"

"I don't know," I said.

"If you've no real reason, I'm going to do it anyway," she said, and went up to the boys' room.

And so the tussle, a long delayed one, began between us. She didn't immediately begin the preparations for the puja. She waited a few days before she went and bought the necessary things. A priest, summoned through the women community's communication system, came to the house to note down the necessary information so as to fix on the auspicious day. The man sat there on the sofa, cross-legged, in his vesti and jubah, munching on sireh leaves and betel nut shavings. He looked an incongruous figure not because he was archaic in a modern setting but because he pretended to know so much and wield so much power over the women.

"You've to fast for a day," Santhi told me after being in consultation with the priest.

"I don't have to do anything," I said, not quite angry. "Do anything you want but leave me out of it."

"But you're the most important person in this ceremony," she protested.

"You make me important," I said.

She went away looking at me as if I was out of my mind. The tension increased between us but I wasn't uncomfortable.

172

I knew I was making contact with her. She was aware of me now in a way she hadn't been before; I had become attentive to her mood changes and thoughts.

Later Santhi informed me, at breakfast, how the ceremony would go on Friday.

"The priest and his assistant will come very early in the morning to dress up the idols and decorate the niche," she said. "They will bring the idols, Ganesha and Saraswathi. All you have to do is to take a bath, wear a white vesti and shirt and do what the priest asks you from time to time."

I was silent, though not in an offensive way.

"I'm inviting my women friends," she said. "Do you want to invite your friends?" I shook my head. "My women friends will cook the vegetable meal in our kitchen. So don't let the noise in the early morning disturb your sleep."

"Why're you doing all this?" I said. "It isn't necessary."

"May be not to your way of thinking," she said, and began to clear the table.

The Friday morning dawned clear and cool. With the women in the kitchen asking for this pot and that stuff and the priest ordering his assistant to dress up the coconut in a certain way, I felt trapped. The light at the window, the herald of another day looking in on my life, seemed to have lost its mystery. The smell of dhall curry, fried long beans and brown sugar rice from the kitchen dispelled any hesitation I may have had. The priest clearing his throat and beginning the practice chants got me out of bed and into the bathroom. Soon I was out in the hall, wearing the vesti and the white, long-sleeved shirt my wife had laid out on the bed.

The various stages of the thanks-giving ceremony wound slowly into mid-morning when the heat, in spite of the fans whirring at full speed, began to seep into the hall. My wife and the women clustered behind the priest's bent figure and acquired an even more devotional expression on their faces. At various points I was asked to scatter flowers at the feet of the idols, which I did meekly. After an interminable time, the air stuffy and reeking with all kinds of scents, we were all given handfuls of yellow rice. The priest and his assistant chanted themselves into a breathless climax and we threw the rice at the idols.

After the priest, his assistant and the guests had fed on the vegetarian meal and gone, I sat in the sofa in the hall, exhausted. My wife bustled about, cleaning up and putting the house into its usual order. The afternoon was calm and peaceful in contrast to the morning's noise and congestion. The boys were upstairs, playing some computer game.

My wife came and sat in the armchair, opposite me, picked up the newspaper and glanced through it listlessly, almost as if she would have liked the ceremony to go on and on. She didn't look like someone who felt that the occasion had been correctly concluded and gratitude properly expressed.

"Not happy with the ceremony?" I asked.

"Did anything go wrong?" she said. "Except for you, everything went smoothly. You weren't thankful at your own good fortune."

"Nothing to do with good fortune," I said. "Has to do with recognition."

"There you go again, talking in a strange manner," she said. "The ceremony was a waste of time and money."

"No, it was beneficial in its own way," I said.

"I've listened too much to you," she said.

"That was in another time," I said.

"Strange words again," she said. "When are you going back to work?"

"When the time is right," I said.

She folded the newspaper carefully and put it neatly on the coffee-table beside the armchair, then got up and went into the kitchen. She didn't talk to me for the remainder of the day. I couldn't help recalling how radiant she had looked in her tightly wound orange-and-blue sari that morning, when

174

she knelt behind the priest and recited some of the prayers. And all her saried friends, clustered about her, seemed equally radiant. What was this radiance? Was it the radiance of those who merely follow? The thought frightened me and I turned away from it for a while.

Santhi was dissatisfied after that conversation on thanksgiving day. She didn't withdraw into herself; she, in fact, became more active in a silent sort of way. She was thinking the whole day, I could see. Hers was also a history of suppression. Why wasn't someone else made to look after her crippled sister? I've seen and know from experience how families can pressure you into doing what they want. I escaped but Santhi has been conditioned for too long to be able to even distinguish between true and false responsibilities.

The boys, Ravi and Sivam, sometimes sit in the hall watching me read or lie there on the sofa, resting. They have exhausted all the games they could play on the computer. Ravi, the older boy, went after a while to the kitchen where his mother was busy. Sivam sat on, apparently preoccupied with some question in his mind. He looked in my direction and then slowly turned his head away. I thought I had not been an affectionate or attentive father to them. But I couldn't believe they were my children, the issue of those lusty struggles between Santhi and me on the nights I came home primed with drink. Santhi had said nothing, only submitted silently. They were the children of a hardly felt or understood ritual.

When Ravi was born, I couldn't keep down my sense of triumph, especially when I saw his tiny penis in erection. All those nights of meshing with Santhi had at last brought into public view a concrete product of my manliness. Santhi too couldn't suppress her smile of victory for she had become a mother and the centre of attention for further rituals. She was no more a girl with virginal, lusty limbs. She had become the source of another life; someone invested with power and dignity. Her child-bearing experience made her not only maternal but also matronly. A severe sense of purpose tightened her face as she went about her motherly duties.

We celebrated. The in-laws came. There were feasts. Friends, colleagues and neighbours were invited. The child cried in his cot and Santhi had to give him her breast, hurriedly, caught as she was between the kitchen and the hall full of guests. Sivam's birth wasn't filled with that kind of excitement but Santhi was quietly happy when she found herself drawn deeper into motherhood.

The birth of the boys renewed me with energy and strengthened my ambition to do well in my business and in the world. Santhi went out with the children more often, showing them off as if they were the badges of her success. Santhi retreated even further from me, as I did from her. The boys made us touch each other as when I held Sivam while Santhi dressed him. We lived vicariously in each other through the children: they brought her smells and presence to me when they ran up breathlessly to me from her. In the same way they touched her with the hands that had touched me. So we felt bonded, even if this happened only indirectly. But as the boys grew up and started to look after themselves, this bond slipped away from us. The thing that we did in the bed, on occasional nights, only emphasized our separateness.

I realized, in my own case, that my personality had been violated: made to be something less than it was. I looked at Santhi to see if she was aware of this violation. If she was, she hid it very cleverly. She would certainly have protested, if she still preserved her self, when asked to give up school to look after her sick sister. Can the sick recognize sickness? I crippled her further when she married me. I was sick myself at that time and didn't know it. Women, I realize, have always shaped their lives and personalities in opposition tothat of their men. This has become a historical phenomenon, so much so that what they bear as children are, in fact, a system of stability for themselves. The woman gives birth to a child out of love for a

176

man; out of a hatred for him; out of a need for self-assertion; out of a desire for independence; out of a hunger for vengeance. The children are conceived through a reaction to some domestic or social force outside themselves; they are not conceived for themselves and in themselves. The break is never made from the action-reaction chain so that children, it would seem, are already influenced at the womb stage to be someone thought of and taken measure of, premeditatively. Centuries of this disability passing through the veins and cells of women must have reached Santhi at a tender age.

"How women allow their nature to be violated!" my father, I recall, said in his moments of clarity. I didn't understand him at that time. The references he made to *The Ramayana* and the stories he selected from it to tell, puzzled me even more. Whenever he got into his rare rages with my mother, he would sit quietly on his bench outside the house, waiting for that spasm of anger to pass. Then, when I thought he had forgotten the incident, he would tell a story about Sita, Rama's wife. The one I remember vividly and which bears some connection with my ideas about women's nature, is illustrated by Sita's willingness to go through the fiery test.

"You know why Sita entered that fire?" my father would ask me but I knew he was also addressing himself to my mother, who was attending to one of my brothers or sisters in the room behind us. "To show her nature was not spoiled by any of the hardships she went through while the prisoner of Ravana on that island. Women have forgotten about the fire that purifies. They've forgotten about purity."

My father spoke in frustration and out of a personal sense of failure. But as I cast my mind over that image of Sita entering the faggot flames to prove her purity, other thoughts and histories come to my consciousness.

It wasn't just wifely fidelity that Rama was insisting on. And Sita wasn't just proving, by immersing herself in those flames, that she hadn't been unfaithful to him. Those flames burned away whatever threatened to un-self her. They burned away the twisted imaginings her captivity had imposed upon her. Burned away the sense of defilement; burned away the sourness despair brought. Burned away all the anguish she had been through; burned away the thoughts that distorted the image of herself. Restored her whole to herself; restored her whole to Rama, without any sense of violation. After that immersion in the fire, she could only act from the centre of her being.

It strikes me that is what women have been unable to do since they entered modern times. And modern times go back to those periods when men began to organize themselves into societies, shape kingdoms, monarchies, the reich, socialism, communism, democracies. To the times when these social systems began to oppose each other and go to war to uphold the purity of their visions. Then atavism came into existence, an atavism centred around the images of women.

The history of women is the history of their atavism: from Sakuntala to Patty Hearst, who loved the man who held her in captivity for ransom. It is a history of the perversion of women's nature. And when I see Santhi I see her bent under the burden of these atavisms.

"When are you returning to work?" Santhi asked again. "There were some phone calls while you were away."

"Money can be made at any time," I said.

"How long will the money in the bank last?" she said and stared at me.

"Until I go back to work," I said.

"You might go away again," she said.

"I've made the necessary journey," I said.

"What did you see?"

"What I missed when I travelled along the same road the first time," I said.

"I could understand you more when you were silent," she said.

"I'll talk when it's necessary," I said.

"You're saving words like you're saving money," she said.

"Too much of anything loses its value," I said.

We looked at each other from the edge of an untraversed land. It was like being with Zulkifli again but with him there had been at least physical motion and therefore a sort of communication. I realized I had to discover some kind of language to talk with her. Or understand her language and destroy its limitation.

I caught Santhi standing in the middle of the kitchen as if she suddenly found herself in alien territory. On the days this happened she retreated into her private room for a couple of hours, when she thought I was taking a nap. When she returned she seemed to have regained her confidence. But as the days passed her visits became more frequent. What was she looking for in that room? I inspected it again when she was out doing the weekly marketing. Nothing had been changed except for the statue of the innocent boy. It was turned directly to face anyone sitting or sleeping on the cot. She had also dressed the boy in freshly made clothes, which enhanced his innocence. She had gone into that room to sit and gaze on the boy's face. I found myself, in a strange sort of way, also attracted to him. But I weaned myself away from the seduction. It wasn't a frozen, simplistic indifference to the world that I needed.

Santhi began to perplex me. Sometimes I lay beside her, on our large bed, thinking about her as if she wasn't there. She slept as soon as she stretched herself out; I had hardly touched her since my return. It began to worry me that I didn't exist for her. How could she will herself so easily into sleep?

She had, over the years of living with me, become the other. As I had become somebody other than myself. Her life had not been her own. First, her parents had had designs and ambitions for her. They had sent her to school for some purpose only they knew; they stopped her from going to school for their own convenience. They had woven the garland of marriage around her neck even before she could work out

179

for herself what she wanted to be. And when she met and married me, she became part of my purpose and ambition. The frightening thing about all this was that she had submitted so easily. But, at the same time, I couldn't help thinking that she had hardly seen herself in her own light. So how could she offer any resistance to whatever plans other people had for her?

She had grown a second skin on herself all those years she lived with me or must have come to me with her own feelings and thoughts stored in some shell inside her. The two halves of the shell had fused into an unreachable sphere. And I had only helped to make irrevocable that inaccessibility. My duty, as I saw it, was to de-fuse that clammed up remoteness.

She already looked wearied, as if worn out by adult duties, when she married me. The first weeks were a reprieve: colour and movement came back to her face and body. She was, if only fleetingly, young again. There was a fragile, far-away expression in her eyes. They looked into the future with doubt but also with hope. When she came to me in the bed some of her habitual gestures were left behind. Perhaps for a brief period in my life, especially during the nights, I didn't allow the consciousness of my self to dominate over my actions. There was an exploratory freshness during those nights of contact between us. But in the mornings, dressed up for work, I regretted my surrender to Santhi. The way she looked as she prepared my breakfast showed she was going through similar feelings.

Those nights, I recalled, had had about them an immense and complex suggestiveness. We were, after we had discarded our familiar clothes and habits of thought, complete strangers to each other. It hadn't been frightening at all. (In the day time, I had, of course, tried to cover myself with all kinds of personal reflexes of identity and separateness. I had acted the up-and-coming husband to a wife who didn't have any resources except her services and her body.) On the contrary, we enjoyed being strangers to each other. Our inhibitions fell away from us. More importantly, the ideas we had had about each other were destroyed by our coming together during those nights. We were equal and unknowable personalities in a world we could hardly begin to know.

Slowly these thoughts about Santhi have built up into a day-time vision. As I gaze into it, I see that the brightness is merely an effusion from the larger, more enveloping arc of darkness. It is like emerging from a cinema and being struck by the immediate light before becoming aware of the sombre sky about to burst into a thunderstorm: a permanence beyond which lies impermanence. The intellectual sky I carved out for myself, before, had had the same effect: that there was nothing beyond the efflorescence that enclosed me.

So I lie now within that deceptive effulgence and hope to penetrate the beyond. But what I see is only human actions, which while clear to the individuals, go to harvest the aftermath of murkiness.

Santhi has been going about the house wrapped up in the remains of herself. When will the righting happen or balance be restored? This question has been plaguing me since I began to see her in her atavistic forms. And I've been looking for ways to be included in the process. For there has seeped into me a horror that I can't exorcise. It isn't a figure that comes to me in a nightmare; it is a real one that the last world war mangled. I may have read about that woman but that makes her no less real. I've seen her during my childhood days, violated and abused and there was no war at all at that time.

Even in my child's eyes - perhaps because they were only child's eyes - she was a beautiful young woman. There is no need to talk of her colour - it was indeterminate, made all the more nebulous because she had married the dark Indian clerk on the estate. I thought at that time that she came from a foreign land, an almost unreal country.

The husband worshipped her as if she was a goddess, bringing or buying jasmine flowers for her hair, every day. She had a bloom on her face that I thought would stay there for eternity. Her behaviour was very different from that of the other young girls who had married and come into the estate community. She had a pail of water ready for her husband when he returned from work and on occasions even washed his feet. If you happened to pass by the window in the evenings, at meal times, you could see her feeding her husband with handfuls of rice mixed with vegetables and chicken meat. The smile on her lips, as she did so, was unmistakably that of a child playing at family. If you had passed her as she hung the clothes to dry in the mornings, you wanted to linger on in the vicinity of her presence for she exuded gentle scents and fragrances. If she hummed a tune you felt it came like the flow of fresh milk.

When she was rounded with her first child, the women in the estate couldn't resist baring her belly and touching with their palms the soft, visible swell. She allowed them their pleasure with a smile on her lips. For us, the boys, who knew nothing of pregnancies, she became the centre of a mystery. But that sense of awe didn't last long. It was the husband who destroyed it for us. His reaction to the arrival of a child in his household was completely different from that of the others. He grew sullen; he grew furious. There were days when he shouted at his wife; there were days when he was away, leaving her to suffer in silence. We hated him but it seemed our hate couldn't match the bitterness he directed at his wife. He neglected her so much that the neighbours had to attend to her needs in her pregnant state.

When the first child was born, the man was briefly happy. But now the wife had little time for him. The bawling baby kept her awake most of the night and when morning came she looked tired and weak. The man, however, wouldn't leave her alone. He demanded his breakfast, fresh clothes for work and commanded that she have a good lunch ready for him. The wife tried to give him her best; the child was unlike any other

182

born in the estate. It was chubby and, except for its constant wailing for its feed, pleasant enough. Most of the afternoons he lay quietly in his sarung cradle and so allowed his mother to get some rest and finish the household chores. But the man wasn't to be pacified.

In three years the woman had given birth to three children; the husband seemed bent on making her suffer. During the first two years there had been a small scale battle between him and the rest of the estate, who took his wife's side. He had started ill-treating her, beating her whenever he wanted to. Some of the neighbours rushed in to intervene. He thrust them away.

"Husband-and-wife quarrel," he said. "No need for you all to interfere."

The woman had lost all her youthfulness. She, in turn, began to beat her children. That was when the neighbours turned away from her. The woman had changed completely. Her clothes were always soiled and her hair, ungroomed, fell across her face and shoulders. She didn't bother to look after herself. Perhaps this was what made her husband take to drink. When he returned home lurching and raging, he beat her, invariably, on her hips and across her breasts with a flat stump of wood.

The children grew up somehow, without sufficient food and sufficient love; the children that came steadily from her womb, conceived during the husband's drunken stupor, were born warped and twisted. I heard her cast the magic spell of deformity upon them as they were about to be born. She sat in the doorway of her house, hugging her pregnancy and saying:

"Little one, you about to be born, listen. You came into my womb violently. I didn't want you. The man put you there while smelling of drink and vomit. Other, worse things are smelling inside him. He has made me smell too. When you come at last into this world, you won't be drinking milk from my breasts. You'll be drinking bitterness, hatred, suffering. You can stop the suffering if you try. You must get the strength for that from the little milk you can receive from my breasts. If it's not the custom for a son to beat his father, you must break that custom. You must break his head and spill his blood. There won't be any brains to spill. So, son, you must be stronger than your brothers and sisters. He buys them sweets, clothes and toys. He makes them soft. You must be hard. Hard like a twisted metal that can't be twisted any more."

By the time I left the estate, her children had grown up, especially that one I heard her talking to, in the belly. There wasn't anything that he didn't leave ravaged: plants, windows, clothes, bicycles. He was defiant for the sake of defiance. His mother had been successful in passing this spirit to him while he was still inside her. But that isn't what I remember vividly. What I can't get out of my mind is the woman herself.

The last time I saw her, she was seated in the doorway of her house. The threshold of the house had assumed a secret importance to her. She sat there at all hours of the day. From that strategic place she kept watch on all that went on outside the house with, it would seem, a fierce desire to keep out whatever she thought was fearful. From that place too, she could see when her husband came and so disappear quickly from his sight. But most of the time she sat there with an air of indifference. She was a silhouette in the doorway which nothing affected. Her children, playing boisterously inside or outside the house, didn't disturb the insularity she had thrown around herself. At that time I had looked at the worn-out face with contempt. But what had been more hateful to me were her protuberant hips and carbuncular breasts. Even strangers noticed that there was something abnormal about these parts of her body. We who knew her history knew also the cause of these unnatural swellings. The breasts were ugly tumours and the hips knobs of extra bone not only because her husband beat her in these places but also because the woman did something mysterious to herself. It was, perhaps, a secret rite of mutation.

184

Had I, together with a hidden tide of history, transformed Santhi in some such way? Ever since I discovered her private room, I had felt uneasy. It was precisely this discovery that had accelerated my sense of doubt and anxiety. When I stood in that room, I felt stripped of everything I knew. The bareness of the room seemed to accuse me.

Women, I feel, have always acted out of a reaction. They are not entirely to blame but they must take some responsibility for what has happened to them. Their breasts and hips have been damaged, say, by the arms of history or by the arms of the men who made history, personal or otherwise. Their loins are soured by the very men-children they have produced. How to stop this line of progeniture? And on what scale? How to restore to the women their innocence?

The other day we met in her room; a shock ran through my body as I saw her come in, falteringly. She stood in the doorway, wondering.

"Sorry to be here," I said.

She didn't say anything, only stood there, feeling violated.

"The one place I can call mine," she said.

"I know," I said.

"Not strange," she said. "You want to be everywhere. Until there is no place for me."

"Not any more," I said.

"Oh, yes. You've gone back the way you came," she said bitterly.

"You don't have to talk that way," I said.

"What other way do I have?"

"You just have to choose," I said.

"I was never given a chance to choose. Never will be," she said.

"It took me a long time to learn that," I said.

"You? Never choose?" she said.

"Chose too much," I said. "Too quickly. You've to burn away all the unnecessary things."

We were silent for a while; I looked around the room, with her watching me. Once again I felt with keenness that I had denied her. Hasn't she denied herself too? I thought.

"It's all very sad," I said.

"There you go again," she said.

"We must go back again and again," I said, "together."

"It's too late," she said.

"You can't decide that," I said. "I can't decide that."

A wild look came into her eyes; she made as if to leave the room. Then the conflict within her was contained and she stayed. She strayed towards the curtained windows, not knowing what to do with herself. That unsteady trailing to her old saris that served as curtains revealed to me the suppleness she had lost. There had been, when she married me, something rearing to go. And because she hadn't too great a hold over language, her body took over the expression of her inner impulses. There was always something quivering inside her and about her body which had irritated me at that time. She had put her energy into all kinds of activities and her slimness remained, mobile and swathed with power.

All this was gone; she had begun to resemble that other woman in the estate. The deformity wasn't so obvious but it was there. While that other woman was outwardly transformed, I guessed that Santhi's change was still internal, the edge of which was beginning to show. Her breasts were not slack or hardened but held, tensed, in response to some inward force. For a woman who still had the fading bloom of womanhood on her, she walked or sat hunched. Her hips bulged with the flabbiness of a woman who had accepted futility. And the flab, at moments, strained, muscle-like, in protest against what she had become - a mechanical caretaker of a husband and two sons.

"I've seen you come to this room many times," I said.

"This is where I feel comfortable," she said, a trace of bitterness in her voice.

186

"I like it too," I said.

"A simple place like this?'"

"I can see what you're trying to do in here," I said.

"And you want to change it?"

"No," I said.

I could see another atavism come to play on her: the startled woman but one who was determined not to let her guard down. There was a delicate moment when I thought of compelling her attention towards herself. Then I changed my mind: one violation could not be set right by another. When I left the room, she followed me out and I saw I had made a sort of impression on her.

The days that followed were awkward for us. We didn't actually avoid one another; whenever we saw each other a strange feeling came between us. As far as I was concerned, I felt I was intruding; she, on her part, stood there, in the living room, as if discovered doing something immoral. At other times I was the one who felt ashamed and she the one who had stumbled upon my secret misdeed.

Some sort of a common ground, not immediately recognizable, was growing between us. I lay on my couch in the study, during the afternoons and sometimes in the nights when I didn't share the bed with my wife, trying to work out what it was. Going over the reactions to each other, I discovered that while guilt was one of the feelings, the greater feeling was one of incompleteness. I, at least, felt that I was covered in ashes, the fire gone out, and wriggling to find out what I had become. (Sivasurian's saying came to me: 'Words don't match up to the actual experience.') Those ashes had, over the years, hardened into a kind of second skin. But this acquired skin was beginning to crack and then crumble to reveal, beneath it, an unformed or misformed creature. Was that how Santhi saw herself too?

The house itself became intolerable to us: it was like a shroud waiting to be rent so that the reality we had long ignored could come through. When the boys were at school, I could hear Santhi moving about the rooms listlessly, a futile, hollow ring accompanying the sweeping and ordering she did. At such times I was tempted to go down and ask her to stop her work but I merely lay on my couch torn between acting and not acting.

The house that had kept us together stood like a massive obstruction between us. Its floors shone with a dull gleam; the carpets, lamp-shades, furniture and cabinets were so many pieces of disorientation. They had merely held our lives together physically. The few women who came to see my wife chatted with her in the large kitchen. All the rooms appeared to be simply blocks of concrete within a larger room, useless, unnecessary and without the stamp of our lives on them.

The thin veil of our personalities that I thought had draped everything in the house, was gone. Resentment set in between the both of us. Almost out of a kind of perversity, Santhi went and worked in the neglected gardens. I sat studiously in my study pretending not to notice her. There was a desperate attempt on both our parts to remain faithful to what we thought we were.

But the shamming didn't hold up. When the family met at dinner, there was hardly any talk. The boys bottled up their complaints about the tasteless food. Santhi religiously, silently, attended to the ritual of serving the food and clearing the table. We sat there in the living room, while she washed up, like strangers marooned on the same bit of shore. And the thought of riding the sea back to familiarity frightened me and them.

The boys, Ravi and Sivam, in their own ways, had begun to sense our disorientation. They had accepted me as a recluse, while I stayed in my room, but they were bewildered by my wandering about the house in my disembodied manner. They looked at me as if they wanted to pin down something in me they could be sure of. The older boy, Ravi, was the more thoughtful and determined. I saw in him a younger version of what I had been and turned away in disgust. Yet, I couldn't totally ignore him. I felt I was responsible for maiming him in that particular manner.

The younger boy, Sivam, showed some fluidity of accommodation: his personality wasn't, like Ravi's, beginning to set. There was a muted wildness about him that chaffed under the rules my wife and I had seen fit, over the years, to impose on our sons. He could be, by turns, rebellious, submissive, opinionated, humble, quiet or boisterous. There was something about him that wasn't quite stable. He had always fascinated me but being busy with work and preoccupied with the ambition of climbing up into status, I had only felt irritated by his behaviour. I had caned him on more occasions than I had Ravi. I had beat him because I had seen in his eyes the flicker of light that had played in Mani's eyes.

"We're doing something to the children," Santhi said one morning, when the boys were away at school.

"We've already done it," I said. "Not just us. All of us through the centuries."

"I'm talking about our boys," she said.

"All boys are our boys," I said. "Only being ourselves not our own, we also made them not our own."

She looked at me, puzzled. But her face didn't set in the old way, lined with intolerance. It was still rigid but not with any particular attitude. Am I seeing a face that is beginning to shed its former masks? I wondered. As she wondered over my words, her face became faintly animated.

"They're not themselves," I said, continuing gently. "We turned them away from being themselves. As I turned you away from being yourself."

"You don't know that," she said.

"I've seen enough signs," I said.

"You don't know me," she said.

"That't true," I said. "We only pretend to know ourselves and others."

189

"We've to know something," she said.

"Yes," I said, "but not to make too much of that something."

"I'm not sure of myself now," she said.

"I was too sure of myself for too long," I said.

"And now?" she said.

"I don't even know you," I said.

"But we're husband and wife," she said, amazed a little that she could say these things to me.

"Only that," I said, "in this house."

"What are we to do?" she said.

"I don't know," I said.

But we were beginning to get out of that numbed state of being we had made of each other. The house and that private room, Santhi's initially, began to take on different meanings for us. If my own study had been a kind of cell where energy and thoughts had collided in confusion, perhaps necessary for a time, the other room seemed to grow, under a different consciousness, into a larger, more liberating dome. (I had a language that identified these features of the house and the room. Santhi had no such language; she merely behaved.) I went in there more often, even while Santhi watched, as if to re-immerse myself in a consciousness that had been over the years eroded and displaced.

For some reason or other, Santhi had hung a thick gauze around the circular fluorescent tube. This darkened the room by breaking up the light. Unable to sleep one night, I went down to the room. The sari curtains were closed. I took the thin pallet Santhi used for a mattress and opened it out on the parquet floor immediately beneath the gauzed light. I lay down and tried to soothe myself to sleep.

But sleep didn't come. I must have lain awake for some time when I began to feel a mixed warmth-and-coolness all over my skin and body. Perhaps it was the light covered with the gauze that induced the feeling, together with the cell-like network of shadow and brightness that fell all over me. While my body tingled with warmth on the outside, it was strangely cool and calm inside. The web of light and darkness lay like a nourishing membrane over me.

Where else had I felt enclosed in such a nourishing warmth? Not in time, I thought, but outside or at the beginning of time. Had it been in my mother's womb? I wondered. Perhaps. And also after birth, swaddled by a kind of timelessness. In my mother's womb I grew towards shape; cradled by the human membrane I was already travelling towards personality. Memory recalled a timeless ante-chamber, where, waiting, I could have become anybody. Lying there under the criss-crossed complexity of light and shade, I realized that the way to the other was through the mortal womb.

Santhi found me sleeping peacefully in that room the next morning. I didn't recognize her immediately. In her night-gown, she could have been any woman I was seeing for the first time. In her sari she had looked stiff and prepossessing. Through that cloth wound around her breasts and hips, she seemed to have inherited a constrained way of moving about. I had watched her during the early days of our marriage go through the intricate process of draping the sari around her young body. She had worked quietly, almost without concentration, at the task. Her hands had moved with certainty and swiftness so that soon her flesh was covered except for her midriff, which was exposed in some kind of reproach. Later when she began to wear slacks, blouses and T-shirts, an insousiance entered the ritual so that her body seemed to acquire certain thrusts and angularities which at that time I thought fitted in with her new station in life.

But that morning she amazed me with a freshness that had lain suppressed within her for a long time. Perhaps she had not put on her guard for the day; perhaps finding me there in her private room she let crumble the stiffness and masks she wore about herself. I thought there peeped through this defenceless-ness a body and a self uncorrupted by time and personal habits.

For the first time in more than a decade our breaths and presences mingled. As she bent over me, I could see myself recovering in the reflections I saw in her eyes. Something quickened inside me. Perhaps she too saw an unmanipulated reflection of herself in my eyes for the blood seemed to go to her face and put there the vitality the years of living with me had drained.

Under my gaze the old scars of her personality were ready to peel off. The sweep of her arm as she rose from waking me seemed to contain in it more than a personal gesture. The morning light trembled on the upper expanse of her breasts. Her uncombed hair, flaming with sunlight streaming through the parted curtains, blurred further the familiarity I had cast about her face. The light expanded and enclosed her entire body in the silky shine of an unidentifiable newness.

That glow followed us out of the room and rested lightly on all our movements, thoughts, feelings and also on the walls, furniture, nooks and corners of the house. Sometimes we, Santhi and I, caught ourselves looking around us and at each other with wonder. We were quite unsure of what was happening to and around us. The boys, Ravi and Sivam, were similarly caught in that effulgence of wonder. They looked at us as if they expected some sort of an explanation or reassurance from us.

But I was wary about insisting on recognition; I didn't want to fix the features of an experience purely in the mind. Something else, it appeared to me, was needed. I wondered if a ritual, similar to the thanks-giving one conducted by the priest, was necessary. But that kind of ceremony created a special place and occasion for itself. The ritual that was needed had to be placed within ourselves and within life itself. How to enter the other womb of renewal? I wondered. To be born again untouched by all the corruptions of man's history and ambitions?

While these thoughts continued to preoccupy me, I went more and more into our room - it had become *our* room. Santhi sometimes came in and sat on the cot, shyly, fearfully. Her face showed that she too wanted to be open to something more than the glow that enveloped us in that room. She wanted to, as I did, cross some invisible barrier into that other land where we could be fully ourselves.

Was it this desire that made her talk to me with some loss of her usual reserve? Or was it the room itself, where she said she felt more comfortable? Talk, she did, hesitantly perhaps, but with an anxiety and openness I hadn't before seen in her.

"I don't know much of the world," she said. "I saw more of it after I married you. But I'm not sure if I like what I see. The world I lived in with my parents, brothers and sisters was a small one. More than that, it frightened me. So when I saw you coming from the other world, I was happy. For a while.

"I didn't think I would need a room like this. As you can see I had to have it. It makes me feel so many things I can't put into words.

"When I lived with my family, I was made to feel that I had to put on a face that was different from mine. A face for my mother. A face for my father. A face for my brothers and sisters. A face for the neighbours. And a face for the town people when I went to the shops to buy thread or ribbons or a bit of cloth. After some time I didn't know who I was.

"There was always this feeling that I lived inside the skin of someone I didn't know. My own self was somewhere far away. It cried out in the night, like a child caught in the womb beyond its delivery time.

"After some time I gave up wondering who I was. My crippled sister helped me to make this decision. My parents let out the story it was the Japanese Occupation that crippled her. Fear of the soldiers paralysed and wasted away her legs. That wasn't the truth.

"My father too had many faces. But the face we saw most of the time was filled with anger. 'Can't bring up the children properly without anger,' he used to say. So he beat us often. Sometimes for no reason at all. As if he enjoyed that kind of exercise. Sometimes for the wrong reason. As happened with my sister.

"Do you want to hear all this?" she said, pausing.

"At one time I used to think the rice grain was more important than the husk," I said.

She looked at me for a while, her face relaxed, soft and understanding. In her eyes I detected that light I rarely saw in people: a clear, outwardly turned brightness. Was I only imagining those things?

"My sister loved wandering about," Santhi said. "So she told me. I wasn't born yet. She didn't think about the danger. Only of moving here and there. Seeing this and that. It was towards the end of the war. The Japanese were already losing. And their behaviour wasn't harsh any more. There was great excitement. Children ran about here and there. My sister joined them. She wasn't to be seen for hours. The soldiers were giving away their food rations. One evening my sister returned with a handkerchief bundle of chocolates. It was then that my father beat her.

" 'So you'll take things from strangers!' he said as he beat her.

" 'They're just giving away things.' my sister said.

" 'Now you're talking back!' he said and beat her all over the body. One of the blows fell on her back. My sister crumpled to the floor. They had to put her to bed, from which she never got up. She never walked after that. My parents tried everything but my sister was crippled for life.

" 'People never want you to run in your own way, for your own happiness,' my sister said. They were almost the last words she said to me.

"My father never admitted his guilt. That made us all more frightened of him. We obeyed him in almost everything.

"When I saw my sister lying there, dying, I saw myself as her. People pitied her. Would they pity me? Did I want pity? When she died, I gave up all ideas of running.

"Where would I run to? In that small world everyone seemed the same.

"And not only in that small world."

She stopped and looked at me. I didn't flinch from her gaze. I knew what she meant.

"And then I brought my world to you," I said.

"Yes," she said.

There wasn't any accusation in her voice, only recognition and acceptance. There wasn't the weariness that there had been when we had talked, desultorily, about our relatives on an uneventful evening. We looked at each other and we knew, through an unspoken language, that the recollection and recognition of ourselves would not stop there.

Something like an expectation hung between us; it lay like a palpable glow over our eyes. As the days passed that brightness over our eyes seemed to strip the world of the familiarity we had known. We seemed to be startled out of our self-assurance and to look about ourselves with new eyes. Was that when the process of recollection and recognition of ourselves really began?

The fire that Sita purified herself in didn't come; instead, something else washed away the changeling mantles from our shoulders. It happened on an evening when the boys had gone to a birthday party in the neighbourhood. Santhi had just returned from the temple but she wasn't her calm, absorbed self such visits made her into. The sombre sari she wore seemed to constrict and suffocate her. She must have looked for me in the study before she reached me in our room.

She looked to me like a traveller who had come through the centuries bearing the weight of an inquiry but not finding the answer. As I sat on the cot observing her, she moved near the sari curtains with something like a new listlessness. She made no attempt to look at me or talk to me. I laid aside the book

I had been reading as if it was an object that didn't have the freshness of a pebble thrown up on the shore by the sea.

Then she came and sat beside me, keeping her face turned away.

"These saris I've hung over the windows," she said. "They were to remind me of my youth. They don't. Not for some time now. Another trap I got into."

Then, as I watched her, she began to sob and then to cry. It wasn't a woman who was crying. Her body didn't just shake; it was convulsed with tremors from a deeper source. Was it because I was so near her that I saw and felt a straining? Was it because I was near the nearness that I couldn't help myself from releasing her from the straining?

Something helped me to begin the unworking. Unworking the sari folds tucked so tightly, neatly, into her flesh. Undoing the cross-stitches of her and my sari-bordered life. It comes to me now, even as I write, this strange, unlooked for energy that dares to undo the network of inhibitions, prohibitions, history and predilections that we have cast about us. Santhi is before me and I before her in all our nakedness: a nakedness that reaches beyond the flesh.

We have entered and live in that white country of convolutions and convulsions. That cell-laid whiteness is an endless landscape the ridges of which lead you into fresher and fresher valleys of discovery. And the woman, the ridges and valleys of whiteness herself, is bathed in her own fluids of creation. Just as we have destroyed history, we move towards that timeless centre where explosions of human consciousness - not nuclear weapons - will build the skies of a yet-to-be-formed world.

"There's work to do," I get up and say every morning.

And she, the woman, the lumps in her hips and breasts removed, doesn't have to say a word; she only has to come forth from that effulgent glow with a smile which is the smile of all things to be.

AFTERWORD
By
Dr. C.W. Watson
Senior Lecturer, Department of Social Anthropology
University of Kent at Canterbury

It is difficult to read *In a Far Country* with any degree of confidence. By that I don't mean that it is difficult to construct some sense out of the words on the page and follow the episodic descriptions conveyed there, although there is that difficulty, too, at times. Where the real difficulty lies for me, is in getting a grip of the whole: feeling confident that I know what the novel is about, that I am properly interpreting and understanding, indeed even correctly identifying, the various levels at which the text is operating.

One easy reaction to such doubts is the familiar one of dismissing them by incorporating them within a critique; thus one argues that the doubts are part of the response which the novel's structure is designed to elicit. The structure in this perspective deliberately seeks to undermine the usual conventions of reading and create uncertainty for the reader. Consequently, I can interpret my own doubts as an indication of the success of the novel's style. Much of this argument is clearly appropriate in relation to *In a Far Country*. It should not be read as a realist novel; its ambiguity is a deliberately intended structural feature of the text, and the conventions according to which it must be interpreted are to be found not in the realism of the late nineteenth century novel, but in the modernist and post-modernist texts of the late twentieth century. Nevertheless, even though I appreciate the strength of this argument, I still feel uneasy, and I want to account for my uneasiness in terms of what I see as a promiscuous use of narrative conventions and tropes which confuses the reader at crucial moments within the text. Let me explain.

197

As a reader I am quite happy to go along with the task of selecting appropriate literary conventions and codes and relating them to *In a Far Country*, and certainly this is a rewarding way to approach the novel. One can, for example, reflect on the surrealist quality of the narrator's confinement to his house in the opening sections of the novel and his breaking with the daily routine of his middle-class family life style, and recall similarly constructed situations in the claustrophobic stories of Kafka or Samuel Beckett. In other episodes where the focus is less on the experience of mental and physical confinement and more on the notion of journeying, pilgrimage and discovery, other parallels spring to mind. The expeditions into the jungle, the return to the northern town and the narrator's second encounter with Zulkifli, and the recurring symbolism of Mani the goat, for example, seem cognate, in a non-specific way with some of the thirties novels of writers like Rex Warner or French novels of the fifties. Closer to Malaysia, I am reminded of the fantasy and absurdism of the Indonesian writer Iwan Simatupang whose protagonist in *Ziarah* and *Merahnya Merah* are not only observers of the unreal world of others, but total participants within it. And, finally, another literary form which invites comparison is the magical realism of Marquez, Isabel Allende and Salman Rushdie, all of whom revel in anecdotes of extraordinary characters and phantasmagoric situations, yet at the same time insert within their narrative a committed historical and political commentary.

The point of making these comparisons is not to transfer attention away from *In a Far Country*; on the contrary, it is to invite a closer reading of it, since by observing the similarities and differences in the way in which the conventions of anti-realism are manipulated, the reader is guided to a view from which she can, ideally, identify and evaluate what the enterprise of the novel is, what it is about. Let me illustrate what I mean by referring once more to the political intentions of the magical realists.

Marquez' *One Hundred Years of Solitude*, Allende's *House of the Spirits* and Rushdie's *Midnight's Children* deal respectively with Colombia, Chile and India, giving powerful and individual interpretations of the recent political history of three nations. In their case the way in which that commentary is conducted is through the retelling of historical events in gross caricature in which political personalities appear in exaggerated grotesque forms which combine the blackly humorous with the horrifically violent. The political commentary is located, then, in the juxtaposition of violence and humour, a juxtaposition which precisely because it is so alienating, forces the reader to reflect more profoundly on the political statement being made - an excellent example of Brecht's Verfremdungseffekt. Here in *In a Far Country* it seems that K.S. Maniam is occasionally trying something similar, but only very tentatively and unconvincingly. In several places throughout the narrative there seems to be an attempt to present specific detailed descriptions of events in the narrator's life and in the record of the lives of the significant others whom he encounters. Now at one level we can read these descriptions as indicative of the transformation of Malaysian society over the past forty years. Thus the narrator's progress from being a junior official in land development schemes in northern Malaysia to his present financial success as a property developer mirrors the economic transformation of the country from being a largely agriculture based British colony at the start of this period to the achievement of modern nation status with a fast-growing economy after forty years. Similarly, the various characters whose life-stories are recounted, or hinted at, throughout the narrative seem intended to reflect the victims and the beneficiaries of that transformation, the victims being those like Lee Shin and Andy the smoke-house man who cannot accommodate to the demands of the new society and the beneficiaries, those like the narrator, Jimmy Kok and Ramasamy, who have adapted and made good. And in between there are those like Zulkifli and the narrator's wife who do not fully adapt, but manage to survive. These characters and the episodes in which they are involved are on this reading to be seen as case-studies. Certainly at one level such an interpretation is plausible, but unfortunately these are only the faintest gesturings towards social comment, and there is nothing substantial which might allow the reader to obtain any real sense of what has been happening to the country.

The same is true of the muted political commentary in the text. In Chapter 10 towards the end of the book, for example, there is an account of a political meeting, but this is filtered through the description of a surreal nightmare, and the narrative of the dream allows the assembling of characters and events from different periods of the narrator's life history: Mani the sacrificial goat, symbolising perhaps the common man; the friends of the narrator, Lee Shin, Zulkifli, Jimmy Kok, Ramasamy, each again perhaps - but this is not certain - representative of an ethnic voice within the nation. At the centre of the dream, however, is the "representative" and it is he who provides the focus for the satire:

'Once launched, the representative rambles on about how the administration has only the welfare of the people at heart. He cites various projects that have been completed, all in the interests of the people. The people, he is referring to, shift restlessly on their chairs and feet. It is when he beings to talk about how the multi-purpose complex represents everything that a society dreams of that we hear a raucous explosion, like a fart. The representative stops talking but the culprit isn't to be found. Security guards walk among the people, trying to identify the mischiefmaker. The speaker continues with his praise of the administration's far-sightedness when we hear a bray, followed by the sound of someone urinating. The representative doesn't stop; he only hurries on and brings his address to a conclusion. Just as he takes the scissors, presented on a silver platter, and prepares to cut the ribbons the air suddenly fills with the stink of a goat's pellet-dung. But Mani is faster than the security guards and having made his comments on the occasion, bounds away. He doesn't show himself for a few days. But he must have been in the administration's black book since then.

As satire goes this is mildly amusing, but all in all it is fairly trite and there is not much substance to it. The figure of the hypocritical politician mocked by the common man has become a stock character in fiction throughout the world, not least in Malaysia. The humour here, then, does not carry us very far. There is a world of difference, between this mild general criticism and the excoriating caricatures of individuals which we find in the other novelists of magical realism.

This is one way, then, in which comparative literary criticism can help us to read selected episodes in *In a Far Country* at a more intense level. And, as I suggested earlier, trying to trace a literary genealogy or locate the novel within a genre can be a rewarding experience. It can never, however, of itself be enough. Ultimately one's evaluation of a work of fiction of this kind depends on an assessment of how far it has succeeded in the articulation of something original within the limits of the conventions it has set for itself. And it is here that the doubts and difficulties arise. I am never sure what the intention of the novel is - where in other words the originality is to be found - and, if the argument is that there is no intention, I am not convinced.

Part of the problem seems to lie in the chaos of a first person narrator, whom the epigraph at the front of the book encourages us to think of in Proustian terms. Like Marcel in *A*

La Recherche du Temps Perdu, the narrator, is searching, or so it would appear, to recreate the past, restoring it, almost, through literary fabrication. Thus the novel opens, like Proust, with a vividly evoked memory of a childhood, in this case the scene of the slaughter of Mani at Deepavali. This opening sequence, and I use the film term deliberately, is to my mind one of the most successful in the book. Very subtly it sets the reader up for a number of the episodes which will follow. The figure of the goat will constantly recur, both as a symbol in itself, a symbol, mind you, which seems to change its referent from ritual scape-goat to peasant rebel, and as dark image within the narrator's mind of the Dionysian spirit which undermines rigid and inflexible control. Above all, however, this introduction alerts the reader, again as in the Proustian case, to the function of memory.

It is therefore somewhat disappointing to find in the succeeding chapters that although the device or recollection, is preserved, the style of the narrative changes and we are led into the absurd and the fantastic. Despite the linking voice of the narrator, the various episodes which follow are dissociated one from another, and striking as they are as vignettes, the life and death of Lee Shin, the Spotted Lady, Sivasurian's chronicle, there is no overall coherence, either in terms of a consistent style or in terms of an overarching narrative structure. To put it another way, the reader is left to puzzle out whether this is a novel about a central character whose reflections on experience are intended as an exploration of individual subjectivity, or a farrago of portraits and stories which taken cumulatively are organised in such a way as to enable us to read modern Malaysian history from the text.

It would be wrong, however, to end on a critical note and one which perhaps says more of my own lack of perceptiveness than of flaws in the novel itself. There is some very powerful writing in the book which should not go unobserved. The description of the narrator's visit to Zulkifli's village and the horror of the transformation of Zulkifli's son, read partly as an allegory of the transformation of Malaysia over the past thirty years, partly as documentary realism, offer fine confirmation, if ever it was needed, of how compelling a novelist K.S. Maniam is. In fact this episode stands out in the narrative not only because of the graphic quality of the descriptions, but also because, with respect to two central issues, the novel here reaches its dramatic climax.

The life of the narrator up to that point, at least this is how it appears in his narrated reflections, has been the accumulation of disconnected experiences, lived through at different levels of intensity, but never providing the security from which an assured self-perception can be achieved. It is precisely this lack of assurance which has led to the withdrawal from the world, and it is the search for assurance which has prompted first the recall of the earlier experiences and then an attempt to revisit the emotion of those experiences for the purpose of greater self-understanding. It is this motive which inspires the desire to see Zulkifli again. Years earlier Zulkifli had tried to help the narrator to see the tiger, a symbol of the quality of Malay life and the Malay vision of the world, but as with other earlier attempts of the narrator to grasp at a subliminal reality beneath the surface, the journey made had ended in failure. The return to the north, then, is an attempt to take up again that earlier frustrated endeavour. In being forced to confront Zul and listen to what has overtaken Zul's family, the narrator does indeed achieve some sort of self-understanding and this is sufficient, not to allow immediate re-entry into the world, but to enable progress in that direction.

The other central issue which is raised here which provides some justification for seeing this episode as a climax is the connection made, for once very explicitly, between the nation's political history and the narrator's desire to arrive at self-discovery through an insertion of himself within that history.

After Zulkifli has described the mental collapse of his son he turns to the narrator.

"He is living and not living," Zul said. "We can accept the results but we still have to look for the cause. You ran away that time. From the tiger. I've become old and wiser, when I look back I see you and others like you as the cause. We lived well, may be too peacefully, before you all came with your ideas and energies. Ideas that can even destroy the tiger, the oldest symbol of our civilisation. You gave up everything to come to this land. We offered you what we had. But you all became greedy and wouldn't share. Saw no other world but the world of progress and money. And we had to make the sacrifices. This time I want you to experience what my son went through."

"I can try, Zul," I said.

"He saw the tiger," Zul said. "I made him see the tiger. Yet, when he went to the city, everything was destroyed."

The ideas here are familiar, the rape of the country, the destruction of tradition, the awfulness of what replaces it, but located where they are in the context of the narrative these ideas are articulated with a poignancy which compels the reader to go beyond a gesture of complacent acquiescence. Although, ultimately, I still feel unsure about the depth of thought here, and how much is really being communicated, I am moved by the style of the statement.

There is, then, much to commend *In a Far Country*. If at times it seems to suffer from a certain lack of control, the experiments it contains were nonetheless worth making and should be applauded. If there is an overall weakness of the novel, then, it lies in its being over-ambitious. Too many different styles and forms, too many literary devices, jostle together, and even though several episodes in themselves come across with a force and vigour which grip the imagination, the success of the whole is jeopardised by the very disparateness of such a kaleidoscopic narrative. Reflections on the literary uses of memory, the depiction of history as surreal, commentary on the nature of tradition and the upheavals of modernisation, are all great themes which sit uneasily together and can only be handled with great literary skill and control. That K.S. Maniam's first attempt in this direction has not been entirely successful is not altogether surprising, but with the experience of having written two very different novels behind him, he is undoubtedly moving from strength to strength, and I eagerly anticipate his next novel.

K.S. MANIAM
The Return
Now Available, P'bk. U.K. Price GBP £5.99

It is a time of both apprehension and hope. The youthful narrator, Ravi witnesses the change in a way of life and the end of a way of thinking. The story depicts the experiences of an immigrant community in Peninsula Malaysia before and after Independence in 1957. It documents the bewilderment and loss of bearings felt within a once secure world coming to an end in political change and cultural fragmentation.

"HOW DOES ONE DESCRIBE THE LAND ONE LIVED IN BUT NEVER SAW? It was more tangible than the concrete one we flitted through every day. Darkness gave it true dimensions. Then it vibrated within our hearts. If we saw, perhaps through some quirk of optics, a flame beside the drain, then it was a dead pregnant woman's soul come out to haunt the real world; if we heard murmurs, echoed voices among the hills, they were the chanting and tinkling of Banana-tree spirits dancing in the courtyard of the night. The quick rush of water in the communal bath-shed signified some unappeased soul's feverish bathing. We were hemmed in our rooms, houses, and in our minds. The tension between good and evil shimmered therefore like an inevitable consciousness within our heads."

K.S. Maniam, *The Return*

K.S. Maniam is a myth-maker, reconciling Malaysian and ethnic Indian consciousness in an organic symbolism rooted in unconscious experience.

The growing reputation of *The Return* is much deserved, and in its appearance in this new edition will allow new readers a rare opportunity to enter imaginatively into a certain kind of Malaysian experience which is paradoxically perhaps, both highly specific and yet universally representative.

Dr. C.W. Watson, *University of Kent at Canterbury*

Maniam was already known as a writer of some fine short stories, and his first novel lived up to our expectations. The Style was impressive, creating and sustaining, seemingly without effort...

This second edition of *The Return* should win it many new readers and, hopefully, raise a crop of novelists in English, settlers moving in to cultivate new terrain, inspired by Maniam's worthy pioneer achievement.

Edward Dorall, *New Straits Times*

Skoob *PACIFICA* Anthology No: 1
S. E. ASIA WRITES BACK !
Publication date: 31st Aug. 1993, P'bk. U.K. Price GBP £5.99

As the advancement of technology exceed our grasp, contemporary culture has reached the juncture between Postmodernism and Postcolonialism to give rise to an entirely new idea of chronology. The 'Post' is a diachrony of periods which are individually identifiable. This is the point where we begin. The principle of Postmodern/Postcolonial writing is to deviate from the tradition and to develop a new direction of thought. Such an idea of progress would lead to the evolution of culture. The understanding of a writer involves anamnesis in psycho-analytical context, the free association of ideas and imagery of the unconscious in situations past to discover the hidden meanings of his life.

The Postmodern/Postcolonial writer is in the position of a philosopher: the text written is not, in principle, governed by predetermined rules nor is it judged according to a determining judgement. Those rules and categories are what the work of art is defining. The writer is working without rules in order to formulate the rules of what "will have been done". Hence, the text has a character of the event which comes too late for the author, it's *mise en oeuvre* is ahead of itself. This could be understood according to the paradox of the future (post) anterior (modo). The achievement of the Postcolonial writers is that they see within the self the possibility of a different history, and stemming from this, the reality of a new *genre*.

Preface by I.K. Ong
Introduction by John McRae
PART ONE: New Writings
Shirley Geok-lin Lim * K.H. Thor * Karim Raslan * Robert Yeo *
Arthur Yap * Philip Jeyaretnam * Alfred A. Yuson * Michael Wilding *
Jan Kemp * W.P. Chin * Paul Sharrad * K.S. Maniam * Latiff Mohidin *
Cecil Rajendra * L.G. Leong * T.P. Lee * Kirpal Singh * Anne Brewster
Siew-Yue Killingley * P.N. Wong
PART TWO: Malaysian/Singaporean Prose in English
Shirley Geok-lin Lim * K.S. Maniam * K.L. Lee * C.W. Watson *
B.E. Ooi * T.C. Kee
PART THREE: Other Literatures of the Pacific Rim
Marcus Richards * Pira Sudham * P.N. Wong * Alan Durant
PART FOUR: The Nobel Laureates
Derek Walcott * Wole Soyinka * Yasunari Kawabata
PART FIVE: Literary Features
* Yukio Mishima - Fountains In The Rain
* Vikram Seth - From Heaven Lake, Travel Through Sinkiang And Tibet

WONG PHUI NAM
Ways of Exile
Poems From The First Decade
Publication date: 31st Aug. 1993, P'bk. U.K. Price GBP £5.99

Until now, this collection of poetic accomplishment has been limited to academic circles. Out of the deepest resources of his heart and life, Mr. Wong has forged an identity in the interaction of cultures and ethnicity. This collection traces the development of the poet from student days to early maturity in lyrical litany, honouring the Malaysian soul as well as the geographical and spiritual ground of his country. We have here an important Malaysian collection being added to Post-colonial Literature of S.E. Asia.

Part One: How The Hills Are Distant * Nocturnes and Bagatelles
Part Two: For A Local Osiris * Osiris Transmogrified * Address from the God
Part Three: What Are The Roots...: Readings From Tu Fu * Taoist Poems *
              Reading of a Tang Poem * A Version From T'ao Yuan-Ming
Part Four: Rumours of Exits: From Chairil Anwar (1922-1949) * A Night Easter
Postcript: Out Of The Stony Rubbish: A Personal Perspective On The Writing
              Of Verse In English In Malaysia.

"THESE POEMS NEED TO BE WRITTEN. They are of a time, of a place, of a people who find themselves having to live by institutions and folkways which are not of their heritage, having to absorb the manners of languages not their own."
Wong Phui Nam, *Ways of Exile* (Introduction to How The Hills Are Distant)

VII
Suggested by Li Po's
Bidding Farewell To A Friend In A Boat

We have drunk ourselves to numbness
becoming mere tissue, mere bone
upon whose damp even the lute's flame
has quenched itself. The night now
infects the light of our single lamp,
smoking it blue, and the moon,
as it turns chill once again, engenders
ice in the marrow. Our shouts, disembodied bits
of song and laughter drift with the mists,
like spirits wandering on the face of black waters.
The egrets are startled in their sleep.
The islands heave with a tumult of wings
as, in the small hours, the flocks rise,
abandon long spits of sand to the night.

Wong Phui Nam, *Ways of Exile* (Part 3: Taoist Poems)

"One of the leading poets who continued writing consistently."
Mohd. Taib bin Osman, *Far Eastern Literatures In The 20th Century*